LOVEDA BROWN
COMES HOME

THE IDYLLWILD MYSTERY SERIES
BOOK 2

JOLIE TUNNELL

GOBSMACKED

Loveda Brown Comes Home

by Jolie Tunnell

Copyright © January 2021 Jolie Tunnell

San Diego, California. USA.

Cover design by Jerusha Foltz.

Map by Micah Tunnell.

Claim a **FREE** book at https://jolietunnell.com/newsletter

Visit https://jolietunnell.com/

IN THIS SERIES

*To Julia, who would take country life over city finery any day,
but handles both with panache.*

1

INHERITANCE

The sun was dropping on another beautiful summer day in Idyllwild. Our ridgeline sat in a dry pine forest a mile above sea level but was still not the tallest part of the mountain. Because we perched just west of Tahquitz Peak, sunset was a moment to stop everything and admire the fiery glow that danced fiercely across the naked granite above us.

Legend asserted that Chief Tahquitz resided beneath the peak with a rattlesnake and a condor for company and shook things up once in a while when he got bored. Thankfully, I had never experienced a California earthquake, but the Cahuilla tribes in this area had long known that, after Tahquitz killed his sweetheart, he succumbed to an evil spirit that locked him deep in the mountaintop as penance. The Cahuilla left years ago, but the fire spirit lived on.

The scene would have been altogether romantic had I wrapped my arms around anything other than a chimney top. As it was, the rounded stones beneath my hands mimicked the embrace of gentle shoulders; steady, reliable shoulders that encouraged me to divulge my darkest secrets.

"I'm stuck," I whispered. "Send help."

They were, unfortunately, the strong silent type, and I looked around again at the wooden shingles that fed down in every direction from my perch on the roof, daring me to slide to safety. The hotel was two stories tall. The oak tree next to it rose another ten feet above my head, and the pine forest across the road mocked me from another hundred feet in the sky. Squirrels raced from tree to tree, taking a leap of faith between branches at my own eye level. I'd been watching them for a while now, wondering what their secret was.

Courage, I supposed.

The ladder used for my ascent perched between the oak tree and the hotel, leaning against the roofline closest to the chimney which was another ten sloping feet up the roof. The climb up had been simple, even with cheesecloth in one hand and my skirt bunched up in the other. The minute I'd turned to descend, however, a wave of vertigo hit so hard I had to cling for dear life to the chimney, eyes closed, until it passed. I'd been enjoying the view ever since.

My arms ached. The shingles dug into my left leg and hip. I debated over which was worse: staying up here in the fast-approaching dark or falling headfirst at the feet of my incoming guest. I looked down the dusty road that disappeared around a bend and led all the way down into Banning. The stagecoach was due any minute, and inside of it was my future.

An unexpected sound rose through the treetops. It

was a bugle, I couldn't fathom from where, saluting the setting sun. The last pure notes of "Retreat" drifted away, a fitting tune for my predicament. It was time to let go.

The ladder top peeked at me, surrounded by pretty oak leaves. I took a deep breath and released the chimney. As I began the slow drop toward the ladder, I scrabbled at the shingles with my hands while attempting to aim my high-top buttoned shoes. My shoes hit the ladder and sent it backwards into the oak tree. My hands caught the edge of the roof, and there I dangled, feet kicking in the air, dark skirt billowing around my white knickers, shrieking for Mr. Hannahs.

Whether it was my screams for help or the incoming thunder of the stagecoach that brought faithful Mr. Hannahs out of the post office was irrelevant. His voice boomed out below me, and the ladder landed hard against my back.

"Grab hold!" he called.

I was too terrified to let go of the roof, and my flailing feet somehow wedged the ladder top firmly beneath my bottom. The ladder swayed dangerously under me, and my arms shook. Mr. Hannahs shouted something, and although other voices mingled with it, his Swiss accent came through clearly. The front door of the hotel slammed shut, and seconds later, the second-floor window at my kneecaps flew open. A pair of powerful hands reached around my legs and yanked me and the ladder forward. My arms gave out, and in one swoop, I'd been pulled through the window and into the arms of the stagecoach driver, Jim Roster.

"Now there's something I've never done before," he

said. His arms drove a team of four horses every day, and they had no problem holding my petite five foot four inches above the ground, skirts bunched up around my kneecaps. I goggled at him and caught my breath for a minute before struggling to the floor.

"Maybe you should build a balcony," he said with a smile.

"Jim," I gasped, rubbing my arms hard, "thank you." I looked beyond him, and the man I'd been waiting for stood in the hotel room doorway. He was rounder by far than Mr. Hannahs, quite a barrel of a man, with a perfectly creased professional suit and vest. His mutton-chopped jowls, shaved at precise angles to adorn his middle-aged jawline, complimented a thick head of salt and pepper hair. His face was full of confusion, but I watched him rally as I brushed myself off and stood up straight.

The man stepped forward and gave me a little bow. "Esquire Milo Craven, attorney at law, at your service," he said.

"Welcome to Idyllwild, Mr. Craven." I smiled weakly at both men, then led them down the staircase and into the lobby on shaky feet. Mr. Hannahs was waiting there, his white handlebar mustache quivering with anxiety. Jim retrieved his hat from the floor where he'd flung it on his way up and, fitting it snugly in place, tapped a finger to the brim and went outside with Mr. Hannahs to finish their business. The post office next door was the only spot on the mountain where the stagecoach stopped. Jim delivered mail, parcels, and people to Mr. Hannahs who held them for the tiny town that scattered for miles along the twisting highway. I would have to thank them both for saving my life when Mr. Craven was gone.

"You are the widow of William H. Dunn?" my lawyer asked.

I nodded. "It's Loveda Brown," I said, attempting to get my bearings. "I use my maiden name now."

I handed him a pen and waited while he signed the guest book on my desk, searching for something that a perfectly calm, rational hotel proprietor who had not recently fallen off a roof would say.

"It's a good thing I've already got your information, Mr. Craven. Your signature is truly indecipherable."

I winced.

"All professionals cultivate signatures that are impossible to replicate," he said, adding another curling flourish to the page. It was hard to tell whether he was offended or flattered. "Certain affairs, you understand, would end in disaster in the wrong hands."

Jim opened the door and set a leather suitcase and a sturdy briefcase inside. Mr. Craven thanked him and collected his things. Jim shot one last smile at me that guaranteed my notoriety in his immediate circle of acquaintances and left.

"So they would," I agreed. "Now, Mr. Craven, your room is, um, actually the one we were just in." I twisted my raw hands together in embarrassment. "I suppose you know the way."

"You mean to say it is only you and I on the property?" He frowned as he looked around the small room. "I expected to find you with your parents. Widows generally return to their family homes. Most unusual."

"No family. No home. Let's just say that Billy and I

had some things in common." It was silly that I felt intimidated, and I shook the feeling off. "Not to worry, Mr. Craven. Your character comes highly regarded in professional circles. If I thought impropriety was an issue, I'd ask Carlos to stay over."

"Who?"

"A man next door who likes to hit things with a hammer."

My attempt at levity fell flat, so I didn't mention that I also had a Winchester under my bed and a Colt revolver under my pillow. The fact that I hadn't had time to get ammunition for them was beside the point.

Supper was a brief and tedious affair. I had begged our nice meal from Mrs. Hannahs ahead of time, but Mr. Craven was intent on impressing me and it left little room for the impression of others.

Mr. Craven leaned back in his chair, napkin in one hand, and said, "Now, Mrs., er, Miss Brown? I know you understand how out of the ordinary it is for me to be here this evening."

I nodded but had no chance to reply.

"Normally, of course, I would remain in my seat in Tucson, but it was of particular personal interest to me when my old colleague, Dr. Prost, asked." He reached for another pickle.

"Such a marvel, this telephone. I can't tell you the pleasure it brought me when his call from Boston came all the way into Arizona to my office." He crunched the pickle with relish.

"The man said you worked with him at one time and were now in need of the best legal advice possible." He left no pause for me to confirm it.

"And he called the right man, Miss Brown, he did. I was there to witness my beautiful territory of Arizona ushered into glorious statehood. Stood at attention as the cannon fired, as our beloved President Taft declared us the forty-eighth state of the Union and inaugurated Governor George W. P. Hunt himself!"

I wondered whether I should rise and sing the national anthem, but Mr. Craven continued unabated.

"Shook hands with Supreme Court Chief Justice Alfred Franklin, Miss Brown, and my own promotion followed thereafter." He lifted his goblet. "Danced until dawn at the Hotel Adams," he said with a nod.

I took advantage of his swallowing and said, "I am grateful that you are willing to travel, Mr. Craven. The ranch in El Paso is extensive and, so far as I'm aware, Billy didn't leave a will. I'm not willing to return in order to settle the affairs."

Billy's ranch—our ranch—covered miles of Texas badlands near the El Paso border with Mexico. We'd run cattle, horses, and sheep on it, a sprawling operation that appealed to me at the time.

Until I caught Billy in our bed with the maid a week after our wedding.

"This is why I asked Dr. Prost to recommend a lawyer willing to travel there on my behalf." I sat up straight. "I want you to liquidate the entire estate. I'm taking the cash money for all of it. Once it's settled, I'll pay your fees and cover your travel expenses, as agreed."

When I first came to Idyllwild, I'd been running from betrayal and a ruined marriage. I was twenty-two years old, and this hotel represented the end of my running. My husband, Billy, was dead now, and if his parting gift was the opportunity to never run again, then I intended to pursue it. Pursue a home of my own. Pursue the chance to stand on my own two feet.

"It appears to be a straightforward probate," Mr. Craven said. "No one to dicker with over the fine china, eh?"

He was a pompous old windbag, but he was all I had.

2

HONEYMOON

Morning found Mr. Craven and I at the dining room table once again. Sunshine lit the room through a large frosted multi-paned window at the back wall and through the door that opened into the lobby at the other side. His opened briefcase displayed several pens and multiple files, and his name was tooled into the fine leather at the top.

He had gone on and on for an hour using phrases like probate code, distribution of assets, party of the first part, estate tax consequences, and other legal jargon that made my head ache. I'd been raised the only child of two intellectuals and worked as a governess for the aforementioned Dr. Prost's progeny. While the terms and wherewithals were, on paper, fairly straightforward, there were entirely too many of them.

Mr. Craven looked up at me and said, "My dear Miss Brown. If you don't begin signing, we'll be here until Christmas. Please."

I picked up my pen and slowly signed each page in

turn until they blurred together. I gave up reading the fine print after three pages and resented a page that required more than a signature. Two wearisome hours later, we were done.

"Mr. Craven," I said. "Would you care for some fresh air? Strawberry Creek is just beyond the sheriff's little office." I stood up and rolled my stiff shoulders.

"Sheriff's office?" He stopped his pen mid-air.

"Yes, there's this hotel, then the post office next door, then the blacksmith shop, and then the office that Sheriff Fuller uses when he's in the area. Beyond that, the road continues all the way down the other side of our mountain to Hemet."

He was less than enthusiastic. It was hard to compete with Tucson. I tried again. "Or, if you like, we could walk next door and get you a newspaper for the afternoon and your return ticket arranged for tomorrow morning. Mr. Hannahs keeps at least three from the East Coast, and if we're lucky, he has a little hot coffee left in his fancy Thermos."

That got him out of his chair. He put on his suit jacket, and together we stepped out onto the board-walk. A busy squirrel had scattered the shredded remains of a pine cone across a corner of the veranda. A raucous scrub jay was making trouble across the road, where a thick stand of pines stretched in both directions.

"The heat is coming along later today," I warned Mr. Craven. "You may want to leave your jacket behind. We aren't all that formal in Idyllwild."

He sniffed and marched across the post office

landing to the screen door. "Miss Brown, compared to Tucson, this mountain is the refreshing Himalayas."

He held the door open for me and I stepped inside to see Mr. Hannahs with his feet propped up and crossed on his desk, the soles of his boots rubbing up against the typewriter keys in companionship. He was reading the newspaper and growled out from behind it, "Looks like you put Idyllwild on the map for good, Miss Brown. I'm not interested in bringing every California tourist up this mountain, and that's a fact. Used to be a quiet, respectable town."

His grumbles turned animated as he thumped the pages. "Now. Your ad for a cook came through nicely," he continued. "Your only requirement was that they 'know how to make a proper cup of tea' and 'must be able to cook for two or twenty people on a moment's notice'. Fair enough. Your address says 'The Nelson Hotel'. You keeping her name on it, then?"

Mr. Hannahs finally peeped over the top of his paper and scrambled to his feet when he realized I wasn't alone.

"Good morning, Mr. Hannahs," I said. "Mr. Craven was wondering whether he could borrow a paper or two today. He'll be leaving on the morning coach for Banning, so you might want to arrange for that ticket while he's here."

Mr. Hannahs glanced suspiciously at Mr. Craven, and Mr. Craven put on his most ingratiating smile.

"My esteemed Mr. Hannahs," he said, "I appreciate a man of intellect such as yourself. The *New York Times*, is it?" he said, looking across the room at the long counter spanning its width.

As Mr. Craven went to inspect the newspapers and magazines, I leaned in toward Mr. Hannahs. "I'm not sure I can even keep the hotel. Legally, it belongs to Elizabeth Nelson."

"You mean Red?"

"Don't call her that, she's a woman who had a hard life, and I'd like to think she's my friend."

"She was scalped by Indians, tortured by her family, and lives by herself in the woods. Tell me how you get a crazy homeless woman to inherit a hotel."

"Don't you call her that, either." I frowned. "I know she won't. She's content where she is. But I can't walk away and let her home fall apart."

"She told you this? I thought she didn't speak?"

"She visits her old room once in a while but never stays more than a few minutes. She doesn't need words for me to know she hates the rest of the place. But if she ever decides to stay, it'll be ready for her." I sighed. "I need it. For both of us."

"The hotel is also an inheritance issue?" Mr. Craven stood at my elbow again, closer than was comfortable.

"Yes," I said. "But I was hoping to look into that problem after we settled my own. The only living heir to the hotel deliberately wanders the woods of Idyll-wild, and I want to keep it up for her."

Mr. Craven simply stood there, frowning at me. "Will you be residing there and maintaining it, then? Will you be paying the property taxes each year?"

"I—I don't know if I can," I said. "But...I want to." It surprised me how much I wanted to. It was 1912, and despite progress to the contrary, a woman of independent means was still an oddity.

He shook a newspaper at me. "Squatters, Miss Brown. You live there long enough and so far as the government is concerned you own it." He pursed his lips. "Exactly the kind of situation you want to avoid in El Paso, I might add." He nodded at Mr. Hannahs by way of thanks and stepped outside.

I CANTERED along the Banning road, more or less northbound. It was hard to tell as the sinuous highway that hugged the mountainside continually doubled back on itself. Although I could have walked the shortcut that took a direct line through the pines to visit Lindley, the session with Mr. Craven left me with a need to move fast in the fresh air. Anxiety usually made my stomach rebel, and my early morning jitters had grown into a bicarbonate-worthy event. The comfort of a horseback ride blew most of my butterflies away.

I brought my mare, Blue, to a trot, then a walk. We passed the local cemetery, then left the road and moved onto the grounds of Lindley's resort, the Idyllwild Inn. A little saloon sat prominently roadside, closed up for now, but available each evening for a couple of hours if the locals or tourists needed a nightcap. The main building sprawled in the center of Foster's Meadow, welcoming me to an alpine paradise in the clouds.

I chuckled to myself as I rode up to the Inn. Lindley's postcards promised tourists the amenities of a resort in the seclusion of a wilderness, and one look at the scenic gingerbread-decorated cottages or the white fairy tale stagecoach pulled by four prancing white horses was enough to lure even the most doubtful tourist up the mountain.

Lindley might be a shrewd advertiser, but he was also a good business man and I needed his advice. I dismounted and a boy appeared and led my horse away to the stables. Taking the wide veranda steps in eager strides, I stepped into the lobby. The plush carpet over the wooden floorboards complimented the window tapestries. The late morning sunshine made the windowpanes sparkle and the high rough-hewn ceiling beams glow. Centered in the incoming square of sunlight was a reception desk, and the girl sitting at it was lit up like an angel.

"Wow," I said as I approached her, "that's some first impression."

She wasn't smiling. "Try sitting here for longer than ten minutes. I feel like I might pass out." She swayed a little and then rolled herself from her chair and stood outside of the sunbeam. "How are you, Miss Brown?"

"Fine, thank you. I thought I recognized you. Aren't you one of Lindley's maids?"

"Was. I'm Charlotte. He promoted me to receptionist this weekend, and honestly," she said, dragging a sleeve across her face, "I'm not sure I'm the right girl for the job."

The door leading to the back veranda crashed open and three boys dashed in. Two of them chased a third, who ducked behind the glowing desk and shrieked, "Base!" The two chasers came skidding to a halt, then looked around the lobby.

"That fireplace is huge," the one said. "We could pitch a tent inside of it."

"How do you get up there?" the second asked, looking carefully at the dried bunches of cedar hung in the rafters.

The third crept from behind the desk and reached out to slap one boy on the back. "You're it!" he shrieked and raced across the lobby and out the doors, the others in hot pursuit. A woman was in the process of coming in and, as the boys streaked by, she threw her gloved hands into the air, her words muffled by the slamming door in her face.

"Oh, no," Charlotte said and reached the doors at the same time the woman pushed through. The lady was elegantly dressed, like a paper doll cut from the *Ladies' Home Journal*. I wondered how she managed it, as her proportions matched my own, and I was much too short to pull off the latest fashions.

She approached me in a yellow dress, a tunic over a narrow underskirt, sashed with a chocolate brown satin ribbon that matched her silky, perfect chignon. I was instantly ashamed of my dark blue skirt and white shirtwaist. I'd removed my old straw hat and left it at the door, and the dust from my ride over still clung to my white, high-buttoned shoes. I gripped my skirt to keep my hands from automatically reaching up and smoothing my frizzy top knot.

I wasn't wearing a single ornament.

"It's unacceptable," began the lady. "You really must keep a barrier of some sort between the nice suites and the campers. Those…" she searched for the right word, "hooligans are taking all the serenity from the place." She looked around the room. "Really, I'd expected more."

"Darling, there you are." Pushing through the doors was a young man, impeccably dressed, his dark hair slicked back with oil. He hurried to the lady's side and took her hand protectively into the crook of his arm. "I did say I'd handle this," he said with the faintest reproach in his voice.

He turned to me. "I say, we'd like to play a game of croquet this morning. It seems fairly warm to try tennis, although later in the week, we may. Breakfast this morning was quite passable, yes, but delivered a bit earlier than we'd requested." He stopped to look at his blushing partner. "We newlyweds need our beauty sleep, you know. Do make a note of it, that we prefer breakfast served to our room at seven thirty for the rest of the week. Now, if you please, direct us to the croquet lawn."

I stood there, speechless, while the woman's frown grew. Their confusion ended quickly as Charlotte stepped forward. "I'm afraid she's not our staff, Mr. Fontaine. We have set croquet up on the south lawn, through those doors," she pointed toward the back, "and turn left. Look for the white awning we've set up."

The woman continued to frown at me. "Then you must be here as part of the band? The brochure said there was fine dining and dancing every evening. I suppose you took last night off."

I laughed outright. "Poppycock. I couldn't play a tune on a kazoo," I said. "I don't work here, sorry."

"We don't keep a band on staff, Mrs. Fontaine," Charlotte said, and her alarm increased as the lady in the yellow dress grew red in the face.

"What in the world?" She pulled her hand from her

husband's grip. "It said dancing. Are we to hum to ourselves as we stumble around on the lawn?" She turned to her young man. "It's our honeymoon! I want romance! I want to be swept off my feet by the handsomest man in the room!"

"Now, my love," the man said as he recaptured her hand, "and so you shall be." He turned on Charlotte. "Let's put this silliness away. Tell me plainly, miss, whether there will be dancing tonight?"

"Oh yes, sir," she said with a bob. "We do everything within our power to make your experience here memorable."

"There, you see," he said to his bride, "all is well. Let's go out for some sunshine and warm those pretty cheeks."

Mr. and Mrs. Fontaine left the lobby, and as their steps echoed away, Charlotte turned to me and said, "We have a phonograph and some records. Let's hope it's enough to keep me from getting fired. Mr. Lindley's in his office."

She walked toward the door. "If you'll excuse me, I have some wild Indians to corral." She shook her head. "I'm not getting paid enough for this," she muttered.

3
———

DANCE

L indley sat at his desk in a tiny office off the front lobby, bowler hat and jacket slung aside, tie pulled loose, and had his short beard resting in one hand as he stared hard at a ledger book. I rapped on the doorjamb as I stepped inside, and startled, he leapt to his feet.

"Loveda! How wonderful to see you!" He leaned forward and shook my hand firmly. "My fellow innkeeper and the toast of Idyllwild."

I rolled my eyes at him and sat in the other chair. He smiled and sat back again in his. "What brings you here on this fine Tuesday?"

"My lawyer's here," I said. "I spent all morning signing papers till I'm cross-eyed."

Lindley glanced ruefully at his desk. "I know how that feels. Good for you, taking a break."

"I need to ask two favors, Lindley."

"Absolutely anything."

"I wonder whether you would mind looking over

the paperwork when I'm done? Before I send him off again? There's a lot of it, and another set of eyes would be smart, don't you think?"

"Yes, of course. A smart thing to do." He nodded approval. "That's how business people think. If you had time, I'd have my own lawyer look it over."

"Thank you. Do you suppose it could be tonight? My other favor was to beg a spot at your table for him."

"You haven't figured out your stove, have you?" He crossed his arms and attempted to look stern.

"I can boil water. I consider it a victory."

"Loveda, you can't go on like this, and you know it."

"I know." I looked down at my hands in my lap. "But until today, until the lawyer gave me any solid footing, I couldn't let myself get too hopeful. I already advertised for a cook. And Mrs. Hannahs is coming by later today to talk about the garden in the back."

"Too archaic for a hotel. You need to look into running purchases from Hemet. I already bring my supplies in with my coach. Why don't I add your orders to my list until you have your feet under you?"

"Oh, Lindley, would you?" I was so grateful for his offer, I wanted to jump up and shake his hand again. "What do men do when they make deals? It's very confusing."

He laughed. "We drink on it. In this case, why don't we add to the awkwardness? I've advertised for a new maid. After I've sorted through all the applicants, shall I save you the trouble and send you the second-best one?"

"Perfect! It took me a week to get a room ready for Mr. Craven. Exhausting."

"Your lawyer?"

"Yes, and he's not a bit enamored with Idyllwild compared to the luxuries of Tucson, Arizona." I narrowed my eyes at him. "Your place could change that."

"Feeling personal about it, are you?"

"I am now that I'm going to stake a claim on it."

"Good girl. I have some newlyweds with great expectations staying here this week. We may as well humor them and pour the good stuff tonight."

"In that case, Mr. Lindley," I said, rising, "I'll be here at suppertime to drink on our deal. Thank you." I smiled at him and made my way out.

The veranda wrapped completely around the outside of the building, with doors that led to suites or the dining room or the ballroom. Strategically placed rocking chairs offered views of pine forest, or Tahquitz Peak, or rolling Foster's Meadow, dotted with ancient oak trees and assorted campsites and cabins. Lindley's resort catered to a variety of mountaintop experiences. Halfway down the steps, I heard a shout.

"Timber!"

The stable boy watching me heard it at the same time and spun on his heel. Circling the stable, we saw an oak tree, boughs spread low, with a dozen legs dangling from various parts of it. Below the tree stood two young boys, and at their feet, was a freshly hewn limb. Shouts of "Hurrah!" rang out, and the stable boy dashed in among them, barking reprimands. Actual barking commenced immediately after as the two resident basset hounds came roaring from the stable to add their own opinions to the melee.

I watched in amusement as a very tall, very thin, very clean-shaven man rushed up and began pulling boys from the tree.

"Terribly sorry," he said. "Only turned my back for a minute. Boys! Come down at once. This is not the tree I meant. Now see what you've done. No, we cannot use this for the fort, but it won't be put back on the tree, now, will it?"

He flustered and fussed and pulled at his suspenders, and the boys gathered around the fallen limb, as if studying it for the first time. In the general hush, the man turned to the stable boy. "Good sir, shall we use it for firewood?"

The boys' cheers were quickly stopped. "Mr. Peabody, it's green as a newborn lamb," the stable boy said with some heat. "Won't be good for anything for another year. You've gone and cut into our shade tree. For shame!"

One of the boys saluted and said, "Sir, we think this will make a fine bench in our fort, sir."

Mr. Peabody wiped at his forehead with a bandana. "Okay, boys," he said, defeated. "Let's clean it up."

Like so many ants, the boys lined up along the branch and, hefting it on their shoulders as one, bore it off in triumph to the far side of the meadow where I saw they'd set up an extensive campsite.

I turned to look at the stable boy who shrugged at me, baffled. "They say they're Boy Scouts. They're up here to earn badges, whatever that means. They showed up in that." He jerked his thumb toward the stable and parked behind it was a first rate covered wagon.

We looked again toward the campsite. The two dogs, Biscuit and Juno, followed the happy procession.

"Their mules are less trouble than they are," he said in resignation. "I'll bring your horse, miss."

MR. CRAVEN WAS HAVING a wonderful evening. His suit was spotless, his manners gracious, his hopes exceeded, from the arrival of Lindley's fancy white coach that whisked us away to the resort to the cabernet now swirling in his crystal goblet. Lindley's chef had outdone himself with a German hasenpfeffer and a Waldorf salad. The creamed potatoes and lighter-than-air brown bread smothered in fresh butter curled my toes. We sat at a lace-frosted table in the ballroom while a maid cleared our plates.

"Merely lacking a few hundred guests," Mr. Craven said cheerfully, raising his glass, "but I expect they will arrive in time. Who knew there was such a gem hidden among the trees?"

Lindley and I raised our glasses to clink with Mr. Craven's and I said, "Idyllwild can surprise you."

Then I clinked my glass to Lindley's again.

"And," I continued, "there are also some things that you can count on. Like friendship."

"Hear, hear, Miss Brown," Lindley said, taking a drink of his wine. "To the establishment of a profes-sional partnership."

I lingered over my own sip for a minute. More and more, it appalled me to think of the amount of work running a hotel meant. Lindley looked quite pleased with himself. I desperately hoped my smile would match his one day. I'd spent all morning signing papers, and my fingers weren't going to forgive me. Lifting my wine goblet was painful.

"Shall we take a turn on the dance floor and seal the deal?" asked Lindley.

"I thought men just clinked glasses?"

"As there's no way around the fact that you are, indeed, female, I think we must make up our own rules."

"You do have a point. Why not? I haven't danced since forever." I looked toward the only other guests in the room. The Fontaines circled the empty ballroom floor to the music, she in a dark blue evening dress trimmed in silver and he in his tuxedo jacket, oblivious to anyone else. "I may not remember how."

"Let me call you sweetheart," crooned the scratchy voice accompanied by its orchestra, "I'm in love with you."

Charlotte stood against the back wall between two large windows. Through them was a view to the moonlit meadow and a starry sky. The phonograph sat on a cherry-wood table, its large open orifice aimed toward the center of the room, and as each record finished, there was a pause while she changed the cylinder out for the next.

"Ahoy there!" called Lindley to her, standing up and holding out his hand to me. "Play the Jones and Murray."

"That doesn't sound like ragtime," I said, joining him on the floor.

"If I have too much fun, I won't have time to go over

your paperwork, remember? One dance, and then I'll leave you to your own devices while I take care of that for you."

"You're incredible."

"True," he said, then sang along with the record as he swung me around the floor. "Oh, say, let us fly dear. To the sky, dear. Jump in, Miss Josephine! Oh joy, what a feeling. Look how we fly through the sky, so high! Come, Josephine in my flying machine, going up, she goes! Up, she goes!"

He exaggerated the up part, swinging our hands high, and I laughed. He had no idea that I'd flown off my roof yesterday, and I wasn't going to repeat it in this lifetime. It was good to see Lindley smile. He'd recently lost his fiancé and buried himself in work afterwards. She had been my friend. It was a pain we both felt. When the song ended, the honeymooners clapped and stepped outside for some air. Lindley escorted me back to my chair and looked at Mr. Craven and me.

"I'll only be a minute," he promised. "Please make yourself at home."

Charlotte seemed glad for the intermission. I watched her slip away, likely for a drink, and I couldn't blame her. The cylinders were tiresome to attend.

"He does have a live band for the weekends, doesn't he?" asked Mr. Craven. "You won't keep a crowd busy with that old thing. Hard to hear, as it is."

I reached for my glass and spent a minute studying the dregs of my wine, hoping Mr. Craven wouldn't ask where Lindley was going. The maid who'd cleared our plates popped back in and scanned the room in all directions. When she realized it was only Mr. Craven and I left, she crossed over and whispered, "Where did Mr. Lindley go?"

I closed my eyes briefly. "He didn't say," I said. "Why?"

"The chef's furious." She glanced apologetically at Mr. Craven. "The dessert for tonight has vanished, right from under his nose, and he's making another as fast as possible." She put her hands behind her. "It won't be delayed by much, but I can promise it's worth waiting for."

She dashed from the room, and I shrugged at Mr. Craven.

"In that case," he said, patting his well-stuffed waistcoat, "I will take my evening cigar on the veranda and admire the stars."

I hopped up from my chair. "Perfect timing. I'm sure it won't be long. We shouldn't make it too late of a night if you're leaving early tomorrow."

He nodded. "Miss Brown, thank you for a most surprising evening." He crossed the room and let himself out through the veranda door.

I followed him as far as the phonograph machine. A wind-up handle that turned the mechanism operated the glossy little box that held the cylinder, much like the treasured watch I carried in my pocket at all times. My watch was all I had left of my parents, and anything to do with machinery or science or inventions reminded me of our time together before they'd gone down in the Atlantic on a return voyage from England. I looked over the selection of wax cylinders, some black, some pink, a couple dark blue, and admired Lindley's taste in music. But Mr. Craven was right. A resort needed a live band to fill the place.

Footsteps pounded by on the veranda outside, and I looked through the window in time to see a couple of dark shadows streak past, followed by a very tall silhouette. I clearly heard it hiss "Stop!" as they passed, and I went to the door just as a scream pierced the air. The scream was very masculine, if several octaves higher.

I yanked the door open and ran outside and collided with Mrs. Fontaine. She bounced off of me and onto the handrail, but not before I caught a scent of her lilac perfume. "Johnny!" she shrieked as she stood upright. "Where are you?"

The veranda echoed with running footsteps. "Lucy!" called Mr. Fontaine. His strides carried him swiftly to us and, ignoring me completely, he took his fainting bride in his arms.

"Dear God!" cried another voice, and the three of us hurried down the corridor to find Lindley standing at the corner. He was staring at one of the rockers, and the size of its occupant froze me in place, several feet away.

"Should we get our first aid kit, Mr. Peabody?" shouted a boy's voice from around the corner of the veranda.

"Boys! I want you all at the campsite immediately!" replied the voice of Mr. Peabody, undeniably the source of the original scream. I heard a scramble and then watched three boys pelting across the meadow toward a distant campfire.

Another scream erupted from behind the corner, and I saw Lindley tear his gaze from the rocker and say,

"Phone down to Banning. See if you can find the sheriff. Ask for a physician." Then he looked at the rocker again. "And a mortician."

Footsteps receded, and the bride moaned behind me. "Darling," she said, "I think I'm going to be ill." Then she turned to the rail and vomited over it.

I forced my feet to move but refused to look toward the rocker. Lindley stood next to an incredibly tall thin man who was swaying dangerously forward and back. Certain that he was about to faint, I grabbed him by the elbow and dragged him the few feet beyond the corner where the stairs led from the main lobby doors and shoved him down on the top step.

"Put your head between your knees," I said. "Breathe."

Then, I did the impossible and returned to stand beside Lindley. The smell of cigar smoke mingled with that of fresh blood. I stared at Lindley. He stared at the rocker. "No," he said. A plea. A denial. The sound of a soft gurgle made my skin crawl, and I finally stared in grim fascination at the figure of Mr. Craven slumped sideways in his chair.

Or rather, his head was sideways. His throat had been deeply slit, his eyes were wide open in shock. In the moonlight, he appeared to have had too much wine and spilled his glass over himself. His vest and jacket were dark where the wetness soaked in, and his upright collar was no longer white but deep burgundy, matching his tie, still perfectly in place. His hands had fallen to either side of the armrests, the wispy smoke of his recently lit cigar drifted lazily into the air from the floor.

4

SHERIFF

The strident call of a bugle jerked me from a fitful sleep. I sat straight up in bed and realized I was still at Lindley's, and the tune of "Reveille" hadn't finished before I remembered Mr. Craven and the mess I was in.

By the time I joined Lindley, the front lobby was full of people. None of us had been able to stomach our breakfast, and we sat or stood, pale and patient, while Sheriff Fuller and a bevy of deputies spread out to do their duty. Even the dogs were taking the news with fortitude and lay sprawled across the cool stone hearth in front of the fireplace.

"Thank you for gathering, folks," the sheriff said from the center of the room. "This is going to take a while, so get comfortable." Sheriff Thomas Fuller was a middle-aged bachelor who patrolled the mountaintop, twenty miles of twisting road to Banning and twenty miles in the opposite direction to Hemet. His was the office that sat empty most of the time next to the black-smith shop near my hotel.

My hotel. I swallowed and kept the tears at bay. I wasn't making any progress toward that goal after all. As a matter of fact, I thought to myself as I looked around the room, today felt like I was going backward.

There were deputies combing all of Foster's Meadow for anything that might lead to the apprehension of Mr. Craven's assassin. The physician and mortician were doing an autopsy and preparing to take the body down to the South Pacific train station in Banning as soon as possible. You didn't bury important politicians in the nearest convenient plot. Telegrams were being prepared.

The Fontaines looked as resentful as any newlyweds could be, interrupted by the world outside their bedroom door. Mr. Peabody sat opposite them, agitated and unhappy. Ten boys sat cross-legged at his feet, and it was apparent that, short of immediate entertainment, their temporary attention would dissolve. At the moment, all eyes followed the sheriff as he moved about the room taking names and preliminary information, and when he came to their group, the boys instantly shouted over each other, jockeying to be the first contributor.

Lindley's staff stood with him, silent and apprehensive. Resorts rarely had murder on the activity list.

I stood aside, wishing I were anywhere else. So far as I could tell, the only person in the room capable of landing a deadly swipe with a knife was the chef. But what could he have against my lawyer? When the sheriff had had enough of the boys, he turned and locked his bloodshot eyes with mine and came directly over. I groaned to myself.

"Well, good morning, Miss Brown," he said. "Imagine finding you here. Spend the night?"

I nodded.

"I suppose the deceased was in some way connected to you?"

I nodded again.

"I may as well begin with you, then." He sighed with a certain amount of resignation and rubbed the back of his neck. It wouldn't be the first time we'd discussed death.

"Morning, Lindley," he said, turning toward him. "Help me out and bring me some coffee, will you?"

Sheriff Fuller led the way into Lindley's office, and his deputy followed behind. The sheriff and I sat down. "Allow me to introduce you to my new deputy, Garrett MacDougall. Deputy MacDougall, Loveda Brown."

The man standing next to him nodded.

"I have decided that Idyllwild, what with its growing tourism presence and certain recent tendencies toward trouble…" I cringed. "…is in need of a perma-nent representation of the law. Deputy MacDougall is your new neighbor, Miss Brown. Later this afternoon, we'll ride down and open up the office. See what we can do about making it more functional."

I looked back at the new deputy as he flipped pages over in his notebook, preparing to take my statement. He was younger than the sheriff, thirties maybe, average height and build with sandy brown hair and mellow gray eyes. His tidy mustache seemed amateurish compared to the sheriff's full walrus-style one, but, where the sheriff had a short beard, MacDougall was clean shaven, and I finally decided the overall look made him appear modern. It added an air of certainty to his unruffled manner.

"Okay, Miss Brown," the sheriff said, leaning back in Lindley's chair and putting both hands behind his head. "Tell us what we need to know."

Ten minutes later, the sheriff was leaning forward on the desk, his hands around a hot coffee mug, squinting his eyes at me. "You realize Mr. Craven was a high-profile lawyer with connections all over the country, Miss Brown? This is going to be a very messy, publicized event. The pressure for me to bring someone to justice is about to turn my life inside out."

"I'm so sorry, sheriff. I don't understand how it could have happened. We're miles and miles from any city, and only a handful of people are on the mountain. He only arrived Monday night and was leaving again first thing this morning."

"Did he seem uneasy at any time? Mention anyone following him? Discuss complications?" He paused. "Maybe he knew someone up here?"

"As far as I know, Idyllwild was brand new to him, and he made no secret that he was less than impressed by it. He was in a hurry to get my business started and finished before winter set in."

"What is a big shot Tucson lawyer doing in a tiny place like Idyllwild all by himself? Isn't it odd for a lawyer to travel distances like that?"

"Yes. I had to call Boston to get a recommendation for one that would."

The sheriff waited.

"I have the money to pay for it, sheriff. Billy's ranch should be worth thousands, at least."

"Where are Mr. Craven's personal effects?"

"He has a suitcase back at my place in his room, and his briefcase," I blushed, "is here in this office." I looked around and saw the leather case sitting on the side table where Lindley had left it.

"Mr. Craven was in this office last night?"

"No. Only his briefcase." There was no hiding my discomfort. "If you look inside, you'll see a pile of paperwork covered with my signature. I asked Lindley to look it over last night, you know, to have another pair of eyes on it before Mr. Craven left, but I was too embarrassed to ask Mr. Craven for permission. I didn't want him to think I didn't trust him, of course, his being such a big to-do back in Arizona, so I sort of," I glanced at MacDougall, but he was scribbling furiously in his book, "brought it along without asking. Lindley was in here, doing just that when the scream happened."

The sheriff sat up and rubbed the back of his neck again. "When Mr. Craven was discovered on the veranda, where were you?"

"Standing over the phonograph, looking through Lindley's records."

"Was anyone else in the room?"

"No. Everyone had stepped out by then."

"So you can't prove you were there." His voice was flat.

"No." I wasn't going to argue with him. If he thought I was a suspect in a murder, so be it. My future was already as murky as a clam chowder. "Although," I added, "when I stepped outside after the scream, I ran straight into Mrs. Fontaine. So, she can tell you that I was inside. And I can tell you that she was outside. How's that?"

It brought him the slightest bit of relief, I thought, and he said, "Thank you, Miss Brown, I have a long day of questions ahead of me. If you'd be so helpful as to see yourself out?"

He looked at MacDougall. "Bring in the Fontaines, one at a time. The woman first."

He smiled weakly at me as I stood up. "Miss Brown, I don't need to ask you to remain in town, do I? A deputy will come by soon to collect Mr. Craven's belongings. Please touch nothing in his room until the deputy makes his report." I nodded. "Later, when we make it over to the office, I'll duck in to see whether you've remembered anything else that might be useful in the investigation."

"I'll watch for you both," I said, and made my way back into the lobby.

Lindley stepped forward and extended his hands. "I'm so sorry," he said, taking mine. "You were so close to getting your things in order. I didn't even have time to look at the paperwork." He glanced at his closed office door. "When we take care of this, I'll contact my lawyer about finding a way to move your papers forward." He put his chin up. "Hell. I'll be talking to my lawyer today, either way."

"I would think the two of you are close, personal friends by now," a voice I recognized said behind me. I pulled my hands from Lindley's and turned around to see John Wyman walking across the lobby. John, like Mr. and Mrs. Hannahs, lived further up the Banning road beyond Foster's Meadow and near Logan Creek. Forty years old, divorced a lifetime ago and living off the land in a solitary cabin, he had a way of showing up at inconvenient times.

It was because of John that I knew Red, the woman whose hotel I was squatting in. Elizabeth, as I called her now, lived off the land as well, a skill she had from her early days living among Indians. John and Elizabeth looked out for each other.

And sometimes, they looked out for me.

"Good morning, John," Lindley said. "You're right about that. My lawyer is happy every time he hears from me. Can I get you some coffee?"

"No thanks, Walt."

"How did you hear?" Lindley asked.

"Hard to keep secrets up here," John said, looking at me. "Even Mr. Hannahs knew about the dance last night. But it wasn't until this morning when I heard the contingency from Banning pass by that I figured something was wrong."

"We're a spectacle," Lindley agreed.

I didn't like the way John was looking at me, and it had nothing to do with the fact that his frame stood a whole extra twelve inches taller than mine. I decided my irritation had everything to do with the stalled paperwork in a leather briefcase, the large pool of blood on the veranda, and my imminent return to a kitchen with no food in it.

"Lindley, I have to go now. I have to meet a deputy back at the hotel. Thank you for everything." I turned to give Lindley a smile and held out my hand.

He took it and brushed the back of my hand with his

lips. "Courage, partner. I'll let you know how things go around here. Would you like the coach or the buggy?"

"Neither. I'm going to walk. It'll be good for me."

"There's a killer on the loose," he said with a frown. "Not for one minute are you going to walk yourself home."

"You can see it coming on her face, can't you?" asked John. "The look that tells you to go straight to hell?"

Lindley gave him a crooked smile. "Doesn't mean she's going to get away with it."

"That's it," I said and stomped toward the front door. To my surprise, neither of the men came after me, and I went down the veranda stairs with determined strides. It felt good to get out into the fresh air, and I refused to look behind me as I headed for the path that connected Foster's Meadow with my little turn in the road. I didn't want to see the deputies taking pictures of the bloody rocking chair. I didn't want to see the Boy Scout camp with its little flag at half-mast. I had brought nothing with me last night except Mr. Craven's briefcase, but it was hard not to look back at a comfortable room with maid service and a chef.

My little storm of thoughts kept me company as I entered the stand of pines, and I ignored the scrub jays scolding and the squirrels throwing pine cone cobs at my feet as I passed. I froze when I heard the footsteps, though. They stopped when I did, and when I turned slowly around, John was leading his horse a respectful twenty paces behind me.

We regarded one another for a few minutes until I shrugged and motioned him forward.

"Looks like you remembered the way," he said when he joined me.

I reached up and patted his palomino, a beautiful golden gelding, then we moved on together.

"I didn't get a chance to ask your partner what's going on," he said. "You want to fill me in?"

"Ha."

"His words, not mine. You spent the night."

I turned on him fast. "I have the right to do anything I want. But I didn't spend the night because I wanted to. For your information, it was my lawyer who was killed on Lindley's veranda last night, and no one has the slightest idea why." I headed down the path again, but John easily kept up. "He was supposed to be halfway to El Paso by now to liquidate my assets and send the party of the first part packing, but no. Instead, he was wined and dined and then got killed while trying to smoke his cigar."

John put a hand on my shoulder, but I shook it off and kept walking. "Loveda. Hey."

I slowed down a little.

"What else?" he asked.

"You mean there's more than that?" I didn't keep the sarcasm out of my voice.

"Yeah. I think so."

I stopped because the effort to march with indignation was too much when combined with the provocation that he was right. "Lindley has money. He has talent. He's a genius with ideas that never stop flowing." John's face remained impassive as he listened. "He's patient and plans ahead and knows how to charm his guests."

I took a deep breath. "And still, he needs a lawyer every five minutes because horrible things happen and horrible people come to stay and they wreck his property and demand crepes served in bed, and there are bills to pay and how do you know how many tins of tomato sauce to keep in the pantry, John? How? Because I don't have any of Lindley's talents! I can hardly boil water! It took me a week to get ready for Mr. Craven and *I* was paying *him* to be there!"

The only indication that he had heard my words was a single raised eyebrow. Maybe the hint of a smile at one corner of his mouth. I pushed at his chest and he didn't budge. "You're impossible," I said.

"No one said you had to take on the hotel, Loveda."

I walked on in silence.

"You can let it go. Just live there yourself if you want to. Red isn't going to mind, either way. I think she has some peace about you being there." He paused briefly when I cut my eyes at him, then said, "I saw her watching you the other day when you were beating out the rugs. She seems at peace."

"And how did you happen to be watching Elizabeth watching me?"

"I might have been passing through."

"And you didn't stop to help?"

"You're fierce when you're hitting carpets. Only a fool would step into the middle of that."

The path opened out onto the Banning road, at the final turn that passed in front of the hotel. We continued on, and I saw Mr. Hannahs step out onto his landing and look our way. Beyond him, we saw Carlos step out of the blacksmith shop. Both men locked their eyes on me and waited.

"You were missed." John's observation was meant to encourage, but I felt in some way that I'd let them down.

"Loveda," he stopped and gathered the reins together. "Your lawyer's dead. Someone has a grudge worth killing over. Was it a grudge against the lawyer or a grudge against you?"

"Who's mad at me?" I held my palms up.

He swung up on his horse. "Did you mean it about meeting a deputy here soon?"

"Yes. They have to get Mr. Craven's things out of his room. And then the sheriff is moving the new deputy into his office later tonight."

"New deputy?"

"Apparently, we tend to have trouble around here."

"I see." He smiled then. "You're surrounded. Try to behave yourself."

I scowled at his receding back as Mr. Hannahs called out to me, "Miss Brown! I am so happy to see you! Come, tell me what's happened!"

"Good morning, Mr. Hannahs," I sighed. "I'm coming."

5

NEIGHBORS

Carlos Peyote leaned against the hitching post in front of his blacksmith shop, arms crossed, battered fedora shading his dark eyes, as I sat on the bench at the front of the post office next door, explaining the events at Lindley's. The post office landing was wide, to accommodate stagecoach passengers and luggage, but almost always deserted. Mr. Hannahs never left his office when he was on duty, so I sat between the two men to save myself the trouble of repeating everything. The post office screen door was a barrier to the flies, but voices moved freely through it between the office and the landing. I'd taken advantage of that feature more than once.

"You mean to say," Mr. Hannahs said from inside, "that he was all alone and no one knows who did it? It happened that fast?"

"It felt like only a few minutes after he left the room," I said, loud enough for Carlos to hear.

"Terrible business," Mr. Hannahs said at his doorway. "I could see plain enough as I rode home last night that the two of you were having a fine time over there. Hard to miss the group of law men riding by early this morning, though. I rode out at four thirty in the morning to open up and heard them coming up the road behind me. After I got past the spook of it, I realized they were all turning into Lindley's place, not following me."

Carlos was leaning forward to catch the words, but he wouldn't join me on the landing. He kept his own boundaries.

"Carlos over there," continued Mr. Hannahs, "was beside himself when I arrived this morning, and that's when he told me you two had never returned last night."

"I was not beside myself." Carlos turned his lips down. "The hotel has never been vacant. It was unusual."

"I count on you noticing, Carlos," I said quickly. "I wouldn't have the courage to stay here all by myself."

"Courage!" Mr. Hannahs said. "That's what's needed around here."

Carlos stood up straight, and he angled his body to peer into the screen door. His single long dark braid twitched back and forth like an angry cat's tail. "Which one of us went to the back porch over there and got rid of the big rattler under it?"

"I knew there was a snake under my porch!" I jumped up. "Carlos, tell me it's gone forever."

Carlos shrugged and crossed his arms again. "Snakes are territorial. It might come back."

"What about bats?" I asked. "Do bats come back?" I

turned toward the screen door. "I think I have bats in my chimney. I keep hearing scratching noises inside of it."

"Is that what you were doing up on your roof?" Mr. Hannahs exasperated face was clearly visible through the mesh.

I shuddered. "They have curling little scratchy claws. If one flies into the lobby, I won't stop running till I reach the border."

"They won't hurt you," Carlos said. "Maybe it was lost."

"They'll live in chimneys, same as any cave," Mr. Hannahs muttered, and I wrapped my arms around myself.

"Well, they won't anymore," I said adamantly. "I covered the chimney with a cheesecloth."

Carlos laughed. "Keep that in mind before your next fire."

I let that sink in for a minute. Hell was going to freeze over before I climbed that ladder again.

"What matters now, is we all keep an eye open." Mr. Hannahs' voice was grim. "Someone out there is not afraid to use a knife. Miss Brown, are you sure you want to stay in that hotel alone? I know the missus would make room for you until the sheriff finds the killer."

"I know she would Mr. Hannahs, but there's one more thing I need to tell you both. We're about to get a new neighbor. A grand total of three residents. What do you think of that, Carlos? We practically live on Main Street."

"Resident? Where?" Carlos looked up and down the deserted road.

I smiled at his confusion. "Exactly. The sheriff's office." I pointed past him to the little one room building. "I wouldn't call the bars on the windows homey, but it contains a bed." I frowned in thought. "And he might just fit it."

"Do you mean they've caught the killer?" Mr. Hannahs asked.

"No," I said, "At least, not as far as I know." I glanced toward Lindley's. "Sheriff Fuller is at Lindley's right now, of course, but later tonight he's coming by to move in a new deputy. I met him this morning. Garrett MacDougall. He seems a sturdy type. He has more important things than bats and snakes to worry about, now. I'll feel safer knowing he's here." I pulled out my pocket watch and checked the time. "I wonder when they're coming for Mr. Craven's things?"

Carlos wasn't smiling. I noticed his hands, tucked beneath his crossed arms, slowly roll into fists. "Sheriff never said anything about needing another deputy," he said. "I've been helping the sheriff out for years. Always been more than adequate for the amount of funny business around here. He's never said otherwise."

"Carlos, I'm sure he needs you as much as ever," I said. I was sorry to upset him. "I'm sure I do. What would I do without you? When Mr. Craven showed up, I wasn't worried about him being in the hotel with me because I knew you were right there. It's a real comfort to know I can call on you any time for help if there's a problem."

There was no moving Carlos' scowl. "I have to go to work," he muttered, and went into the blacksmith shop. Soon after, I heard the hammering of metal from inside and decided he was as settled as he was going to be about it.

I turned to the screen door. "Mr. Hannahs, I wonder if you can get something for me?" The silhouette behind the screen relaxed a little. "I need the Sears Roebuck catalog and one from Montgomery Ward."

"Have you not purchased cartridges yet?" Mr. Hannahs had a right to be frustrated. He had been asking that question for a while, now. He walked away from the door grumbling, "I may have a copy here, somewhere. If not, easy to bring up."

Mr. Hannahs' assumption was only partially right, but ammunition wasn't at the top of my list. If there was a minute shred of redemption from the posturing Mrs. Fontaine, it was the reminder that I needed new clothes. The few things I had were more for traveling than for hosting guests in the lobby. Nothing I had was suitable for horseback riding, let alone dancing in Lindley's elegant ballroom.

There was nowhere to shop in Idyllwild. No cobbler, no milliner, no tailor. Certainly, no department stores. The only jewelry I owned were two abandoned wedding rings strung on a fine gold chain and hidden beneath my shirtwaist, and I owned a single straw hat. I would have to get at least a few things before winter set in and slowed down the stagecoach.

I stared across the road at the rustling pines as I thought it over, then shook my head in regret. I would order only the basics. The small supply of cash locked away in my trunk would not last forever. Frivolous, pretty things would have to wait. I sighed, and .45s moved back to the top of the list.

"Don't have 'em here," Mr. Hannahs called from behind his door. "But I can have em up tomorrow evening for you."

"Thank you, Mr. Hannahs. I suppose there's no rush."

I turned to the road at the sound of hooves, and a single rider came up to the landing. He tapped his hat and said, "Miss Brown? Sheriff Fuller sent me to collect Mr. Craven's things."

"That's me. I'll talk to you later," I said at the post office door as the deputy dismounted and hitched his horse. "Thank you for coming so soon," I told the rider. "I haven't even been inside yet."

Not that I was looking forward to it. He nodded and gathered his kit from a saddlebag, and when he was ready, I led him over to the hotel and showed him up the stairs. Mr. Craven had not locked his door, and his trust had me ashamed all over again for taking his briefcase without asking. The room was tidy enough, he'd not been in it very long.

I stayed in the hall in case the deputy had any questions. He took copious notes in a little book, inventoried all of Mr. Craven's property, and asked for my input in deciding what was which. Once he was satisfied, he gathered everything he needed and carried it back down the stairs to his patient horse.

"Is there any news yet?" I asked him as he mounted.

"None I can give," he said. "The sheriff is still questioning folks." He nodded. "Miss."

I watched him ride away; the suitcase swaying against his saddle girth and then pushed back through the front door into the lobby. I glanced at the stairs and shook my head. I wasn't ready to face Mr. Craven's room again. Why had Mr. Craven been murdered at Lindley's, surrounded by people, when my place was more isolated? Nothing made sense, but I felt a guilty gratitude that Lindley had been present when it happened. That I had not had to face it on my own.

There had been so much blood.

The kitchen was in disarray, and I picked through the jumble of pantry items and discovered a jar of peach preserves. I popped the lid and spooned them out for my lunch. It was good to feel hunger again, instead of numbness.

I looked over the basket of vegetables that Mrs. Hannahs and I had harvested from the garden the day before. Carrots, potatoes, and radishes. Cherry tomatoes from a dead-looking vine and barely ripe apples from the twisted trees beyond the garden bed. Gravenstein apples, she'd called them, with excitement in her voice. Her home had Pippins and they wouldn't be ripe for another two months.

The Hannahs' raised their family and homesteaded on a hundred acres before selling off portions. Years ago, they had sold all of Foster's Meadow to Lindley and regretted it ever since. When I saw the way Sarah Hannahs went after the radishes, I asked her if she missed cultivating on a massive scale.

"Not at all," she'd laughed, both hands in the dirt. "Gardens are best worked by a passel of children."

It was another sign that gardening had no part in

my future because, so far as it stood, children had no part in my future. It may have briefly crossed my mind in El Paso, but, if the two activities went together, I was content to leave both in the hands of professionals.

I was snapped from my thoughts by a fast rapping on the front door. The large plate glass window in the lobby revealed no one on the veranda, but the knocking was imperative. I swung the door open, and the boy standing behind it gave me a swift salute and said, "Ma'am, I need to know if the apple trees in the back are yours?"

"Apple trees?" I stepped out, and he ran to the corner of the hotel veranda and peered behind the hotel.

I followed him as he pointed and said, "Those trees. We need the apples for the horses, ma'am."

There were two boys climbing an apple tree and two more in the corral behind the blacksmith shop chasing Blue, Carlos' pinto, and Mr. Hannahs' chestnut gelding. A fifth boy stood on the rails and yelled, "Wait for the apples, they'll come to you, I said!"

Carlos exploded from the back of his shop shouting, "Let those horses alone!"

I hurried behind the boy with the yellow bandana as he joined his friends. The two in the tree dropped down, apples in their trouser pockets and in their hands. The two in the corral managed to catch the halter of Carlos' pinto and the boy on the rails climbed to the top so he could hop aboard.

With one glance at Carlos, the boy leapt from the top of the corral to the pinto's bare back. I watched in horror as the pony jerked free of his captors and made three spectacular bucks, jettisoning his rider several feet away. The boy sat up and rolled his shoulders, then smiled at his audience. Blood poured from his mouth.

"Get out of there!" Carlos said, stepping into the corral. The three boys scattered, leaving Carlos to calm the horses.

"What do you mean, running amok like that?" I scolded. "Don't you know you could get hurt?"

The boy with the bloody mouth stepped up. "I ain't hurt," he said, feeling around with his fingers. "Just a busted lip is all." One of his friends clapped him on the back.

All the boys looked about the same age. Ten or eleven years old, at the most. They reminded me very much of the twin boys I'd been a governess for in Boston. Dr. Prost's sons had been full of energy and curiosity, and not always for the better.

"We have one week to earn our badges," the clapper said. "Mr. Peabody didn't let us do first aid on that dead man, and the stablemen back there won't let us in the stable."

"Yeah. This kid in New York already got to the Eagle Scout level," another said, eating his apple.

"You gotta have twenty-one badges to make Eagle Scout!" This from the apple-eater's twin brother, who reached over and snatched the half-eaten apple from him and proceeded to eat the rest.

"Does Mr. Peabody know you're here?" I asked, looking around for a chaperone.

"Nah. He's too busy making the other kids do clean up duty."

"Yeah. They got caught stealing a basket of dough-nuts from the kitchen last night."

"They were so good!" One twin jabbed the boy with the yellow bandana in the ribs, and the other kicked him in the shin.

"We already got our pioneering badge."

"We made up some knots for Mr. Peabody that he couldn't figure out!"

"We're real adventurers!"

The multiple voices spoke over the top of each other, but the only message I understood was that the boys had broken out of Lindley's place and somehow made their way here without anyone noticing.

"But we can get two more badges right here!" Yellow Bandana said. "We need one in horsemanship and one in blacksmithing! This is gonna be the best day ever!"

"Hurrah! Hurrah! Hurrah!" With the final cheer, the boys poured into the blacksmith shop, and Carlos, with a strangled sound, leapt after them.

Morbid curiosity made me follow near enough to peek inside. The boys had scattered, investigating every square inch of Carlos' workspace. Some stirred up the fire with the bellows, and some found hammers and went around knocking on anything they could find with them. A crash announced a tipped over a shelf of horseshoes, and several hands reached out to sort them back into piles.

"Hey mister," the boy with the fat lip said. "I think my tooth is loose."

Carlos watched helplessly while the boy wiggled it back and forth.

"Stop!" Carlos had a big voice when he needed it, and even I shrank back in the doorway. The boys froze in various positions and waited for his follow up. "This is where I work. You can't touch anything. Put it all back."

"How will we learn blacksmithing? We need to know how it works to get our badge."

"Yeah. We need to show Mr. Peabody that we can shoe a horse."

"And ride a horse," added another.

"Do you really cut the horse's hoof? We have knives in our kit back at the campsite."

"We have a hacksaw and some axes, too!"

"Uh oh," the boy in front of Carlos said. He held up his tooth in his fingers.

Carlos looked around him, fists on his hips, and shook his head. I watched him take a long, deep breath. Then he bent forward to meet the boy's eyes and smiled.

Carlos had the exact same tooth missing.

6

SCOUTS HONOR

The Boy Scouts punctuated the next hour with muffled shouts and multiple clanking noises that were mostly shut out by my closed lobby door. I'd extracted a 'scout's honor' promise that the boys would stay out of the apple trees and the corral and left them milling about in the blacksmith shop with a confused Carlos. I stood now, with my back to the lobby window, squinting in speculation at the desk placement.

The lobby had puncheon wood flooring covered by a thick, dirty burgundy and navy-blue carpet. The walls were covered with a dull yellow patterned wallpaper in an attempt at cheerful first impressions. Hung near the bottom of the staircase were a handful of framed old photos of different historical buildings in Idyllwild.

I'd dragged the behemoth of a desk away from the wall with the kitchen door and put it below the staircase, facing the large plate glass window and the front door. The third wall contained an unused fireplace and a door leading to my small bedroom behind it, and my back was to the fourth.

The heavy oak desk was hollow, every single drawer removed, contents spread across the lobby floor, to prepare for a task designed to take my mind off what was happening at Lindley's. When faced with chaos beyond my control, I sought order with something manageable. It helped me think.

The desk was the hotel office on legs, the heart of the operation, and I was about to make it mine. I'd already found the tiny key that unlocked the drawers tucked away behind some decorative pine cones on the narrow fireplace mantle—not the cleverest hiding spot in this place of secrets. Now, each item pulled from the desk was up for scrutiny, and what puzzled me the most at the moment was a missing cash box. The ledgers were all in order, written in the tidy script of the previous owner. A handful of receipts. But no money. I stood with my back to the window and surveyed the room again.

I didn't sleep well in this empty building, though it carried the intimate feel of a home that had simply added a few extra rooms to it. Which it was. This home had been built for seclusion twenty years before and held the story of a family plagued with madness. Apparently, it held some mysteries still.

There was a rapping on the window at my back, and I jumped.

"Yoo-hoo!" called a woman's voice from the veranda.

Turning to look through the window, I saw a woman

who was taller than I was—really, most people were—but her dark brown eyes were merry in her smooth olive-skinned face and they matched the elegant crushed hat perched on her head. It was short brimmed, chocolate brown, and trimmed with tiny beads. I devoured it with my eyes and was only dimly aware that she was dressed in a tidy suit, quite appropriate for making calls.

A small buggy stood hitched at the boardwalk, and I wondered that I didn't hear it pull up. Purple, white, and green bunting decorated the driver's seat.

As I hadn't moved, she went to the door and let herself in.

"Hello, Miss Brown," she said, extending her hand. "Mary Keen. We met last month at Lindley's, remember?"

"Yes," I said, shaking her hand. "I do. And your husband, I think?"

"William. Yes." She looked around at the mess on the floor. "I wanted to stop by and see for myself how you're getting on and bring you some news. I can't stay but a minute." Her eyebrows went up, but her smile remained in place. "You appear to be making progress."

"I'm afraid I can't call it that, Mrs. Keen." The Keens lived in the Hemet direction of the road, two miles away in Mountain Center, where the stagecoach and its driver, Jim Roster, stayed. As the coach alternated its route between Hemet and Banning every other day, the Keens also kept the horses required to change out for the arduous trips. "You must not have heard yet what happened last night."

She smiled behind a gloved hand. "Jim may have mentioned an incident with your roof."

"No, something else." Jim was going to get a piece of my mind next time I saw him. "I hired a lawyer to come up so I could get my estate paperwork started."

"An excellent beginning to any good enterprise."

"Yes. Well, he and I were at Lindley's place last night and—"

"There's a fellow with a good head on his shoulders," she said. "He has plenty to teach you, I'm sure."

"Yes. Mrs. Keen. Last night, my lawyer, Mr. Craven, was murdered on Lindley's veranda." I hated to put it so bluntly.

"What? Murdered? Have they arrested the killer?" She clenched her hands together at her waist and swiveled her head to look out the window. "Is there someone locked up in the sheriff's office? Who's that?"

She recoiled from the window and I saw that a very tall, narrow man had ridden up on a mule. From his perch, his boots could have touched the dirt road without much effort. We watched him dismount and tie up next to Mrs. Keen's buggy.

"I think that's Mr. Peabody," I offered. "He's a camping guest at Lindley's, and his Boy Scout troop is running rampant across the mountain ridge. I'm shocked that anyone would think it a good idea to take on ten-year-old boys for a week in the wilderness."

Mr. Peabody stepped up to the door, took off his hat, and rapped. Mrs. Keen stood aside, and I opened the door. "Hello, Mr. Peabody, please come in."

He looked inside with uncertainty and said without budging, "Hello. I'm not sure we've met?"

I held out my hand. "Not formally, no. I'm Loveda Brown, and I was staying at Lindley's last night."

He started to reach for my hand, but when he heard that, he clutched his suspender instead and said, "Oh, a terrible business, that. Horrifying." He looked sideways at Mrs. Keen. "We've been at the campsite. No idea who was staying at the lodge."

"This is Mrs. Keen, Mr. Peabody," I nodded her direction, "but she lives up the way and only this minute found out what happened."

"How do you do?" His Adam's apple bobbed in his throat. "Some of my boys have gone missing. I can hear their voices in the blacksmith shop over there, but before I collect them, I figured I owed anyone in the vicinity an apology." He frowned. "The boys can be a bit…rambunctious."

Then he focused on the wall-to-wall mess on the lobby floor. "Oh, no! Did they do this? I can make them clean it up. They really don't mean any harm. They move faster than I can find them."

"I see." I couldn't help my smile. "No, this mess is all my own. But they did have a run in with my apple trees and my horse. The apples, they are welcome to, but not my horse."

"I'm so sorry."

"My only real worry is that someone will get hurt. I'm afraid there's already been a lost tooth today, but surprisingly few tears were shed over it."

He looked toward the blacksmith shop in alarm. It was hard to decipher what the various noises coming from it meant.

"Are you leading a Boy Scout troop, Mr. Peabody?" Mrs. Keen asked.

"Yes, ma'am," he said, straightening up. "Theodore Roosevelt believes in building character through outdoor recreation. We have a troop in every state now." His voice was full of emotion. "Only think of the inspiration that young boys will gain. Many of them don't have strong father figures at home, you know."

Mrs. Keen looked skeptical. "And are you, sir, a father?"

His face flushed. "No, ma'am. But I hope to provide these boys an opportunity to find their strengths and become good citizens of these United States of America."

"And what of the girls of these United States of America?"

"Ma'am?"

"The girls. How are they to find their strengths and become good citizens?"

The poor man was so flustered that I felt sorry for him. Mrs. Keen leaned forward. "It's my opinion, Mr. Peabody, that organizations such as these would do well to include the female perspective. I'm a member of the Political Equality League, and we secured equal suffrage only last October in this glorious state. Women who expect to own property, hold jobs, and *vote*, sir, ought to have an early start in their disciplines and apprenticeships with strong women leaders."

I watched Mr. Peabody take the blow and wind up for the return. "Mrs. Keen, is it? Yes. My troop earned their badges in pioneering this week. We traveled by covered wagon, and they built their own lodging by learning how to splice and knot ropes together with wood from the native environment. This week, we'll study everything from stars to stalking. We're even climbing Tahquitz Peak. Is the wilderness truly an appropriate place for ladies of refinement, such as yourself?"

Mrs. Keen drew herself up even taller. "Mr. Peabody, it is the exact place for ladies. The American West was tamed with the blood, sweat, and tears of our pioneering foremothers. We are but the sixth state to give women the vote, and we are certainly not going to let them down now. Our daughters will have a voice."

"You have daughters, Mrs. Keen?"

Mrs. Keen's face grew pale and her chin went up. "No, Mr. Peabody. But if I did, they would not, at this very moment, be racing down the road on an obviously stolen horse."

We all turned toward the road as Carlos' brown and white pinto streaked past the hotel with two boys emitting great whoops of joy and clinging to it like burrs. Mr. Peabody ran to the road, calling after them, and Mrs. Keen and I followed. I heard the door on the post office slam as Mr. Hannahs came out to see, and Carlos stood in front of his shop, a file in one hand, while the rest of the Boy Scout troop around him cheered.

"That's not how it works!" cried Carlos. The boys saw Mr. Peabody marching toward them and quickly formed a straight line and saluted. Carlos wasn't sure what to do with himself, so he backed slowly into the blacksmith shop doorway and Mr. Hannahs vanished altogether.

"Boys!" began Mr. Peabody sternly. "This is absolutely not how it works, as Mr., uh," he looked toward Carlos.

"Peyote," Carlos said.

"Mr. Peyote says. You left camp without permission. You trespassed on private property. You have stolen goods."

There was only one boy left with an apple in his pocket, and he shifted slightly to hide the tell-tale bulge.

"The horse that just went by is definitely not Boy Scout troop property. I'm disappointed, men."

"Sir," Yellow Bandana said, "we're earning our blacksmith badge. Mr. Peyote was showing us how."

"So you took his horse?"

"Sir," added a twin, "it was an accident. Marvin and Frank wanted to work on the horsemanship badge first. Said it was easier, sir."

Mr. Peabody hung his head. Then he looked at Carlos. "I apologize on behalf of our troop. After we bring your horse back, we'll put in the time for restitution."

The boys groaned.

"One of the biggest lessons in life, men," Mr. Peabody said to the lineup, "is the idea that we leave things better than we found them. That we go out of our way to serve our fellow citizens, and if we don't have the time to earn the other badges, you will have earned the pride of a job well done. We must each do our part, gentlemen."

"How are we gonna make Eagle Scout?" a tall boy with freckles said.

Mr. Peabody glowered at him, and they all managed to look acceptably ashamed. He motioned for them to follow and unhitched his mule. He turned to the row of people along the boardwalk and tipped his hat generally to all of us.

"We'll be back. Please be prepared to accept whatever compensation we can offer when we do." He turned to the boys. "Let's go find the horse."

He led his mule and his troop down the road; the line merging into one loose group. The boy with the apple pulled it out and began eating quickly. One twin punched Yellow Bandana on the shoulder. The boy with the fat lip gave it a gentle swipe with the back of his arm.

"Ridiculous," Mrs. Keen said. "This is exactly why we women have to come alongside of them and clean up their mess." She turned to me and smiled, but it only reached her tight lips. "Miss Brown, I wanted to let you know that Mr. Keen and I have decided to open a general store on our property down the road. It's time Idyllwild had somewhere that stocked supplies for sale, and it will be a good business with the tourists coming through."

"Oh!" I couldn't contain my delight. "It's a wonderful idea. I was only asking yesterday about—"

"Yes, it is. At the moment, we will focus on being grocers, but in time, I imagine we'll grow into a mercantile with a diverse range of items. It will depend entirely on the demands of the region. We'll still host the home station for the stagecoach, of course, but I wanted to be sure we had your support. A hotel needs regular supplies, and we'll have them at your fingertips, dear."

She unhitched her horse even as I thanked her.

"I really don't understand," she said with a sniff as

she climbed into her buggy, "why the man had to get personal." She gathered up the reins. "Just because I've never been able to have children doesn't mean I don't have a fervent interest in the future of this country." She turned her horse to the road. "Don't waste your life in a kitchen, Miss Brown."

I watched her trot past the post office and the blacksmith shop, but she only took notice of the yet-empty sheriff's office as she disappeared around the bend in the road.

Carlos still stood in his shop doorway, arms crossed, deep in thought.

"Carlos!" I called, taking a step in his direction. "Are you all right? What about your horse?"

"Nothing I can't put back," he called. "The other horses are safe."

I stared at him, puzzled. I wouldn't have left my beloved Blue in the hands of rascals. A wicked smile spread across his face, and I wondered what horrible thing the boys had done to him. He looked unhinged.

Then I heard it. The slow hoofbeats of a walking horse. Swiveling around, I watched his pinto come back past the hotel riderless and stride purposefully up to Carlos. Carlos reached out and stroked its mane, murmured quiet words into its ears, and, gently taking the halter, he led his horse around to the corral where the other horses whinnied in greeting.

I stood for another minute on the veranda, appreciating the quiet. An afternoon breeze moved through the pines across the road, and their whispers and rustles lent a sumptuous hum to the sunshine that filtered between the branches. I turned to admire the massive oak tree that grew directly in front of the hotel. Its thick, spreading boughs extended beyond the corner of the building and above the roofline, shading the ground floor and second-story bedroom windows and lending a deep shade to half of the hotel.

With a sigh that matched the trees, I let myself inside and went back to work.

7

GUESTS

The desk would have to stay below the staircase. I made the executive decision, knowing that anyone coming down the stairs would be above and behind me, but it was worth trading for a direct view out the window and anyone approaching the front door. I didn't like surprises.

As the afternoon wore on, I'd replaced the drawers, each one examined for secret panels or stray keys that might be taped beneath it. All the contents were gathered up in a single wooden crate on the floor next to it, and I slogged my way through the pile, crunching on the carrots from the kitchen, deciding what to keep.

Four filled ledgers and two empty ones went into a side drawer and the pens, pencils, blotter, and three stamps went into the narrow one above it. The guest book remained open on the desktop and beside it went the small lamp and a large leather desk pad. I held a silver letter opener in my hand, admired my initials on the handle, then placed it in the rubbish bin.

I considered everything for a minute, then rose from the chair and, crossing the lobby, went through the far door into the bedroom I'd claimed. I didn't linger. I got my revolver and brought it back to the desk. It was cool and heavy in my hands and reminded me of the good days in El Paso when I'd learned to shoot it.

With today's conversations fresh in my mind, it made more sense to keep the gun handy in my desk.

A movement out the window caught my eye, and I congratulated myself on the view from my seat as four white horses brought a white coach past my hotel and pulled up at the post office landing. Lindley's coach was a spectacular sight. I rose and went to the window to look at it. The wheels were white, the trim was gold, the driver wore white, down to his leather gloves. My hand moved nervously to the chain at my neck as the driver climbed down from his perch. He was breaking a very strict rule about Lindley's coach.

Sure enough, I heard Mr. Hannahs shouting and debated whether to go out and investigate or stay hidden behind my door. I chose the latter; I'd already had a long day of it. Mr. Hannahs' grudge against Lindley went all the way back to the day he sold Foster's Meadow to the entrepreneur. The Hannahs were not in favor of progress or tourism as a rule. The Hannahs never went near Lindley's hotel, and Lindley was never, ever to park his white coach in front of the post office.

I wondered what the special occasion was and pulled back from the window. It was time for tea. As I stepped in front of the door, it was pushed open, and Mrs. Fontaine barged into me.

"For heaven's sake!" she cried, untangling her parasol and silk purse strings from the small valise in her hands. I took two steps back to steady myself.

"Are you hurt?" asked Mr. Fontaine, directly behind her. He dropped the suitcase in his hand onto the veranda with an undignified thump and reached for her elbow, but she shook him off.

Her hat was almost as wide as the doorway, a fine white muslin with black peacock's feathers floating over it, and as she reached up to feel for her hat pin, her eyes met mine. "You," she said. "Where have I seen you before?" Her eyes swept the lobby, and her nose twitched. "This is a hotel?"

Mr. Fontaine reached back for his case and came inside, nudging his wife forward. "Hello, there," he said. "We've come from the Lindley Resort, which has closed down, and the man himself assured us that we could find accommodations here. That's his coach outside, you see," he nodded toward the door. "Our trunks and things are being unloaded. I say, are we in the right place?" He paused and looked at the dusty mantle, the dingy carpet, the faintly spotted window, my box of flotsam next to the desk.

How had I not seen this coming?

"There's been some mistake," Mrs. Fontaine said. "I can't stay here."

"But darling," the husband said, with a careful hand on her sleeve, "a man's been murdered. You were in hysterics only an hour ago over staying anywhere near the crime scene, and the sheriff made an enormous concession allowing us to go even this far away until the killer's been caught." He frowned at me. "Is this or is this not a hotel?"

"Yes," I said, "the only one left. I'm afraid I wasn't expecting you, but as there are no other guests here, you may have the pick of any room upstairs that suits you." This was not going to be good.

Lindley's coachman stood on the veranda, a large case in each hand, and Mr. Fontaine said, "There you are. Let's pop up and see what we make of the place. On you go, darling."

Darling's lips were pressed tightly together to keep from crying, but she stuck out her chin and led the way up the narrow staircase, followed by the gentleman and the coachman. I listened as they bustled from room to room, their endeavors punctuated with agitated statements. "Only five doors? Why, the rooms are smaller than our closets back home. No windows! None! I would suffocate in my sleep!" After a few more minutes, Mr. Fontaine came back down and said, "We will take the rooms on the right."

"Rooms?"

"Yes, the corner one for sleeping and the one next to it for our luggage. They are the only rooms with windows."

The coachman passed empty-handed and returned again with a trunk in his arms and hefted it upstairs.

Mr. Fontaine bent over the desk and signed the guest book. "But, I thought you said there were no other guests?" He pointed to the extreme curves of the signature above his.

"No. This gentleman checked out last night." If the Fontaines didn't recognize me or connect me to Mr.

Craven, it was all for the better. I didn't need any more drama on my doorstep.

"I see," Mr. Fontaine said. "Now as to the matter of payment." He reached into his breast pocket for a scrap of paper and handed it to me. "As we had already paid Mr. Lindley in full for the week, he assured me that you would agree to the transferring of funds from himself, and we could continue as paid in full through this Saturday."

I opened the paper and realized it was a blank receipt on which Lindley had scrawled, "I'll square it with you tomorrow. WL."

I closed my eyes briefly. I had no idea what to charge for guests and no idea what Lindley charged, but I imagined there was a big discrepancy based on actual amenities, and even with two rooms taken, Lindley was going to give me more than I deserved.

Lindley's coachman passed again with another suitcase and a leather hatbox.

On the other hand, maybe Lindley was going to owe me.

"Yes, Mr. Fontaine," I said, "this will do. Thank you. I'm Loveda Brown." I rose from my chair and extended my hand. He shook it affably. "Here's the key to your rooms. Make yourself comfortable. I'll just step out and help the coachman."

I followed the man in white as he exited the hotel yet again and followed him to the landing. Mr. Hannahs stood there, red in the face, having run out of words, fists on hips, waiting for the abomination to move on. The coachman lifted down yet another hatbox, this one made of white card and elaborately trimmed with brocade ribbon, and I took it from him.

"Is this the last of it?" I asked.

He nodded and climbed into his seat. "But, is there no other message from Lindley?" I called up, trying to keep the desperation from my voice. He shook his head, took off the brake, and turned his team for home.

I stood next to Mr. Hannahs with both arms hugging the hatbox, willing myself to stay calm.

"There's been some mistake," I said aloud. "She can't stay here."

Mr. Hannahs looked at me.

"What am I supposed to do with them?" I asked. "What am I supposed to *feed* them?"

"We've had more excitement on this road in the last few hours than we've had in years," Mr. Hannahs said, disapproval in his tone. "I'm going inside."

I went back to the hotel and set the hatbox on my desk. The upstairs hall echoed with angry sentence fragments that I tried to ignore as I fished out the last few items from the wooden crate that I wanted to keep and then carried the still half-filled box into the kitchen and set it on the floor. I was up a creek.

THE STOVE LOOKED INNOCENT ENOUGH, but I knew that it would take a solid hour to simply get the wood fire down to a set of coals that could heat water. I held my breath as I opened the back door and stepped gingerly over the wooden porch and down to the corner of the hotel. We stored stacks of firewood beneath the front veranda where it opened at the side, and I took an armful back into the kitchen without waking up the snake.

Several matches later, the fire caught. I had just opened the kitchen door to get rid of the smoke, when voices in the lobby began calling out. Closing the stove door and silently begging the fire to hurry, I stepped back into the lobby to see the Fontaines waiting for me.

"Are we on fire?" asked Mrs. Fontaine. "Should we run up to save our things?" She drew one entire side of her face up in derision as she pulled on her second glove. She stared pointedly at her stray hatbox left on my desk.

"No problems at all, Mrs. Fontaine," I said. "Preparing for supper." The forced smile on my face fooled no one, myself included. "We serve it fashionably late here. Around seven or so."

"Your chef follows the Paris customs, does she?" Mrs. Fontaine softened the slightest bit.

"We're going out for a stroll," Mr. Fontaine said, "to clear our heads and see whether we can put the recent events behind us. Are there any places of interest immediately nearby?"

My sooty hands crept behind my skirts to hide, and I bit the inside of my lip to stay focused. "Yes," I said, "if you follow the road past the buildings and turn to the left, you'll find a very pretty spot where Strawberry Creek forms a little waterfall." I blinked several times as they turned to the door. "It's not much taller than six feet high, but you can get quite close without wetting your shoes."

"Thank you," he said, and he ushered his wife out into the late afternoon sunshine.

I swiped my nose without thinking and streaked my face. With a sound of disgust, I went back into the kitchen. The place was absolutely medieval. The last time I'd worked in a kitchen, I'd been giving a chemistry lesson that ended in an explosion. As a governess, I understood that hands-on education, especially in the area of science, required the chemical elements usually found in a kitchen. Cooking was simply further experimentation. I sincerely hoped I would be able to keep my eyebrows during the process.

I pulled a heavy dutch oven from below the sink and pumped water into it. When I hefted it onto the hot stovetop, water slopped over the edge and created a hissing smoke, running through the cracks around the several pothole covers along the backside. The only knife in the kitchen was as long as my forearm, but I didn't have time to go looking for anything smaller.

Tipping potatoes out of the basket onto the table, I whacked at them. An ax would have been a more dignified tool. Most of the potatoes went into the warming water. I was on my hands and knees retrieving the runaway pieces, when a loud knock landed on the door behind me. I looked up to see an inquisitive face peering in, riding quite high in the doorframe, and topped with a crown of thick, silvery gray braids.

"Hello in there," the woman said. Her voice was low and guttural, and as she leaned in, her person filled the entire available space. Astonished, I stood quickly and wiped my hands on my skirt.

"You didn't answer my knock outside," continued the woman. "This may be the right place, but you might not be the right person." She backed up as I approached, and I pushed through the door to stand in the lobby with her.

She was easily a foot taller and a foot wider than I was, but completely in proportion. Her traveling cloak pinned over her dress added even more bulk to her presence. At her sensible sturdy shoes was a carpetbag and a suitcase, and in her hand was a black umbrella.

"May I speak with the hotel proprietor?" she asked with a smile.

"It's my place at the moment," I said, frantic to collect my thoughts. "Loveda Brown, and I'm terribly sorry, but I have to work in the kitchen right now, and the only rooms available are on the left side upstairs." I was breathing hard, but I couldn't help it. "And supper is at least an hour away." I frowned. "Although I have no idea what it will be."

"Ah me, but you misunderstand."

I shook my head. "No. No, I'm sure I don't know what we'll have, but potatoes are on the menu!"

She tipped her head to one side in consideration, but I had no time for a discussion. Pointing at the staircase, I ducked back into the kitchen. I was lifting a double handful of carrots out of the basket when another set of hands reached over my shoulder and took a pot from the wall. I spun around to see the newcomer in the kitchen, cloak removed, apron donned, setting the pot onto the stove.

"You need to knock the fire down a level," she said, and taking the poker from beside the stove, she opened the oven door with her apron-wrapped hand and did just that.

I stood there another minute, clutching the carrots to myself, until she rose again and put the poker away. Her presence filled the breadth and width of the area so that I felt pinned against the little table. She held a square, calloused, and self-assured hand out for the carrots.

"You need a cook." Her statement carried a hint of accusation.

"Aren't you a guest?" I stammered.

She rummaged in her skirt pocket. "Here we are," she said, then pulled out my newspaper ad, crumpled and sweaty, the print already worn off along the edges. "This is you?" she asked, waving it around in my direction. "Asked the coachman three times if it were you, and he guaranteed to take me to the right spot." She pocketed the ad again and took the carrots away from me, then turned to wash them in the sink.

"Nice place, sure. Small for a hotel. But you said up to twenty folks, and that's on the smaller side of what I've done back in the day." She gave a brisk nod. "It'll do just fine."

"Um. Well." I almost knelt back on the ground to pick up my errant potatoes, but thought better of it. "I was expecting applicants to write me with their qualifications, not show up on the doorstep."

She chuckled and turned back to the table, and I hustled out of her way. She shook her head over the size of the knife but began to cut up the carrots with a deft rhythm of her wrist. The pretty orange buttons were a mockery next to my potato lumps.

"How many for supper?" she asked, her back to me again as she peeked into the Dutch oven.

"Four, counting yourself. But…"

"Out you go, then. Set the table or some such thing, and we'll let this supper be my calling card." She smiled when she turned to see my face. "The coach brought me in the nick of time, I see. You might want to have a wash up."

I put a finger to my cheek and rubbed at the soot. Torn between thanksgiving and deep misgivings, I backed out of the kitchen and nearly tripped over her luggage. She'd tossed her cloak over my desk next to the hatbox, and I lifted it to see her clear, tidy signature in the guest book.

Karine Halvorsdatter Torkelson. San Francisco.

The carpetbag at my feet shifted, and I jumped. Horrified, I watched the handles twitch, and I picked up the umbrella. Reaching forward as far as my arms could stretch, I released the catch with it. A pink nose parted the carpetbag, followed by the whiskers, eyes, and body of a giant gray striped tabby cat. It came out of the bag in a single, fluid bound and stretched itself, bowing low and unfurling its tail several inches in the opposite direction, before sitting back up to look around the lobby.

From within the kitchen, a low humming accompanied the sounds of clanking pans and crackling fire, a melody I was unfamiliar with. The cat sat down in the middle of the carpet and gave its complete and dedicated attention to grooming itself, putting every hair into its proper place, purring low and contentedly in accompaniment with his mistress.

8

KARINE

The Fontaines sat outside on the veranda, lingering over their after-supper drinks and watching for the moonrise. The dusk had deepened into the blackness only a mountaintop wilderness could offer, but the couple had requested no lights on, even in the lobby at their backs. Mr. Hannahs had locked up the post office and ridden home while we dined. The blacksmith shop was closed for the night as well, and I imagined Carlos in his little room above it, content with his simple meal for one.

"That," I said as I brought the last fork into the kitchen from the empty dining room, "was amazing. Magic."

The large woman chuckled and continued washing up. She moved with amazing efficiency. "It was nothing but good, honest food," she said. "The fresh air up here would give anyone with the sense of a butterfly a healthy appetite."

The two of us had eaten in the kitchen between the

courses that I'd served the honeymooners in the dining
room. I'd delivered crisply fried salmon patties decorated with sprigs of carrot top, potatoes in a white
sauce, puffed rolls that resembled popovers, and baked
apples stuffed with prunes and wrapped in pastry. The
drinks in their hands were a combination of some
alcohol from the pantry and fresh sprigs of mint, and I
hadn't yet tasted the one in my glass on the sideboard. I
surrendered the fork and took a tentative sip, feeling
the cool liquid warm my throat as I swallowed.

"Miss Torkelson," I said, "as surprised as I am to
meet you, I hope very much that you are going to stay."

Her laughter boomed across the kitchen and out the
open back door. "Ah me," she said, washing the fork
and setting it with the others drying on a cloth, "none's
called me that since the grand day I left Minnesota
township, and that's going on thirty-some years. No,
dear, call me Karine, my solid, given, Christian name,
and leave off the Miss if you please, as I've been going
with Mrs. for those thirty years in question."

She wiped her hands on her apron and surveyed the
room. "I'll be giving this place a going over tomorrow,
and that's certain. Seems to be all here, but not in a
place that's handy, if you know what I mean."

"Well, just Karine, is it? I haven't cleared out the
little room where you put your things earlier, but you
must tell me what you need and toss out whatever it is
that doesn't suit you. I suppose you agree on the
payment amount I posted, or you wouldn't have simply
hopped on the coach and come." I took another long sip
of the cooling drink. "That might have been an actual
issue for me, though, if this couple hadn't arrived on

the doorstep ahead of you. They'll provide your first paycheck. Although, I think they'd rather be anywhere else after the murder last night." The words had rolled out unbidden, and I gasped at my own crassness.

She rested her hands on her wide hips and considered my statement.

"Sounds like you've a story to tell." She took off her apron and hung it by the open door.

"Let's sit in the lobby," I suggested. "It's dark, but cooler, and I need to watch for the sheriff when he rides by."

"That'll do," she said, following me through the door. She pulled up the only other chair in the lobby next to my desk, and together we looked out through the big unadorned window into the Idyllwild evening. The thick stand of pines across the road held up a sky full of stars, and the single oak tree bough that graced the top edge of window displayed a handful of perfectly still leaves. Framed in the window's bottom were the backs of Mr. and Mrs. Fontaine's heads, bent toward each other in quiet conversation.

After I explained the crisis with Mr. Craven, Karine sat for some time thinking it over. The moon was up and cast shadows into corners.

"And this couple here, were on the veranda, too?" she asked, nodding at the window. "We aren't suspecting either of them, are we?"

"Yes. And no. That is, I can't picture them violent over anything more important than a missing glove." I tapped the hatbox in front of me with a finger. "This needs to go upstairs immediately." I considered doing so, but my legs felt heavy, and I remained in my chair.

"It was a knife, you said," Karine's hushed voice was quite matter of fact. "Easy enough for anyone to get. The one in your kitchen would do, as well."

I startled in the shadows. "Surely you don't think…?"

"No," she said after some deliberation. "You needed him alive. But I must wonder why anyone would kill someone new to town so quickly."

"Please don't leave!" It terrified me that she might, if she felt as though she were in danger herself. "The sheriff will be here any minute with our new deputy. He'll be right here." I hiccupped.

I heard her softly chuckle. "I'm not easily frightened," she said, "and you'll not be used to liquor." My glass was almost empty.

She shifted on the overstuffed armless horsehide chair. It was a couple of inches too narrow for her on either side, but it had not collapsed beneath her yet. "A spinster of thirty has but two choices in the town of my childhood," Karine said. "It was spend the rest of my days on the farm feedin' my brothers, or head West." Her smile was attractive in the night light, creases smoothed in the dark, and her large eyes were mischievous in a broad, approachable face. "I was a mail-order bride."

My silence encouraged her. "Exchanged letters with a gentleman in San Francisco, and I put myself on a train. Never looked back. If the man turned out to be other than he'd advertised, and he did, well, I had some considering to do. A married woman has more options than unmarried, as you likely know, and taking on his name was a business decision I don't regret."

The Fontaines were having heated words on the veranda, and I had to force myself to listen carefully to Karine. Her voice sounded far away, and a sour smell came from her general direction. Cooking was a thankless task.

"But," she said, "it was business. Husband on paper only, and I became the cook for a conglomerate of gold miners. Went on well enough, ended up in Chinatown later. Thought I'd retire there. The earthquake destroyed that dream. Went up in smoke."

"Earthquake?" My head felt thick. I thought about chief Tahquitz.

Karine looked at me like I had two heads. Maybe I did. "The earthquake of 1906? Brought the entire world down around our ears. Barely made it out alive. Been on my own since, working my way south. Haven't found a suitable place until now. I think I'll enjoy a winter with a little snow to remember home by."

Her enormous hand landed on my shoulder. "And good it is to find you here, exactly as advertised, may I add. Miss Brown? Are you okay?" She shook me gently.

I mumbled an affirmative.

"Were you waitin' for the sheriff?" she asked. "I think he just rode by."

I rubbed the cobwebs from my eyes and tried to focus out the window. The moon was overhead, and I saw the figures of the couple on the veranda get up from their chairs. They raised their voices to the point where we could clearly hear their words.

"What were you doing on the veranda with the maid, then?" Mrs. Fontaine said.

"Nothing, I say, the dark must have confused you," he replied.

"I saw what I saw! Right before those wretched boys ran into me, I saw you and the maid kissing!"

He snapped at her. "I was walking along the veranda for some air. You gave me leave to do so. I did see a maid out there, but we never even spoke. Perhaps it was a trick of the lights coming through the ballroom windows. Shadows and such, you know."

Mrs. Fontaine began to weep, but her voice was angry. "Your heads were together. The minute you noticed me, you walked away quickly, and the maid approached to ask if I needed something." Her chin went up. "I don't interact with the help. This was squarely on your shoulders. I sent her away on some fabricated errand and got rid of her. But you…" Her tone was icy. "You need to explain yourself."

Mr. Fontaine stood erect. He could have been carved from marble in the moonlight. "I am many things, Mrs. Fontaine. Faithful is at the top of the list. I will not stoop to argue my fidelity when I have only just pledged it to you for eternity. If you will excuse me," he said, choking on his words, "I'm going to get some air."

Mrs. Fontaine stood for some minutes, watching him walk away. She took a couple of deep breaths and opened the lobby door. She stepped inside and startled, surprised to see us sitting there in the dark.

"I'm retiring," she said abruptly, and marched past us up the stairs.

"Lover's spat," Karine said quietly. "Praise be to God I never had to have one of those." She took my glass and stood up, saying, "I'll make you some tea."

She went into the kitchen, flicking on the lights as she went. The sudden brightness was overwhelming, and I had a hand over my eyes when I heard the front door open again.

"Miss Brown? Checking in with you like I said I would this morning."

I parted my fingers and peered between them at the sheriff and the deputy. They removed their hats and stepped inside, and I attempted to shake off my lethargy. I smiled brightly at them and got a look of concern for my effort. It occurred to me that the deputy was incredibly handsome.

"Hello, Deputy MacDonnell," I said. "I'm so happy you'll be living with us."

The deputy went very still as the sheriff said, "Miss Brown, we've finished questioning everyone on Lindley's property. It's a fair amount of people, but there are others we need to think about. Do you have a few minutes to talk to us?"

"Oh, yes," I said, "Karine and I were just discussing it." I leaned toward the deputy and lowered my voice. "Do you know I have a knife in my kitchen as long as my arm?" I nodded sagely. "Anyone could've done it."

I'd leaned too far over and used the edge of my desk to pull myself upright again.

Karine walked in with a hot mug, which she set in front of me. "Drink."

"Karine Torkinson, this is the sheriff and Deputy MacDingal. They're here to talk about the murder." I nodded and reached for my tea. "And this is my new cook, sheriff. She's amazing."

The men and Karine sized each other up as I sipped.

"I suppose we'll take her word for it," the sheriff said. "Are you aware that a man was murdered last night right down the road?"

"Yes," Karine said, "and I'm thinking a lawyer like that must have some friends in high places. Some enemies in low places, too. Unless," she said with a glance in my direction, "Miss Brown does. Does she?"

They all looked at me, and I attempted to look as innocent as possible and then gave up the effort and went back to my tea.

"We can't rule out a political crime," the deputy said. "We have a lawyer coming up tomorrow to go over his papers, and we still have the rest of the community to talk to. Sometimes the politics are so close to home, they are overlooked."

"The deputy is new to Idyllwild," the sheriff said. "He thinks everyone is a suspect, including his own mother."

The deputy smiled. "I'll take that as a compliment."

"That's right," I said approvingly. "Never trust anyone except your dog."

The sheriff smiled then. "Miss Brown," he asked, "do you think that the local, um, wanderer, Red, might have a part in this?"

I sat up straight and stared at the hat in his hand. "No. She wasn't anywhere near there."

"Yet she is known for wandering through. You have to understand that, with her history, it's not a stretch to include her for consideration."

I felt very defensive. Why was the sheriff picking on Red? "You couldn't find her to ask, anyway. John might be able to explain better." I ran out of words. If they wanted to know more, they would have to talk to John. I watched the deputy write something down in his notebook. Were his eyes gray or were they blue?

"And was anyone else in contact with Mr. Craven while he was here?" asked the sheriff.

A vision of Mr. Craven's arrival popped into my head, and I laughed. I leaned back in my chair and laughed until tears were in my eyes. "Yes," I finally got out, "he saw Mr. Hannahs and Mr. Roster and he saw me in my knickers."

No one had a response for that information, and I returned to my tea.

The deputy murmured something as he scribbled away in his book.

"Miss Brown," the sheriff said, "can you think of any unusual, suspicious, or threatening behavior around your place in the last few days?"

"Yes," I said at once. Everyone leaned in. "Yes. There was a theft right here today, took my apples and then stole Carlos' horse. I can't understand why no one's done something about it." I shook my head. How could the sheriff chase after people who had done nothing and ignore the rapscallions right under his nose?

"Who, Miss Brown?" The cute deputy had such a passion for fighting crime.

"The Boy Scouts. They're a danger, deputy. You really must look into it."

I didn't know what they thought about my revelation. I didn't even remember going to bed.

9

MACDOUGALL

W hen I walked gingerly into the kitchen the next morning, Karine clicked her tongue at me and handed me more tea.

"What you want is nothing stronger than cooking sherry," she said. "I'll remember that in the future. How's your head?"

"Pounding, thanks," I said. I started to lean against the table and jumped up again. Karine's cat was lying there, stretched out across most of it, eyes rolled up in its head, motionless.

Karine saw the look on my face and laughed. "Come along, Spoon, let's get." She lifted the sleeping feline over her shoulder and deposited him in the lobby. She chuckled as she came back in. "I know how to cook a lot of things," she said, going back to the sink, "but I draw the line at cats."

When I recovered sufficiently, I asked, "The Fontaines must still be asleep?" The hotel was eerily quiet for having guests in it.

Karine shrugged. She was systematically scouring every pot and utensil in the room. "I wouldn't expect otherwise," she said, "with Mr. Fontaine not getting in until the wee hours this morning. Must've been some walk he went on."

My stomach heaved, and I stepped through the open back door and breathed in the fresh morning air. Carlos was feeding the horses across the way, and I noticed a new horse among the others, black, with three socks. The steady tapping of a typewriter came from the post office window.

"There are muffins in the dining room. You might get yourself one before you go to your appointment," Karine said.

"What appointment?" I wondered if I was expecting something on the coach and pulled my pocket watch out to check the time. "The coach has come and gone already."

"The one you made last night with Deputy Doodle." Karine gave me a quick look over her shoulder. "When you agreed to help him solve the murder." She enjoyed the horrified look on my face. "I believe you two are going to begin with the Boy Scouts."

"Oh, Karine, no. I made a fool of myself last night!"

"You were, to be fair, completely honest."

"Did I really call him that?"

"And several others. I got off easy, I'm thinking."

I hung my head and swore to myself that I'd never drink again. What must he think of me?

"Chin up, dear," Karine said. "I believe he's quite looking forward to seeing you."

I determined to turn over a new leaf as of that

minute. Was I running a respectable hotel, or wasn't I? I was a local now, a member of the community. I was a pillar of support. The new deputy had to look to me for guidance. The ticking watch in my hand was a gentle reproach from my father, admonishing me with his favorite line.

"Look to the future, darling girl!"

I glanced at the inscription on the inside of the watch plate. "My dear colleague, from Dr Prost", it read. Dr. Prost was the man who hired me on as a governess after my parents died. The man who recommended Mr. Craven. He believed in me, too.

Somebody had messed with the wrong girl.

I thanked Karine and went into the dining room for a muffin. The apples and spice in it melted in my mouth, and for one moment, as my eyes rolled up in my head, I understood the cat's position. I stepped back into the lobby to look for the misjudged creature and discovered it lying on top of the forgotten hatbox, teasing at the ribbon. Here was my first step toward a more conscientious life.

"Apologies," I said, waving my hands in his direction. "I have to put that away." The huge cat stared at me in defiance.

Tucking my watch safely away into the desk, the cat and I had a skirmish that extended across every inch of desktop as I lunged and feinted, trying to avoid nips and the swiping claws. Finally, with an insulted hiss, Spoon leapt to the floor. I didn't command the respect he gave his mistress, but at least I wasn't bleeding.

"Sometimes you have to get the job done," I told him, "and you don't have to make a fuss about it."

The cat accepted my apology by wrapping around my ankles, purring, as I lifted the box. "You're apologizing, too, are you?" I asked. Cats were bizarre creatures.

It was no simple task to walk upstairs with a cat under my feet, but I made it to the first door on the right without stepping on him. When I swung the door open, I almost shrieked out loud. I dropped the box on the floor inside and grabbed the cat before he could follow. I tiptoed backwards and quietly closed the door, then padded quickly back down the stairs. Mr. Fontaine was sleeping in the second room. After waiting for my heart rate to slow, and hearing nothing, I decided I hadn't woken him up.

Blasted honeymooners. Even the cat walked away, offended.

I took another muffin to bolster my courage, and stepping out to the veranda, walked toward the sheriff's office, eating it. It was going to be another long day.

As I approached the small one-room building at the end of the boardwalk, a voice carried through the propped open door. Deputy MacDougall sang a tune as he stepped outside and gave a shake to the bed quilt in his hands.

"When Irish eyes are smiling, sure tis like a morn in spring," he sang before he caught sight of me. He hesitated, then, gathering the quilt under one arm, he stepped forward and held out his hand. "Good morning, Miss Brown," he said, curiosity plain on his face. "How are you?"

I shook his hand hard to emphasize my words. "I'm fine, Deputy MacDougall, thank you. I believe we have an appointment for today?"

"You remembered! Excellent! If you'll give me one minute, I'm just putting myself to rights." He turned to spread the quilt over the small bed inside. Normally, the room held a bed, a cane-backed chair, and a desk with its own wooden chair. The original purpose of the sheriff's office was to hold criminals until they could be taken down the mountain to the Hemet jail. The two windows had bars across them, and the door could only be locked from the outside. Now, there were boxes and bags piled in the corners, and the remains of his breakfast and his shaving kit on the desk. He'd tacked a small mirror to the wall. A pipe sat on a narrow shelf beside it.

"Sheriff Fuller is staying at Lindley's place," he was apologetic. "He has considerable more space there. Not," he hastily assured me as he shifted some boxes onto the bed and cleared the desk, "that I'm complaining. This is an excellent opportunity for me. Willing to put up with anything for the chance to solve a murder, you know."

"Deputy MacDougall..." I began from the doorway.

He immediately stopped and turned to me. "You must call me Mack. After last night, it's the least you can do." He watched the color rise in my face with satisfaction and said, "Easier all around, and it's what my friends call me back at the Hemet station, so I shall feel more at home, you see. Caught a lucky break, interviewing with the sheriff right as this case came in. Can you pop that chair inside? We should attempt some discretion, even in a quiet place like this. There we go."

He'd moved around to his desk chair, and I pulled the other inside, letting the door close with a thud. The open windows were the only relief in the tight space.

He waited for me to sit down, then sat down himself. He had pleasant manners, and now that we faced each other properly, I could confirm the color of his eyes. Gray.

With his notebook open, he leaned forward, a pencil in hand, and said, "Miss Brown, we shall let ladies go first. You were adamant about the Boy Scout troop. Can you tell me why?"

I blushed again. "They were more of an annoyance than a criminal presence, uh, Mack. While I believe them capable of almost anything, murder isn't one of them."

"We questioned their leader, a Mr. Peabody," he consulted his earlier pages, "who hails from Beaumont, on the outskirts of Banning. Says the Boy Scout troop gathered from the local areas, a variety of backgrounds. He seems to feel a strong male role model is essential to American youth. Committed to this vision." He looked up from his notes. "Mr. Peabody discovered the deceased first. His shouts brought the others to the scene of the crime."

"That's right, I saw him run past the windows, chasing the boys. Why?"

He turned a page. "Mr. Peabody says three of his boys snuck over to the resort and pilfered a basket of doughnuts. He noticed them missing from their campsite, the remaining boys confessed to knowing about the plot, and Mr. Peabody came to retrieve the errant boys. Witnessed them exiting the kitchen, basket in hand, began a pursuit that ended at the veranda corner where the victim sat. The boys were sent back to the campsite at that point. Assumed the basket went with them."

"What did the chef say? The knife had to come from somewhere."

"Chef claims he and a maid—Molly is her name—were working in the kitchen at the time of the murder, when a basket of doughnuts was taken from the kitchen table." He looked up at me. "As you pointed out last night, the knife could belong to anyone. But the chef claims that all of his knives are accounted for. None were missing."

"Molly came into the ballroom and told me that the dessert was missing," I recalled, trying to avoid the mention of last night, "and that was between the boys' theft and Mr. Craven leaving the room."

"What was she doing out of the kitchen?" Mack flipped through his pages, and I congratulated myself on the detour.

"She was trying to report the theft to Lindley, but Lindley had gone to his office," I said.

"Yes. Here it is. The maid exited the ballroom into the lobby and approached the office, which was open but empty. She returned to the kitchen through the dining room. Claims to have never been on the veranda until screams began and everyone had gathered."

"And the other maid? Charlotte?"

"My notes indicate that Mr. Lindley has only two maids at the moment, one recently promoted to receptionist, and an advertisement placed to hire a third."

"Yes," I interrupted, "the receptionist is Charlotte."

"The one in the kitchen then, this Molly, is acting as a general maid for the resort. Apparently, help in the kitchen is only a small part of her duties. I assume you are asking about the receptionist?"

"Yes. Charlotte was running the phonograph."

"Ah, a fun contraption. I have a secret fondness for mechanics, Miss Brown, if you must know, I've got a kit here," he leaned over and looked around the room, "with the very latest crime solving tools. Can't wait to use them. Have you heard of the fingerprint technique?"

My estimation of Deputy MacDougall went up several notches.

"Yes," I said, leaning forward, "It's said to be a vast improvement over the Bertillion system."

He looked at me with an entirely new appreciation, and I felt as though I'd redeemed myself from last night's debacle at last.

"Fingerprint identification is a hundred percent accurate and accepted now for scientific evidence in court. A match can determine who the criminals are, and the prints can be lifted from almost anywhere. A goblet stem, a door latch. A knife, Miss Brown."

"You haven't found the knife."

"But we will." Confidence filled the little room. "As for the receptionist—Charlotte, that is—she says she stepped out onto the veranda for some air, was accosted by Mrs. Fontaine for some complaint in her suite that she went to attend to. Mrs. Fontaine corroborated the statement, added that she found the resort to be below expectations, and as soon as the maid left, three boys ran madly past her, knocking her into the veranda rail and," he paused to read the note again, "she will send a bill for the replacement of a beaded bangle which lost a moonstone when it was bashed against it."

I looked up at the ceiling. "The Fontaines are staying at my hotel. This has to end soon."

"Yes, she finishes by saying not one minute after, the woman dining with Mr. Lindley came blasting through the door from the ballroom and sent her reeling all over again." He looked up at me and smiled. "Did you, really?"

"Anyone who heard that scream, started running. I had no idea she was there." I sighed. "At any rate, her husband was there to catch her."

"To be exact, Mr. Fontaine was taking some air along the veranda, and Mr. Lindley had exited the front lobby doors onto the veranda, caught three boys in mid-flight against his person, none of them hurt, but was arrested almost instantly by a scream from Mr. Peabody, who noticed the victim in his rocker."

"You keep very precise notes, Mack. I'm impressed."

He jumped up from his chair. "Oh, you must see what's in my boxes!" He inched his way around the desk, and I stood up, wondering which way he was going. "I've got them here somewhere," he said, reaching for a pile.

I had pushed my chair up against the door, and, as there was nowhere to go, I plopped back down in it again. He brushed by me and found what he was looking for in the second box. Triumphant, he lifted a handful of old magazines and spread them on the desk over his notebook.

"Original *Strand Magazines*," he said, flipping through one. "I'm a great fan of Sherlock Holmes. He's my inspiration for the minutiae. Have you read him?"

"I have, yes," I said and realized I hadn't a single

book or magazine in the hotel. Not even a Sears catalog. The thought was a sad one. "But it's been a long while ago. I used to read all the time."

"The man presents scientific method in all of its glory. He imagined forensic science before the tools to implement it had been invented. We are living in the Age of Science, Miss Brown, terrifically exciting. Holmes makes the most fascinating deductions. He's the reason I'm here." The deputy was directly in front of me, leaning over the desk. "I knew all along that Holmes faked his death!" If I encouraged his enthusiasm at all, he'd land in my lap.

A hard knock on the door at my back saved me from a speech on poisons and boxing. It occurred to the deputy that he would have to sit around back at his desk again before I could rise and shift the chair from the door, and we each struggled for a minute with the logistics before he called, "Open and enter!"

The door swung out, and Mr. Fontaine stood with his hand on the latch, unable to get farther than the doorway. I put a hand to my mouth. He must have been face down on his pillow when I barged into his room. His blue serge jacket and light trousers were immaculate, but the straw boater hat on his well-oiled head could not distract from the blooming black eye he sported.

"I say, are you the deputy?" he asked, his eye almost swollen shut.

Mr. Fontaine was having a miserable honeymoon.

10

FONTAINE

"Here now," the deputy said, rising up from his chair. "What happened?"

Mr. Fontaine was in an exceptionally foul mood. "It would do you well to know what's happening. Are we in some Wild West where everyone takes the law into their own hands? Where were you last night when all hell broke loose in the saloon?"

"The saloon? Back at Mr. Lindley's place?"

"Yes. I took a stroll down there last night and thought I'd have a late drink. Full of troublemakers. Should have turned back when I saw them inside. Instead, like a fool, I thought the place had better decorum. I had to defend my wife's honor, right there at the bar. I don't know why the lot of them aren't locked up right now. I made my way back in one piece, more or less," he touched the side of his face with a fingertip where it turned purple and green, "but if they are still to be found, I demand they land behind bars for assault."

"Excuse me, please," I said, motioning to the road behind him. Mr. Fontaine retreated and allowed me to pass onto the boardwalk so that the deputy could come around his desk and speak face to face. I wasn't sure whether I wanted to stay and listen or get back to the hotel.

"Mr. Fontaine, the sheriff is staying on the property. Didn't he appear?"

"Not that I'm aware of," Mr. Fontaine sniffed. "I am quite determined to quit this place altogether as soon as possible. Please let me know the moment we are allowed to leave. I assure you, we won't be back."

He spun on his heel and walked back to the hotel. As he passed me, the impulse to run in the opposite direction was strong.

"We haven't a moment to lose," Mack said, putting on his hat. "Will you come with me to investigate?"

"Don't you think the sheriff can handle it?" I asked.

"Holmes always needs his Watson."

"You do know that Sherlock Holmes is a fictional character, don't you?"

He stepped across the road. "That is up for debate and doesn't matter in the slightest. The game's afoot, Miss Brown."

Carlos stood with his arms crossed and didn't offer to help Mack saddle up. When Mack finally rode away on his black horse, I turned to him and said, "You aren't very welcoming."

"We understand each other," Carlos said. He turned and went into the blacksmith shop.

I dawdled down the boardwalk toward the hotel, delaying the inevitable. Mack had drawn a more complete picture of Tuesday night, and it left me with a couple of questions that felt almost irrelevant. Whoever had been on the veranda in the dark with Mr. Craven had to have had a very good reason for being there. This was no accident. The violence came too close to the people I cared about, and the thought spooked me. Idyllwild was a place where residents were alone more often than not, and we preferred it that way. One of the prices we paid for solitude was vulnerability. I stopped and looked at the hotel.

My hotel, if I was willing to fight for it.

A voice hailed me from the road. "Hallo, Miss Brown!" Coming around the bend that Mack had just traversed, the Boy Scout troop appeared before me in a row, perched on the backs of mules. Leading the procession was Mr. Peabody, as solemn and dignified as it was possible to be with one's feet about to drag in the dirt. A long rope connected each mule with the one behind it, and the boys rode doubled up so that the last two mules could carry large bundles of supplies.

I waved at the boys, who waved excitedly back at me. "Mr. Peabody," I called, "where are you off to?"

"Climbing the peak," he said, chin up, staring straight ahead. "Sheriff agreed that we were less trouble up there, and we were going, permission or not."

"Won't that take all day?" I asked from the boardwalk.

"We're staying the night!" called a freckle-faced boy.

"We're getting our astronomy badge!" shouted another.

The twins were riding on a mule, and they both held their clasped hands in the air, first on one side of their mule, and then on the other, mimicking a victory parade. The boy with the yellow bandana reached for a bugle that hung at his side and put it to his lips. The ears of his mule, mere inches from the blast, never twitched as the boy called Assembly.

"But, do you know how to get there?" I didn't know of anyone who had climbed to Tahquitz Peak, and it didn't sound like a good idea. I walked back down the boardwalk, keeping pace with them.

"Easy!" a boy said. "We have compasses and maps and everything!"

The boy riding behind him said, "We follow Strawberry Creek all the way up to the saddle, then turn right. You can see clear to Kansas from up there!"

"Yeah! We're gonna pee off the dome!" another boy said, and the boy behind him slugged him in the back.

"Mr. Peabody," I said as they passed the deputy's station, "please be safe."

"No need to worry," he called back, as he began the turn into the pines, "we'll be back tomorrow in time to pack up. These boys are due home on Saturday. Never keep parents waiting, Miss Brown."

The last mule disappeared into the forest at Strawberry Creek, and, although I could no longer see them, the voices of the happy Boy Scouts echoed in the trees for a few minutes longer. The sheriff was right. They would be less trouble in the wilderness.

The rumbling in my stomach told me the morning was almost over, and I marched down to the hotel and found the lobby full of commotion. The delicate Mrs. Fontaine stood next to her new husband, seated on the horsehide chair, giving him a proper scolding over his black eye.

"I don't understand how you can say that with a straight face. I only wish I'd known who you really are before we married." She dabbed at her eyes with an embroidered handkerchief. "You never went to saloons or got into fights during the entire time we courted. What would my mother think?" At this, she did begin to weep, and I slid along the wall behind her and ducked into the kitchen.

"Karine," I whispered, "do you have any muffins left?"

Karine mixed something in a large bowl, and her wooden spoon never slowed as she said, "Yes, there on the sideboard. And if you ask me, you ought to charge them double." She nodded toward the door. "The lady is as shrewish as I've ever seen."

I made some tea while Karine poured her cake mix into a tin, and we breathed a sigh of relief when the lobby went suddenly quiet. I peeked through the door, and, finding the place empty, brought my tea out to the desk. The sounds upstairs were peaceful.

Whatever the issue had been, it was clearly settled between them. Mrs. Fontaine came down the stairs, all business, carrying the hatbox by its ribboned handle. Dropping it unceremoniously on my desk, she turned to me and said, "You." She looked at me closely. "I know you now. You're the woman who ran into me on the veranda over there." She turned her eyes heavenward. "I've been crashed into more times in the last two days than I ever did in my entire life. You're terribly clumsy. Why can't you look where you're going?"

"Darling, is the box strictly necessary?" asked Mr. Fontaine meekly.

Mrs. Fontaine wore a dark green riding skirt topped by a cream-colored blouse and wore a sleek little black cap on her head. As she pulled on riding gloves, I noticed the bruising along her forearm and wrist where she'd fallen against Lindley's railing and I had a pang of remorse. "You certainly don't think I'm going to come back wearing a white silk hat covered in pink roses on my head, do you?"

"I'm going to the resort to fetch my hat," she continued, looking down her nose at me. "I require a horse."

"I'm sorry, I don't keep horses for guests," I said. "A bit smaller operation than Lindley's, I'm afraid."

"I say, how is that possible?" Mr. Fontaine appeared to be at the end of his rope. He heard his wife's intake of breath and circumvented her words with, "I will buy a horse, Miss Brown. Name your price. My wife wants to fetch her hat."

I couldn't bear the desperation in his eyes anymore. "Mrs. Fontaine," I said, "I'll have my own horse saddled and ready for you in ten minutes." I marched out the door before I could change my mind or hear his gratitude or see the entitlement in his wife's eyes. I was never more sorry for someone in the state of matrimony.

Love made people crazy.

When I came back with Blue, Mrs. Fontaine stepped outside with her hatbox, closely followed by her repentant husband. Blue had a work saddle, one used for roping or riding through the desert. It was beautifully crafted and tooled with my old ranch brand and decorative trim, and the bridle was the best money could buy. Blue was all I had left of my estate, and I no more wanted Mrs. Fontaine to ride her than a Boy Scout.

Mrs. Fontaine had to take a minute to collect herself. "This is not a sidesaddle."

"No. But it's a lady's saddle, and it's all there is."

"Am I to sit astride?"

"If you like." Her boots were tall beneath her skirt, I was sure. She would look more dignified than I'd ever been.

Mr. Fontaine had begun another panic, but had the sense to keep his mouth shut. His wife looked Blue over again, shrugged, and allowed him to boost her up.

"Darling, you must be quick. It isn't safe for you to be out alone."

"We've already discussed it," she snapped, and Mr. Fontaine wore the face of surrender.

She sat sidesaddle, with her knee over the saddle horn, and reached for the hatbox. "I won't be long," she said, and offered her husband the hint of a smile. She moved Blue toward the road.

"Your wife appears to be a capable rider," I said. It was the first time I'd offered a compliment, even if I had been ogling her wardrobe all along.

"She really is a sweet girl," he said, watching her ride away. "Her parents passed away right before our wedding, and she hasn't been herself."

He turned to me, and the discoloration from his eye had spread to his cheekbone. "Thank you for the horse. She left a hat behind when we shifted here, and it's annoyed her ever since. I should have retrieved it for her when she asked me to. It's my stubbornness to blame." He was all remorse. "Now that that's taken care of, we'll try not to make any trouble for you. Hopefully, the sheriff's business finishes today, and we can go home."

We turned back to the hotel. "And where is home, Mr. Fontaine?" I felt a pang of longing as I reached for the front door. Home was a very important word, and it hovered at the edges of my day as I struggled, step by step, to make it a reality. I envied Mr. Fontaine's casual use of it.

"We're getting a little bungalow in Riverside," he said. "I am quite looking forward to domestic life. Lucy said she always wanted to see the mountains after a lifetime of desert." He looked around as we entered the hotel. "I say, this place delivered in spades. I don't suppose you have anything for my eye, do you?"

WHEN I RETURNED to the kitchen, Karine was pulling a heavenly coffee cake out of the oven.

"I need a cool cloth for Mr. Fontaine's eye," I told her. "Can I take this one?" I pulled the last dishcloth from a box, and she nodded. I planned to be very careful to ask her opinion on everything. I wanted her to stay.

"Thank you for the cake, it smells amazing," I said, wetting the cloth under the hand pump. The ground water it brought up was delightfully cold. "Mrs. Hannahs made me a full supper when Mr. Craven came into town Monday night. How fun it is to be able to return thanks to her with a cake!" I was going to put it in a basket with the apples from my tree that she had fussed over. "I don't expect she'll leave her house again until they catch the killer."

I shook my head. The locals were getting jumpy. It didn't help that the sheriff was letting a new deputy question every person on the mountain, and it certainly didn't help that they couldn't clear the tourists yet, and send them home. When I asked myself who I thought murdered Mr. Craven, I had to admit that I had no suspect. Holding still, with my hands in the sink, I went down the list again. Everyone seemed to have an alibi, and that was frustrating, because, of course, someone had to be lying.

Unless, the thought hit me, there was someone we hadn't questioned.

I took the cloth to Mr. Fontaine, and he went upstairs to rest. Then, I walked across the way to let Mr. Hannahs know I was making a basket for him to take home.

Halfway down the boardwalk, I had the distinct feeling that I was being watched. I stopped and turned slowly around, taking in the hotel, the road, the stand of trees beyond it. I looked between the buildings to the garden and the corral. Nothing seemed out of place, but the feeling persisted and sent a shiver of dread up my spine. I didn't believe in ghosts and I wondered if, somewhere in the trees, Red was watching the confusion. I wondered what she thought of it all.

And, I wondered, if she was as ready as I was for peace and quiet on the mountain.

11

HEADLINES

W hen I ducked into the post office, Mr. Hannahs was standing behind the counter that spanned the entire back of the building. Below it, facing his kneecaps, were innumerable cubbies for holding the flotsam and jetsam that circulated through the post office, and behind him on the wall next to a large ticking clock hung the skins of a cougar and two giant rattlesnakes, rattles intact. Arresting his attention on the counter in front of him was a newspaper, and he didn't look up as I entered.

"Good morning," he said. "As usual, the news is grim, glorified, and going to send people up to Idyll-wild in droves." He looked up at me without his usual smiling greeting.

"What is it, Mr. Hannahs?" I joined him across the counter but couldn't read well enough upside down to discover the source of his agitation.

"There," he said, planting a finger on a column of

fine print and reading it aloud. "Prominent Tucson Lawyer Murdered in Mountain Resort. Autopsy findings are still pending, but rumor insists that his throat was slit by an assassin as yet unapprehended." He looked up at me.

"And that is only the beginning," he said as he reached for another paper and laid out the front page. "Political Slaying? Milo Craven, Attorney at Law, Decapitated in Alpine Resort. Known for work in estate settlement, inheritance law, asset to criminal cases. Instrumental in the recently established governing body of the newly formed state of Arizona."

"How could they have gotten this in the paper so quickly?" I asked, "There weren't any reporters up here."

"Remember the telegrams I had to send through first thing yesterday morning?" He was clearly irritated. "Those go down to the city, and if you think they remained in the hands of the receivers, you don't know the vicious delight people take in being the first to tell sensational stories." He peered over the columns in disgust. "This is yesterday's paper. They made up what they didn't know, and I imagine sold newspapers as fast as they could print them."

"I suppose they'll come up for the rest of the story?"

"Doubtless. And expect some powerful people to ask some hard questions."

"I hope the sheriff hurries. He needs to catch whoever did this."

"Mmm. Your catalogs should arrive on the coach tonight, by the way."

"I told you there was no rush."

He folded the newspaper back into proper order. "None taken. They're easily gotten." He cut a look at me. "As are cartridges."

"Thank you, Mr. Hannahs, I appreciate it. And speaking of being thankful, I've got a basket to send home with you tonight. I'll bring it by before you leave. A treat to thank your wife for the supper Monday night."

Mr. Hannahs finally smiled. "Well, that's neighborly of you."

A rap on the door heralded another visitor to the post office. We looked up to see John Wyman walk in, and I bit my lip hard to keep from saying anything foolish.

John's eye was exploding in red, purple, and green hues, and was swollen half shut. He didn't look particularly talkative.

"Mr. Wyman!" Mr. Hannahs said. "What's happened to you?"

"Minor skirmish, George, nothing to worry about." He looked at me. "I was told to report to the deputy this morning, but the place is empty. You know where he might be found?"

A smile spread across my face despite my determined attempts to suppress it. "He took off for Lindley's," I said. "Apparently, your condition is contagious. Deputy MacDougall was overcome by a fit of justice and rode off into the sunrise to investigate the cause."

"Will he be back anytime soon?"

"I have no idea." It didn't offend me when he turned and went out the door again.

"Never known him to get into trouble," Mr. Hannahs said. "When would he be in a position for someone to get away with that?"

"One way to find out," I said and, with a wave goodbye, I went out the door after John.

"John, wait," I called. He had unhitched his horse and turned toward me reluctantly.

"I'm not in the mood for company," he said. "I'll talk to the deputy another time."

"John, what happened? Please tell me. Mr. Fontaine is upstairs right now with a matching black eye."

He looked up at the hotel windows. "They're staying here now?" He shook his head in disbelief. "That's not going to work for me. I thought they were at Lindley's."

"It's not my fault. Well, maybe it is. It's my fault Mr. Craven was here, and he's the reason they're here, so… And then, Mr. Fontaine's eye is the reason Mack isn't here, but now you're here and…"

His long-suffering look brought me to a stop.

"Mack?" he asked.

"Deputy MacDougall."

"The one moved in here?"

"Yes."

"And he left?"

I hesitated. "Yes."

I could see whatever esteem John might have anticipated for a new deputy evaporated with the deputy's absence.

"I need to talk to the sheriff." He turned to mount the horse.

"You won't tell me?" I folded my hands behind me to keep from reaching out and stopping him.

His hesitation belied an almighty internal struggle I knew he was having, and I was rewarded when I saw him shake his head subtly and toss the reins over his horse's head. "All right," he said, "we'll walk as far as the turn in the road. Then you're going back inside and staying there until we catch the killer."

"We?" I asked as I walked beside him.

"I've decided that I don't like killers on the loose in Idyllwild. Especially when it results in cops searching through my land and reporters nosing around my cabin." He took a breath and blew it out again. "When it results in strangers getting too close for comfort."

"Do I know which stranger got too close to you?" I asked. "That's quite an eye."

"The last time I had a fist fight was twenty years ago. What is it about marriage that makes a man want to fight? Why does matrimony send a man directly to the nearest saloon?"

"Does it hurt?"

"Yes. A reminder about the wages of weddings ought to hurt. It ought to keep a man's attention."

I had nothing to say about that. John's early marriage had ended badly, and his reprieve in the mountains had left him with old scars and a strong opposition to repeating the mistake.

"Last night, Mr. Fontaine needed a drink, and he needed it bad. I was already at the bar in the company of five reporters and Lindley's stable boys. And I know to stay out of the way of a man when he wants to brood. Thought maybe it was the murder getting to him. But at the bottom of his second drink, Mr. Fontaine told the entire group of us that his wife lit into him over a hat and then accused him of cheating on her. During their honeymoon." John shook his head, then winced. "I'd never met him before. I've never met his wife. But over his next four drinks, we found out more than any of us ever wanted to know. We got all the words he didn't dare say to her. It was nonstop bile. I finally told him to cut and run."

"John, you didn't!"

He turned to me. "If a woman causes that level of grief in a man, he needs to move on. Don't tell me you disagree."

I didn't. I'd run from Billy, myself. "But I do think they're in love. And misunderstandings happen. Drinking never solved them, though."

John grunted his agreement. "Guilty men don't need to drink." After a few more steps he said, "He took offense at my suggestion and slugged me before I realized his intention. Several hands became involved. I might have let him off if he hadn't dragged you into it."

I stopped right there in the middle of the road and waited.

"He might have mentioned that Lindley's dance partner was the only charming face on the property." He stared at me. "By way of proving his innocence."

"Well," I said after a beat, "he was pretty drunk."

"I don't like that he noticed you. I don't like that they're staying at your place. I don't like that the deputy is missing already. There's a lot of things I don't like right now."

"John, I don't know what to say."

"I'm going to find the sheriff and his worthless deputy. By the time he showed up last night, I was the only one left, helping the barkeep put the place back together. I guess the deputy is in charge of taking all the local reports now." He climbed up on his horse. "I want you to pay attention. Fontaine has some respect knocked into him for the time being, but if something doesn't sit right over here, you speak up to someone."

I nodded. He rode away, and I walked slowly back to the hotel. Mr. Fontaine had eyes only for his wife, I was sure. The story John told me explained Mr. Fontaine's behavior this morning, right down to his late-night arrival and sleeping in the second bedroom.

Perhaps there was something I could do to restore tranquility to the Fontaine honeymoon.

KARINE WAS HUMMING in the kitchen, and, although the scent of fresh cake wafted into the lobby, I didn't disturb her. With Mr. Fontaine upstairs resting and Mrs. Fontaine gone, the quiet wasn't so much peaceful as it was foreboding. I wondered about Mr. Craven and whether he had a wife or family waiting for him in Tucson. I wondered what was happening back in El Paso. I wondered what was happening over at Lindley's, and one small sigh escaped when I remembered dancing in his arms, the world our oyster. Before the roof crashed in.

I shook myself and sat down at my desk. This wouldn't do. I pulled out the ledgers and set myself the task of making out a list of supplies for whenever things got back to normal. Karine was organizing the kitchen the way a general prepared for battle, and I was hoping to keep up with her rations. I planned to take Lindley up on his offer to bring them in on his coach.

I was bent over the ledger, engrossed with tiny numbers, when a loud rapping on the window startled me.

"Hello in there!" A man looked through the window, then opened the door and with a thorough scan of the room took in every detail of the lobby as he came in.

"This the hotel where Mr. Craven was staying?" he asked, peering up the stairwell.

He wore a felt cap above his young, clean-shaven face and wore a checked vest over a shirt tucked into jodhpurs. His dusty boots spoke more of driving an automobile than horseback riding, but another look out the window revealed neither. Dragging the lobby chair right up next to my desk, he spun it around and strad-dled it. "You the proprietor?" he asked, arms crossed along the chair back.

"Can I help you?" Had the day come already, when I was to forcefully evict someone from my lobby? I closed the ledger in front of me.

He chewed his gum in my face like a cow chewing its cud. "Looking for the facts on Mr. Craven's final days," he said. "Thought I'd arrive ahead of the pack and get the goods myself. So, he stayed here, huh? Not at the Lindley place?" He tried to look up the stairs again. "Wonder why he chose this dive? No offense, but a man like Craven belongs down the road. What's your involvement in the case?" He squinted his eyes at me.

"Anything exciting happen over here? Can you tell me why Craven was up here in the first place?"

I sat there, wondering how to deal with him.

"He never left home, you know." The gum snapping continued. "Never. What was he hiding from, miss?"

"I don't want anything to do with the papers," I said, leaving no room for argument, "and you need to leave right now."

"Oh, miss," he said, standing up again, "don't be upset. Have a heart. All the other boys are buzzing around Lindley's place like flies around the molasses jar, but here you sit, all quiet and mysterious-like, and you probably know more than everyone over there combined. Give me something, anything at all. I've got a wife and kids to feed."

I stood up as well. "You aren't married by a long shot," I said. "Now get out."

"Did you know about his shady deals?" The man walked casually over to the bottom of the staircase and put a hand on the rail. I could smell the mint from his gum. "Did you know he had ties with the uppity-ups in the courthouse back in Arizona and was charged with fraud? Who was after him, miss?"

He saw the momentary distraction in my eyes and was up the staircase like a shot.

"Stop!" I cried and was about to run after him when I remembered my gun. I reached into the desk drawer and pulled out the Colt. At the same time, Karine came out of the kitchen with the big knife in her hand. She saw my gun and smiled.

We both looked up as a door slammed, and the booming voice of Mr. Fontaine rang out. "Stop thief!"

The reporter came barreling back down the staircase and, without pausing, shot between Karine and myself and flung himself through the door. We ran after him as far as the boardwalk. His checkered vest quickly blended in with the trees across the road, and he disappeared from view.

"Who in the bloody hell was that?" Mr. Fontaine said behind us. His hair was sticking up from where it had rested on a pillow, he was barefoot, and his shirt was untucked from his pants. His eye didn't appear much improved.

"I beg your pardon," he said, as Karine and I turned to him.

"A newspaper reporter," I said. "That explains why I thought I was being watched earlier. He said there are others at Lindley's right now, maybe we'd better be ready for them."

Karine nodded to the gun in my hand. "I believe we are."

"Mr. Fontaine," I asked, "did he steal something from your room?"

He looked even more flustered, if that were possible. "No. No, I'm not sure, but I'll check. It happened so fast. Perhaps I imagined it. What was he doing in my room?"

"Trying to get a sensational story ahead of everyone else. If something is missing, Mr. Fontaine, we need to let the sheriff know right away. Can you check?"

"Yes, of course." Mr. Fontaine's confusion transformed to horror on his face. I spun around and saw his wife riding toward us on Blue. Her hatbox hung from the saddle by its ribbon. Condemnation shone plainly in her eyes.

She stopped in front of us and took in my gun, Karine's knife, and the state of her disheveled husband.

"I'm sure you all have a perfectly logical explanation," she said.

12

SUFFRAGETTE

M r. Fontaine took the hatbox from his wife, and Mrs. Fontaine marched stoically inside with her husband trailing behind her, talking fast. This was not a fairy tale honeymoon experience.

"How am I supposed to create an alpine paradise in the clouds when people insist on being outrageous?" I hissed at Karine.

She gave me a shrug and followed them inside, and I took Blue along the road to the blacksmith shop. Carlos was standing out front already, alert and looking in all directions. There was no sign of the reporter. We both checked Blue over from her hooves to her ears, saying nothing. After one last feel around Blue's fetlocks, Carlos nodded and unsaddled her.

"You know how to fire that?" he asked, sliding the saddle off.

"Yes, when it's loaded." The fact was, I never wanted to be in a position to actually shoot someone. Even reporters.

He gave me a wry smile and carried the saddle inside.

"Easy, girl," I murmured to Blue. She gave an opinionated stamp, and I heard the source of her unrest coming up the road. Before it rounded the corner into sight, we heard the distinct sound of an automobile engine. The motor car was black with white-rimmed tires, and open to the air with a black tenting roof that secured overhead in the front and wrapped down around the back seat.

The driver's goggles were thick with dust despite the windshield, but he must have still been able to see Blue start to back and pull at her ties. The automobile pulled up in front of the hotel slowly and parked.

Carlos reappeared, and we both put a hand on Blue and watched as the driver exited the car and walked around to open the door to the back seat. A woman stepped out and after a cursory look at the hotel windows, she removed her veil and marched inside.

"This had better not be more excitement," Carlos said.

I looked down at the gun in my hand. "Too late for that," I said. "This'll be hard to hide."

"I'm here if you need me," he said, with a disparaging glance toward the empty deputy's office.

"Thanks, Carlos."

"And stop looking at the motor car like that. Blue will get jealous."

"I'm just looking."

I passed the automobile and nodded to the driver who had returned to the front seat, but he didn't acknowledge me. His eyes stayed fixed on the gun in my hand, although I held it straight down by its frame against my skirt. I gave him a tentative smile and went into the hotel, tying to appear as harmless as possible.

I was none too soon. The woman stood in front of the desk, one hand on her hip, head cocked, listening to the muted voices upstairs.

"Can I help you?" I asked.

She turned to me and, without preamble, asked where the Boy Scout troop was.

"They left this morning," I said, pointing out the window. "They're gone."

She turned to follow my gesture, and she didn't like my answer. I shifted around her and slid open a desk drawer without taking my eyes from her. I was sure she didn't notice the gun as I put it back into place, and I smiled as I closed it again.

"What do you mean, they're gone?" she asked, irritated. Her fashionable day dress accentuated her generous curves, and the deep gray cotton print brought out a beautiful shade of silver in her hair. A little black feather curled down from her hat and flirted with her cheek. The cheek, however, was turning scarlet.

"The paper said there was a murder up here this week. I know it said it was a lawyer or some such person, but I've been worried sick ever since. This is no place for children to be. I had my misgivings about letting Tobias come in the first place, but he was so happy about it. Talked about it for weeks. Wants to be an Eagle Scout, whatever that is." She realized she was babbling and stopped to collect herself. "Please tell me where to find the scouts' camp, and I'll take him home now."

"I'm sorry," I said again, "but the troop is spending tonight on Tahquitz Peak, and they should be back sometime tomorrow. There aren't any roads up, only a trail. They took mules. You'll have to wait for them."

Her shoulders slumped, and her lips quivered. "That's what they told me at the resort back there. You're sure they might not be further down the road? Is there anywhere else they might have gone?"

"No. The last stop before the road turns and drops down to Hemet is the stagecoach home station. I watched Mr. Peabody lead them away myself, this morning. They followed Strawberry Creek, so this is the closest you can get to them by automobile." I waved vaguely toward the trail exit.

Her disappointment was palpable. "It's already past the lunch hour. I simply can't take the ride back down and do it all over again tomorrow." She thought over her options. "They aren't due back home until late Saturday. I know it's only the difference of a day, but my nerves won't stand for the delay, and my body wasn't prepared for the abominations of this road."

I nodded in agreement. "The road from Banning is new, but they blasted it out of the mountainside with dynamite. If you ask me, they forgot to fill in some of the blasting holes."

"It certainly feels that way." The woman looked around the lobby for the first time. "Is this a hotel?"

"Yes. Mine. I have rooms upstairs, if you'd like to

stay overnight. It's not fancy," I felt the need to point out.

"It will do," she sighed, "if this is the closest I can get to Tobias. And I can be here the minute they return." She made a little frown. "But I didn't pack a thing."

"You won't need much for a single night. You are welcome to rest on the veranda, if you like. I can bring you tea or some lunch, if you can stomach it."

She spied the lobby chair and perched on it. "No, thank you, at least not this minute. Tea might be nice. And this, this Mr. Peabody, seems competent, does he?"

I smiled. "So far as anyone can keep ten boys contained. I think they're having fun, if that counts."

The woman attempted a smile. "I suppose you think I'm an overly nervous mother. I guess I am. He was my baby sister's only child, you see, and when she passed away, I adopted him. The murder wasn't here, was it?" She looked up the staircase with dread.

"No. The resort you just came from is where the murder happened."

"Oh, how dreadful! No, don't tell me about it! The men there showed me the troop's camp but insisted the boys were nowhere near the, um, incident." She looked at me for a confirmation, and I didn't have the heart to tell her that at least three of the boys had witnessed more than they should have.

"The boys are safe and out of trouble." I stood up and called out, "Karine, could I have some tea, please?"

"Yes, indeed!" came her voice from the kitchen, and it was like the sound of angels. I had a cook.

The woman stood up, too, and I led her out onto the veranda for a seat and had a closer look at her automobile. It was sleek and glossy underneath a layer of road dust, and I very much wanted to sit in it. Only a very resolute woman would have taken the bumpy, winding twenty-mile road to Idyllwild in this machine.

"After you're refreshed," I said to her, "I can show you your room, and the chauffeur's as well. If you think of anything else you might need, please let me know, and I'll try to get it for you." I turned to her with an ingratiating smile. "I'll trade you for a peek under the hood."

She did smile then, and Karine came out with two cups of tea.

"Help yourself," the woman said, accepting the tea from Karine with thanks.

I took the other cup of tea and approached the driver who sat in the driver's seat, waiting. He frowned in suspicion when I offered it to him. After he contemplated the easy way his mistress and I were getting along, he relaxed and accepted it.

"My uncle sells automobiles in Los Angeles," I said. "Mind if I ask you some questions?" I reached out to touch the gold-trimmed glass lanterns mounted to the frame.

I HAD my hands under the hood of a 1910 Overland Touring Automobile, admiring the four-cylinder engine. I'd investigated everything from the radiator to the tailpipe when a familiar voice came from the road.

"Yoo-hoo!" called out Mrs. Keen, riding up in her little buggy. "What have we here?" She attempted to place her buggy close enough to peer into the engine, but her horse was having none of it. She finally hitched him several feet away and came purposefully down the boardwalk where the chauffeur and I were putting the hood back in place.

"What a beautiful machine," she said, walking around it. "Wasn't it awfully dusty coming up, though?"

"We have dusters—" began the chauffeur.

"The white wheel spokes are a shame," Mrs. Keen continued, "but then, it's made for city streets, not wild mountain trails." She smiled at me. "Miss Brown, I hope we never see the day when Idyllwild is covered with automobiles."

"Actually—" I said.

"I do hope I haven't come at an inconvenient time," Mrs. Keen said. "It occurred to me last night that I had completely forgotten myself when I came by yesterday and neglected to ask all the important questions." She noticed the woman in gray sitting on my veranda. "Is there somewhere we can discuss business, Miss Brown?"

I walked away from the machine with reluctance. "Yes, now is fine, can—" I said.

"Excellent," she said and marched up to the door. "Running a grocery is no small feat, and I shall rely on you heavily."

"Rely on me?" I paused at the door as Mrs. Keen pushed through it.

"Yes, indeed." Mrs. Keen surveyed the lobby, and I

wondered what she had in mind. Quiet murmurs drifted down the stairway, and I could hear Karine humming in the kitchen.

"Mr. Keen is busy building the mercantile as we speak," continued Mrs. Keen. "A smaller affair at first, of course, but as we better understand what the needs of the community are, the style he's applying to the construction will allow us to expand later without having to close down. Better for business, you see. Mr. Keen is quite a visionary."

The odd noises upstairs began to register, and I quickly realized that they were friendly ones. Mr. and Mrs. Fontaine must have kissed and made up.

"How can I help you, Mrs. Keen?" I asked, all in a single breath.

She carried a small ledger in her gloved hands and waved it at me, saying, "I'd like to know what sundries you'd like stocked. I'm to place an order in another day or two and, well, my dear Miss Brown, it's no use ordering pickled herring if you don't in fact, eat it."

The sounds from upstairs grew louder, and I tossed open the kitchen door and practically shoved Mrs. Keen through it.

"Karine, this is Mary Keen," I said, closing the door behind me. "The Keens are opening a grocery down the road where we can purchase supplies. Perhaps you can tell her what items we'd like stocked for the kitchen." I paused. "If we were to have regular guests, that is."

Karine stopped humming and held out her hand with a smile. I doubt Mrs. Keen had ever had a sturdier shake.

I didn't know how I was going to tell Mrs. Keen that I would not use her grocery if Lindley had a coach buying directly from town for free. "I'm new to this, Mrs. Keen, and not entirely convinced I'll make a go of it yet."

"I have all the confidence in the world in you, Miss Brown," she said, opening her little book and licking the tip of her pencil. "Now where shall we begin?"

"Will you keep hens?" asked Karine.

That stumped Mrs. Keen, but only momentarily. "Goodness, no. Too many coyotes, I'm afraid. But we can bring in eggs, and I see no reason why we couldn't bring live chickens up if you were to collect them right away." She brightened and wrote 'eggs' at the top of her page.

I remembered my own ledger, still on my desktop. "I started a list for us, Karine," I said. "I think I recall most of the basics, but maybe you have your own recipes? I want you to let me know what's needed." I rubbed my arm, surprised that it was still sore from Monday. "I want you to be happy with the kitchen."

Karine's smile was generous. "Thank you, Miss Brown. The pantry is full of so many spices, I wouldn't know the name of them all." She looked at Mrs. Keen. "I know Chinatown cookin' isn't the same as country cookin' but chicken is chicken everywhere. What about fish? Can you get your hands on fresh fish? I made salmon patties from a tin yesterday."

"Fresh?" Mrs. Keen's eyes darted around the kitchen. "There's pickled and salted and dried and tinned. We aren't near the Pacific."

"Not the same at all," Karine said, her voice vaguely

reproachful. "In San Francisco, fish was dependable. Squid. Scallops. How about cats?"

Mrs. Keen dropped her pencil, then bent to retrieve it again, discomfort plain on her face. Karine winked at me over her head. I scolded her with a shake of mine, and when Mrs. Keen was upright again, Karine smiled and said, "I'm teasing, Mrs. Keen. Let's see where I am with the cornmeal."

"I do have a list," I offered, hands still on my hips. "Let me give you the list of tins we should probably keep."

I ducked into the lobby and snatched the ledger from my desk. I sent one wild look up the staircase where noises confirmed Mr. Fontaine's forgiveness and his wife's wedded bliss. The cat sat on the top stair, grooming his whiskers as though there was nothing at all going on.

The front door opened. The woman in gray stepped inside with her empty teacup and paused, looking up at the ceiling in confusion. Her face went bright pink and, wide eyed, she handed me her cup and went right back out onto the veranda again.

"Karine," I said, walking back into the kitchen, "please stop for a minute and make up a late lunch tray for the two new guests on our veranda." I had interrupted Mrs. Keen's recital for a hush puppies recipe, and she paused in confusion.

"Please excuse us." I handed the empty teacup to Karine. "If you'll step outside, I can give you the rest of the list. Anything else should wait a few weeks until we know what we need."

I led Mrs. Keen past the oven, through the back

door, and around to the veranda again, and Karine watched in bewilderment. If I were going to be a pillar of support for Mrs. Keen, we would have to learn how to hold a two-way conversation with each other.

And if I was going to run a hotel, I was going to forbid honeymooners from now on.

13

COMPLAINTS

The woman on the veranda was fanning herself with a white lace fan, and one look at the upstairs windows explained why her cheeks were still flushed. They were thrown wide open to the afternoon breeze.

I gestured to one of the veranda chairs and said, "This is Mrs. Keen, she lives up the road. And you are...?"

The woman in gray extended her hand to Mrs. Keen. "Rose Alden," she said, "pleased to make your acquaintance."

Mrs. Keen shook her hand. "Mary Keen," she said, taking a seat. "How do you do?"

"You arrived in the buggy." It was more of a statement than a question from Rose. "I couldn't help but notice the bunting decorating it. Are you, by chance, a proponent for women's suffrage?"

Mrs. Keen lit up. "I am, indeed! Are you also an advocate of the noble cause?"

"Nothing short of a miracle," Rose said, hands in the air, "that we got the vote in October."

"It passes all rational thought, the number of women I've met who were opposed. Can you believe it? Women refusing the vote. Encouraging their men to vote against it?" Mrs. Keen sent a scathing look toward the chauffeur, who had the good sense to ignore her.

"Yes, well—" I said, sitting down.

"Yes. We marched in Banning and—" began Rose.

"Oh! You were at the march! I was there as well, last year!" Mrs. Keen was on the edge of her seat. "Magnificent turn out. Not a single nay-sayer broke our ranks that day." She nodded briskly. "The men aren't laughing so loudly now, are they?"

"Arizona will be next, mark my words. This November will be every bit as historical." Rose smiled as Karine stepped out with a lunch tray. "We have a solemn duty, Mary, to raise our sons to treat the women in their circles with equality."

It surprised me how fast Mrs. Keen had pulled Rose from her nervous reverie. I would never have guessed Rose had it in her. I hurried to take advantage of the pause in their conversation.

"Mrs. Keen," I said, "would you like a tray as well?"

"No," she said quietly, the wind torn from her sails, "I've eaten, thank you."

"What is it, dear?" asked Rose.

Mrs. Keen took out a handkerchief and dabbed at her eyes. "I apologize. It's been upsetting me ever since yesterday." She glanced at me. "There's a Boy Scout troop up here, and I ran into the leader and," she dabbed some more, "I was placed in a position of defending my beliefs about Girl Scouts."

"And an intelligent and worthy one, it is," Rose said.

"It's just that," Mrs. Keen wiped her nose, "I myself could never have children, and, until yesterday, had made an uneasy peace with it. Without a child of my own, with which to prove my sincerity, he refused to take me seriously."

"Oh, men will never understand," crooned Rose, and took the tearful Mary into her arms.

I sat there, stunned by the instantaneous display of affection in front of me. Two suffragettes had bonded over men. I was confused, uncomfortable, and invisible as the women wept.

Rose untangled herself after a minute and reached for her own handkerchief. "My very own brother made the same mistake," she said, wiping her face. "Couldn't understand why I never married. But even after I adopted little Toby, he refused to believe why a woman would want a voice in politics when she could be in the kitchen making supper. He's a terrible example, and I forbade him to come around the house."

"You didn't."

"Yes, I did. I fought hard to adopt Tobias. His father —my sister's husband, Mr. Ecton, that is—is a cad and tried to get custody. The man had no business at all being with my sister, let alone a baby. What we don't need, Mrs. Keen, is a cad raising up another cad on this planet. I mean to see that Toby, at least, is raised a gentleman."

She put a comforting hand on Mary's arm. "Boys

and girls both need educating, and I see no reason why you can't advocate for it, whether or not you're a mother. You did the right thing, I'm sure."

Mrs. Keen sniffed. "No. I was spiteful. I owe Mr. Peabody an apology." She sat up straighter. "A woman in a role of leadership acknowledges her mistakes and rectifies them."

"That's the spirit," cried Rose. "Is this the same Mr. Peabody who's taken my boy up the mountain?" she asked, turning to me.

I nodded.

"And did you find him to be less than civil?" Rose turned back to Mrs. Keen and smiled, but her eyes were hooded. "The school assured me he was a model citizen."

"He had opinions of his own, I suppose," sighed Mrs. Keen. "Didn't you meet him yourself?"

"No. Toby insisted I let him wait with the gathered boys without me hovering." She huffed. "Oh, I know Tobias is in a hurry to grow up, but this is the last time I allow him to go somewhere without me. Especially with a man of questionable character. My nerves can't take it."

"Your boy is with the scout troop?" asked Mrs. Keen.

"Yes, and I don't understand why it was decided to run off into the wilderness where the parents can't reach them until tomorrow. That's a man's leadership for you. Someone was killed here. The man should have packed up that very minute and brought our boys home. I will make a complaint after we return, make no mistake about it. I'm sure I'm not the only parent worried."

"You are here waiting for them, then?"

"Unfortunately." She remembered me then and said, "No offense. I'm simply not myself."

"None taken." I meekly held my ledger out to Mrs. Keen. "Would you like to copy the short list I made?"

"Oh. Certainly." Mrs. Keen opened her notebook and, taking my ledger, began at eggs and added various tins to her list.

The storm appeared to have passed.

"If you're done with your lunch," I said to Rose, "I can show you and your chauffeur your rooms." Rose and I both glanced up at the windows. We heard nothing but peace and quiet.

"I suppose it's safe," she said.

The two of us stood, and she motioned to her driver to follow us in. At my desk, they each signed the guest book, and, making as much noise as possible, I walked them up the staircase and opened two of the three doors on the left. The rooms had been unused for weeks. "The rooms on the right are occupied," I said, "and these are dusty, but you should be comfortable enough until tomorrow."

They thanked me, and I left them to sort who was sleeping where. Mrs. Keen entered the lobby. I met her there, and she handed me my ledger saying, "Thank you for a fascinating afternoon. I am delighted to have your list." She called up the staircase, "Yoo-hoo, Rose, perhaps I shall see you tomorrow."

Rose and her driver came back down, and she took Mrs. Keen's free hand in both of her own. "I would like that very much. No idea when to expect them," she looked my way, "but not likely to be too early in the morning."

"I don't believe I will apologize to Mr. Peabody after all," Mrs. Keen said. "He has a disregard for women, maybe, but utterly lacks common sense, for which I have no tolerance."

"I'm sure you'll do the right thing."

"Do you smoke, Rose?"

The woman laughed, and the driver went back outside. "I do. However did you find me out?"

Mrs. Keen smiled as she turned for the door. "It's a great country, Rose. Give me a minute." She went outside, and the two of us followed her in curiosity.

"Here you are," she said, with a bounce in her step. "Something to enjoy your evening with. Hopefully, you can relax. I'm sure the boys are fine."

She handed Rose a cigar from a case. "Miss Brown?" she asked, offering one to me.

"No, thank you, Mrs. Keen. Never acquired a taste for it, I'm afraid."

She shrugged and went back to her buggy. "I'll be stocking them at the store, either way." She gathered herself into her buggy, and with a smart crack of the whip, trotted for home.

THE AFTERNOON PASSED in relative quiet. The Fontaines never left their room, and Rose went up to hers for a rest. Her driver went into the post office and passed the time with Mr. Hannahs and a newspaper. I took advantage of the respite by ducking into the kitchen and getting to know Karine a little better. She'd arranged the boxes and crates on the floor, and already the kitchen appeared twice as big as before.

"Karine, it's amazing," I said. "The place is taking on a sparkle."

Karine beamed under the praise, but neither did she assume an air. "It's been a long time since I had a kitchen of my own," she said. "A kitchen properly arranged makes the cooking a joy and the cleanup easy."

She peeled potatoes at the sink, and I offered to help. She handed me a small knife, and I took a couple of swipes with it. She smiled at my technique and patiently showed me how. "You'll want the potato," she chuckled. "Don't throw it out with your peel. The compost heap is full enough."

I slowed down and practiced.

"I found a row of small tins," she said, "that I think contain seeds for the garden. I recognize some, but the others will have to be a surprise when we see what sprouts up next spring." Hearing her mention next year made me happy.

"How clever of you to get the oven going so early in the day. It took me forever to get the kindling lit in the first place."

Karine laughed. "You sure enough don't understand how a kitchen works. The fire never goes out, Miss Brown. It's only ever banked at night so you can get back to heat quick when you need it."

"Banked?"

"You bury the live coals in the center of the ash pile,

and if you do it right, the coals stay hot and perk back up with some kindling the next morning."

It made perfect sense when she said it out loud. I didn't waste any time feeling embarrassed; I was too pleased with the smells coming from the black beast in the corner.

Karine already had apple pies baking and a stew bubbling on the stovetop for the evening supper. "You'd best decide about gettin' more food stocked up in here," she said, "if we take in new guests every day." Hearing her use the word 'we' made me even happier.

"Agreed," I said, "we have five guest rooms, and I can't see having over ten guests or so at the most at any one time. I know my ad said twenty, but you never know. I've seen some men eat enough for three."

"That's the truth."

We had the back door propped open with a broom to let out the heat and let in the air, but the afternoon was warm either way.

"I have to tell you about the porch," I said, peeling the last potato and setting it into her bowl. "There used to be a big rattler living under it. Carlos said he got rid of it, but they sometimes come back. I almost never go through this door unless it's at a dead run or on tiptoe."

Karine laughed. "Why not look down there and find out?"

"Not a chance. The only way I want to meet a rattlesnake is on horseback with a gun in my hand."

"Have you had to do that?" She looked at me curiously.

"Twice. I used to have a ranch in El Paso. Not for very long, but long enough to know how to kill a snake before it kills you." I wiped my hands on a towel and looked through the door. "My horse is the only thing I have left from El Paso."

Karine joined me in the doorway. "Which one is yours?"

"The blue roan mare." I pointed. "The chestnut gelding is Mr. Hannahs from the post office, there, and the pinto belongs to Carlos, the man who lives above the blacksmith shop on the other side. The new deputy has a black gelding with white socks. That's a lot of horses for Carlos, I suppose, but not as many as the Keens have to keep for the coach."

Karine smiled and went back to the sink. "Mrs. Keen is expanding her horizons," she said. "A stagecoach, a grocery, and the women's vote."

"And cigars."

"The lady has ambition," she agreed.

Another look out the door showed me Deputy MacDougall had returned from Lindley's. He was unsaddling his horse, and Carlos was nowhere to be seen. I wondered whether Carlos took care of that for me because I was a woman. It rather diminished the gesture for me. I would much rather think Carlos did it because he was my friend.

I considered it and decided that, yes, I would do the same for him.

Mack turned his horse into the corral and saw me watching. "Hello!" he called. "Miss Brown! I have something very interesting! You must join me in my office to see."

I waved at him. "Yes, be there soon."

"New deputy seems to have a bit of ambition, himself," Karine said.

"He's eager to prove himself to the sheriff," I said, "if you know what I mean."

Karine raised her eyebrows by way of not knowing what I meant.

"Mack needs to prove that he's necessary up here. The sheriff used to ask Carlos for help with things. I think Mack wants to be sure the sheriff doesn't change his mind, and I think Carlos would be happy if he did."

"How can such a little place have so much intrigue? It's like living in San Francisco all over again."

I shrugged. "It would be nice if everyone got along."

14

WATSON

When I stepped through the deputy's open door, he had placed a large bundle on his cleared off desktop and was rummaging about for the box containing his fingerprinting kit.

"We found the murder weapon," he said excitedly. "Amazing that we overlooked it. We searched the campsite thoroughly yesterday, of course, but something you said this morning simply refused to be put from my mind. Capable of almost anything, you said. Certainly, you can't dismiss a child out of hand, merely on account of youth."

His thought shocked me. "Deputy MacDougall…"

"Mack."

"Mack. They're children. I was around them myself. Hardly a nefarious group."

"No stone unturned, Miss Brown. And as it happens, turning over a tent is what was needed. The knife had been hidden beneath one of the tent floors, you see. Stroke of luck, that."

"After Sheriff Fuller and I interviewed Mr. Wyman this morning, I took myself on a private stroll around the premises, a la Holmes. Surveyed the land. Took in both the details and the ambiance."

"So you did meet up with Mr. Wyman?" I asked. "He came here first, looking for you."

"Yes." Mack was thoughtful for a minute. "Mr. Wyman gave a thorough account of what happened last night. He was not as cooperative as I would have hoped with my questions regarding the wild woman. Red, I believe she's referred to around here. He spent a considerable amount of time explaining her background and current lifestyle. Mr. Wyman seems to think we have no business questioning her possible involvement."

"I have to agree. She wasn't anywhere on the property. No one saw her or expected her."

Mack patted my hand. "There, you see? Assuming innocence without proof. You really must keep with the facts, Miss Brown. The facts are that anyone is suspect until proof is provided. You consider both children and wanderers to be exempt from murder, and yet you have no positive evidence either way."

I closed my eyes and counted to ten. There were very few things that set my temper off. Being patronized was one of them. If he would spend half as much energy on the people that were actually present, he might have caught the killer by now.

"Mack," I said calmly, "you said the knife was beneath a tent. Whose tent?"

"We can't say for certain until the troop returns, but it would appear to be the leader's based on its shape."

"Its shape?"

"Yes. Long and narrow, Miss Brown. Well, that, and the fact that it was the only tent left in the camp. I could see the imprint of the other tents where they had been removed. I noticed that the stays for the remaining tent were lax. The peg recently shifted and then set back in place. Why leave a tent behind, eh, Miss Brown?"

My hand went to my stomach. "Mr. Peabody?"

"His virtuous act was too good to be true."

"Mack! That man is alone in the forest with all those kids! Shouldn't we do something?"

"Once again, Miss Brown. Assuming guilt without proof. If he is guilty, however, it's a crime against an adult he committed. The children would be his cover. I believe the children are safe. No need to fret, whether he is innocent or guilty. He would have no idea that he is under suspicion."

He nodded to himself. "And this, Miss Brown, is where science comes to our rescue."

He pulled on a pair of thin calfskin gloves. A long bundle was removed from his satchel next and carefully unbound on the desk. He took great care not to touch the knife as he revealed it. I pulled back instinctively. The nasty blade was still covered in dark, dried blood, and the coagulated remains of whatever substance was opened along with Mr. Craven's arteries.

"You see, Miss Brown," he said, reaching for his kit, "the handle is quite sturdy. Large enough to take prints nicely, if any remain. We shall hope for the best."

"Won't you have to take fingerprints from everyone who was at supper if Peabody didn't do it?"

"We can't justify that unless we have some prints to match them to. The prints of the villain come first!"

I crept closer despite myself and watched as he carefully dusted the handle with a soft bristled brush.

After several minutes, his frown grew ferocious. "Nothing at all. Impossible." He was so disappointed. "The perpetrator must have wiped the handle before ditching the knife." We both could see the handle still had smears of blood on it. "A messy job. But the marks indicate a wiping was made."

I was staring at the blade. "Why would someone wipe the handle and not keep going and clean the entire knife?"

"What do you mean, Miss Brown? The person obviously didn't want to leave his traces on the weapon. I don't know any other reason why a murderer would feel compelled to be tidy. We know there were many people in the immediate vicinity. Whoever it is was in a hurry."

"Well, a perfectly clean knife would remove all traces of suspicion. Anyone can have a knife. What makes one knife a murder weapon and not another?"

"Well, for one thing, this isn't any knife. Not a knife one would find in the kitchen. Not used in a blacksmith shop. Not a shaving razor. This is a bowie knife. Nine-inch fixed blade, all steel tang, bone handle, no embellishments. The handle appears to be worn, old, but the blade is obviously well honed. Generally used in hunting, camping, and fishing. Not in a kitchen or a dining room."

We stared at it for another minute.

"What's this on the blade?" I pointed from a safe distance. "That's not blood."

He leaned down and scrutinized it. "Hm. Blood.

Yes. Traces of soil from the ground. To be expected." He sniffed. "There seems to be a peculiar sour scent about it. Quite faint." He used the fabric below it to once again flip the blade over. We both drew near and stared. "Perhaps...paper?"

"Something stuck to it from the tent bottom? Fabric?"

Mack turned his face to mine, and he was close enough that his intense gaze, only inches away, distracted me entirely. I stood up quickly, but not before a smile developed beneath his tidy mustache. "Perhaps," he said. "These flecks appear to have absorbed the blood, but the edges here and here," he indicated with a finger, "appear light in color. As if the blood dried and stuck to it. The tent, as I recall, is a regulation olive green." He gingerly bundled the knife back up, and I looked over the fingerprint kit, lying open and ineffective, next to it.

"I refuse to picture a child wielding such a weapon," I insisted. "Mr. Peabody could have done it, though. Mr. Craven was a large man. Even with him sitting down, the murderer would have to be fast, strong, and practically invisible to catch him by surprise."

"Miss Brown," Mack said, lifting my hand and inspecting the fingertips, "you have described a ten-year-old boy. However, we believe the knife was under the man's tent, and it is Mr. Peabody who will be detained for questioning the very moment the troop returns. Now." He smiled at me. "How would you like to have a card with your own delicate fingerprints on it? I'd love the practice."

THE FINGERPRINTING process was as fascinating as I'd expected, and Mack was a gentleman and never once commented on my blunt nails or the small callous on my right index finger where I gripped a pencil. Perhaps if I wore gloves all day like a lady, my fingers would have been pale and tender. But running the hotel was not a job for the one pair of elbow length opera gloves I had from years ago, now wasting away in my trunk. The next pair of gloves I purchased were going to be for riding and the next, for winter.

As my last little finger rolled carefully across the card, a brisk rap on the door interrupted us. It opened as John's voice called out, "Deputy?"

I bumped into Mack since he was standing directly at my elbow. Mack kept my hand in his and wiped the ink away with a wet cloth.

"Mr. Wyman," Mack said, "Good to see you again."

John tapped his hat but didn't remove it. "Just come from Lindley's place," he said to Mack. "Guess you wandered off before he could send this back with you."

John looked at me. "He asked me to deliver it," he said, and held out an envelope. "Karine said you were over here."

I pulled my hand from Mack's and wiped it dry on my skirt. "Hello, John, how are you?" I asked. "For me?"

John stepped back onto the boardwalk after I took the envelope, and Mack said quickly, "Obliged to you for our conversation earlier." He wiped his own hands on the cloth and set it aside. "I wonder if you would humor me for a couple of questions?"

"You don't seem to run out of them," John commented.

Mack smiled. "Could you tell me, please, if you happen to own a bowie knife?"

"I do. Three."

"I would expect so. Excellent for hunting and fishing and the like." Mack carefully repacked the contents of his fingerprinting kit. "Are any of them missing at the moment?"

"Missing?"

"Now wait a minute, Mack," I said, not liking the direction he was taking.

"I'm only curious," Mack said, closing the lid on his box, "whether you could produce them if you needed to?"

"Will I need to?" John stood relaxed on the boardwalk, but there was a new tightness around his jawline.

"Maybe. We found the murder weapon this morning. A bowie knife. And it belongs to somebody."

"I was nowhere near Lindley's place on the night of the murder."

"And yet, when I was in the lobby procuring Mrs. Fontaine, I overheard you say you knew about the evening's events."

"Anyone riding by on the road can look directly into a fully lit ballroom window on a dark night and see what's happening inside."

Mack crossed his arms and looked John in the eye.

"Anyone on a horse can ride in, kill a man, and ride away again."

"Anyone would see something as big and noisy as a horse ride up to the resort, including the victim."

"What were you doing riding by the resort on Tuesday night?"

"I don't have an alibi, if that's what you're fishing for," John said, and his brown eyes were dark with anger.

"And neither does that Red person."

"Neither do most of the residents on this mountain." John didn't hide the fact that he was livid. "Am I free to leave, deputy?"

"For now," Mack said.

I turned on him as John turned to go. "Mack! Why would you accuse John?"

"No stone unturned, Miss Brown." He gestured in frustration at the knife in its bundle.

"What about things like motive?"

"Do you know Mr. Wyman's past well enough to affirm he has no connections to Mr. Craven?"

I rolled my eyes and walked out after John, but not before Mack called after me, "See you tonight at supper, Miss Brown."

I let the door shut behind me with a bang. John looked over his shoulder at me, and my first thought was that, on closer inspection, his black eye was healing. It was tinged in shades of yellow.

"Does it still hurt?" I asked and lifted a hand halfway up to touch it before I stopped.

"Yes." It was a growl.

"Thank you for this," I said, not sure what to say. I fiddled with the envelope and wondered why Lindley hadn't come, himself.

John shot a look at Mack's closed door. Then I walked with him down the boardwalk to the hotel where his horse stood waiting for him. It was a minute before he spoke.

"I assume Deputy Doodle takes all of his meals at your place, now?"

I blushed to my ears and stopped. "Where did you hear that?" I looked around, hoping Carlos hadn't over-heard John's words.

John's face softened slightly. "Karine told me you were over here. She also explained—once I stopped laughing—that those were your words, not hers."

"I should sack her!" I stomped forward again. Nothing was private for long in a small town.

"I wouldn't. She has two pies and a cake sitting in that kitchen."

We passed the post office and arrived in front of the hotel. Rose waved to us, and I returned a smile while John unhitched his horse. He walked it around the automobile, giving it a wide berth, and I followed him into the road.

"It's none of my business," he said, "if you're getting friendly with your neighbors." He paused to consider his words. "Hell, I want you to find your place. But damned if I stand by and let them throw doubts on my character."

"He's new. He doesn't know you like we do."

"We?" He cut his eyes at me. "You trust me implic-itly, do you?"

I started to answer him. I did. But the truth choked the words back. The truth was, I had trusted more than one person and lived to regret it. The longing to trust him warred with my bitterness and fear, and it left me speechless.

"He made you doubt when he brought up my past." John nodded once. "I watched it. You don't know me, Miss Brown. Not enough to defend me." He stopped in the road. "How could you?"

"John, Mack thinks Mr. Peabody is our killer." I felt wretched. "They're going to arrest him the minute he comes back. He doesn't really suspect you."

"What was that song and dance back there, then?" He rubbed his chin and looked at me. "He took your fingerprints." His gaze was steady. "Maybe he suspects you."

"Why would I kill my own lawyer?" I threw my hands into the air and his horse took a step to the side, wondering where the excitement was coming from.

"Why would I?" he echoed, swinging up onto the horse and calming it. "I want you to stay."

I watched him ride off and turned to walk slowly back to the hotel. The tightness in my stomach was not the usual foreboding, but a sensation wrapped up in the pleasure of knowing John wanted me in Idyllwild.

Rose nodded companionably at me as I joined her on the veranda. I opened the envelope. Inside of it was a large sum of money and a note from Lindley.

Dear Loveda,

Please find enclosed payment for the Fontaine's room, and my apologies that I can't deliver it in person. Don't argue over the amount of either. You've gone over and beyond by taking them in, and I've had

such a day of it that I won't be able to
see you personally until tomorrow.
Forgive me.

    I must ask you for another favor. I've
had several applicants interested in the maid
position, but the news of a murder on the
premises drove them all away save one. The
girl is determined to work but is, you will
agree when you meet her, more suited for
your situation by far. Please give her a
chance and see what comes of it.

    I remain your faithful partner,
    WL

15

CATALOGS

S upper was coming on. Delicious smells slipped under the closed kitchen door and tickled at my nose, even with the lobby door thrown wide open to the reluctant late afternoon breeze. I needed to hurry if I was going to get my letter in the post. I looked through the window to the pines across the road and tried to gauge the timing of the evening stagecoach by the angle of the sun through the branches.

Someday I was going to be local enough to master that.

I looked over the letter I'd received from my uncle in Los Angeles.

Uncle Orin had forgiven me. My first letter to him, explaining my reasons for staying in Idyllwild instead of coming to live with him, had been brief but adamant. It wasn't the first time that I'd had to write those words. When I'd left Dr. Prost in Boston, I was on my way to my uncle's Los Angeles home. Aunt Mae had passed away two years before and left him all alone with his little girl, Maria, and he'd invited me to join them. I'd made it as far as Texas, where I'd been swept off my feet, and wrote Uncle Orin that I'd found the man of my dreams and a home of my own.

Well, I thought, looking around me, try, try again. I would have a home of my own, at least.

Uncle Orin understood my independent streak. He was my mother's brother, after all, and the Montgomerys tended toward entrepreneurial fits and intense inquisitiveness. To us, new ideas were like sparkling baubles. And we were stubborn enough to pursue them.

From the front of the envelope, I carefully copied the address of his automobile dealership into one of the empty ledger books, then added the barely decipherable phone number from his original telegram. The telegram was falling apart after months of riding around in my pocket, and though I didn't need it anymore, I put it into my desk drawer, anyway.

Uncle Orin had tucked a brochure for new motor cars into his letter, and I poured over it, imagining the control switches and gear box intricacies, the pistons and brakes. I wondered how the tires would fare on the bumpy Idyllwild roads. What would he say if he knew there was an automobile parked right outside my door? I would have to tell him all about it some other time.

I hurriedly signed off my reply letter, letting him know that I was safe and happy. I supposed he read newspapers, but I didn't plan on giving him details unless he demanded them. Poor Mr. Craven. It was a mess, but I was going to sink my heels in and make this place my home.

I sealed the envelope, put my things away, and stood up.

"Karine, I'm ready," I called to the kitchen.

She handed the heavy basket through the doorway and went right back to whatever magic she was conjuring over the stove. I'd set the table this afternoon, shocked to realize that it was seven people we were feeding. Those people were, for now, behaving themselves, and I looked forward to a peaceful evening.

"Mr. Hannahs!" I called, stepping into the post office. "I've brought your basket. I think Sarah will be pleased, I've given her more apples."

Rose's driver stood up and carefully refolded the newspaper that he'd been reading. He thanked Mr. Hannahs for the loan and left it on the counter, then tipped his cap to me and stepped outside.

"Thank you, Miss Brown," Mr. Hannahs said, looking up at the large clock on the wall behind him. "Stagecoach ought to be here soon."

"Good." I set the basket on the countertop. "I've got a letter for him, too." I handed over my letter, and Mr. Hannahs cancelled the red two-cent stamp and added it to his small collection of out-going parcels.

"Just in time," he said as we stepped outside to meet it.

Jim Roster brought his team up to the post office, set the brake, and hopped down. He had a four-day-old beard going, and his hat and his clothes held forty miles of round-trip road dust. He smiled at me before turning to his seat and hefting down the lock box. I worked up my courage.

"Evening, Miss Brown," Jim said. "How pleasant to find you on your own two feet."

"Hello, Jim. I confess to avoiding you for the last couple of days and don't think I don't know that you told Mrs. Keen about Monday's rescue." I put my hands behind my back as he faced me with the heavy box on his shoulder. "But the fact is, I owe you both my sincere thanks." I looked at Mr. Hannahs. "You both saved my life."

Mr. Hannahs was sheepish. "Now, Miss Brown, I've said it already, nothing a neighbor wouldn't do."

Jim, however, looked mischievous. "I rather enjoyed it. Will you be climbing any trees in the near future?"

"Not at all." He was a tease, and I refused to smile at him.

He shrugged his free shoulder, and the two men went into the post office to exchange the lock box's contents. I stood on the landing, listening to their voices inside, the sound of Carlos tinkering over some work in the blacksmith shop, the clank of pots coming through my open kitchen back door. The Fontaines sat on the veranda chatting quietly, and Rose sat near them, fanning herself and enjoying the view. Her driver was taking a slow survey of the car, walking in a wide circle around it.

"Hello there, Miss Brown," called Mack, stepping out of his office and closing the door behind him. He walked down to join me, saying, "I want to go on record as having officially thanked you for your hospitality." He took off his hat. "Sheriff Fuller promised me he would have the office fitted with everything, including a cook space, but there's no telling how soon we can arrange it. I appreciate the meals."

"You are more than welcome," I said, as the post office door opened.

"So long, Jim," Mr. Hannahs said, "see you tomorrow."

Jim came out and nodded to Mack and replaced the lock box. Mack nodded back and replaced his hat.

Once Jim was back up on his seat and gathered the reins, he gave me a parting wink.

"Good night, Cinderella," he said. As he pulled the coach away from the post office and back onto the road, I motioned Mack forward and led him down the boardwalk to the hotel.

"Cinderella?" he asked.

"I lost a shoe once." I shook my head. "He doesn't let me forget it."

There was a growing list of things Jim wasn't going to let me forget, but so far, I only had to tolerate it for five minutes a day.

"Miss Brown!" called Mr. Hannahs from his doorway, "don't forget your catalogs!"

With a sigh, I left Mack to enter the hotel and retraced my steps to the post office landing. "Mr. Hannahs, thank you."

"They sell cartridges," he said. "Check the back pages."

I smiled meekly, took the catalogs, and, leaving him to lock up for the night, went in to supper.

My guests had scattered for the evening. Once Rose had ascertained that Mrs. Fontaine leaned rather against petticoat rule and was not interested at the present in children—"the noisy little beasts"—she had very little to speak about. Mr. Fontaine had his entire faculty bent upon seeing his wife happy, a full-time job in itself, and therefore took no interest in engaging the driver in conversation.

It was left to Mack to entertain at the supper table, and he went on at great lengths about aircraft, machine guns, and ocean liners with only general return commentary from me. He finally introduced the Titanic, and at last everyone seemed to have a thought on that dreary subject. I was impressed by how well he kept all talk of the current case out of his words. He never brought up the murder or the knife or the suspect of the moment. I was grateful.

After he went off to his office, walking in the starlight, I could smell his pipe all the way back at my veranda. It was a friendly scent that reminded me of my childhood. Papa had always smoked a pipe. Mack was in good company, as Rose was sitting next to me, smoking the cigar that Mrs. Keen had given her. Her driver turned in early, possibly in protest. The Fontaines went up soon after.

I sat for a little longer, but Rose's cigar smoke made my stomach contract with nausea. The smell was indelibly imprinted in my mind with the vision of Mr. Craven, dead in his chair. But that wasn't Rose's fault. I excused myself and went inside.

I sat at my desk again, and the lamp cast a cozy glow over the pages of the Sears Roebuck catalog.

Karine was washing up in the kitchen, humming a tune that constantly evaded me. Her cat lolled on the stairs behind me, and I felt judged by his unblinking stare as I flipped through the pages looking at the lady's fashions instead of turning to the hardware pages near the back.

"Well, I do need something to wear besides this shirtwaist," I told him. He would probably give me more respect if I dressed the part. I turned another page and was lost in visions of silks and satins, velvets and lace. Buttons and collars and hat trimmings that went on for pages.

It occurred to me, as I browsed the happy pictures, that many were familiar. A hat on page 125 was identical to the one I'd seen on Mrs. Fontaine the day before, as was the one next to it. "Most becoming medium high crown, white muslin," I read, "mushroom style, 17" wide, including roll. Folded band, tailored bow, black velvet binding. A cluster of fluffy single ostrich feathers containing seven pieces in jet." I turned to look at the cat. "I would look nice in pink, though, don't you think?" He had no opinions on it.

"Oh," I said, returning to the catalog, "an entire section of switches and rats. What if I never had to wet my hair down? I could pin it up and wrap this coronet braid around it. Done. Oh!" From there, it was all downhill through the jewelry pages, the clocks, and the bicycles.

"Mr. Hannahs wasn't kidding," I finally muttered. "The cartridges are on page 908."

I turned back to the dresses. I found Mrs. Fontaine's day dress on page 157, white with emerald trim and kimono sleeves. Her yellow dress with the brown sash.

Her black silk messaline with wine colored silk trim. White percale polka dot summer frock. The deep blue evening dress trimmed in silver. Fine, sheer lavender lawn. Her silk gloves and beaded bags. Tailored navy satin-lined wool suit. Salt water pearl buttons. Embroidered stockings.

I envied Mrs. Fontaine's shopping spree. She'd obviously gone on one for her wedding. I had left all my finery in El Paso, and there it would stay. After staring at page 908 for a while, I pulled out the order blank and a pencil. I wrote down the cartridge number for the Colt and found the Winchester's on page 912.

Karine popped her head out of the kitchen door. "I made gingersnaps," she said. "Can I bring you some with your tea?"

I looked up. "Not now, Karine, but you can do me a different favor."

She was all curiosity.

"Somewhere in your room is a sewing box. There must be a cloth measure inside of it. Could you find it for me?"

She noticed the catalog. "Having some clothes made?" she asked with a smile.

"Yes, and until you help me get my measurements, I'm not sure I'll eat the cookies."

She chuckled. "You're a tiny thing. You eat as many cookies as you like." She left for her room.

Feeling virtuous, I flipped back quickly to the front pages and found the directions for proper measurements. I put down two dresses on the order blank and filled in the colors. I knew I would regret buying a white dress, but I didn't care. It was summer personified. It said so, right on page 162. Persian lawn, lace and embroidery. The other was a navy-blue striped lawn with a large sailor collar and three-quarter sleeves. It was exactly what an elegant innkeeper would wear. Unusually attractive yet serviceable dress, it said. Perfect.

The total added up fast, and I hadn't even gotten to hats or shoes. Rose walked into the lobby, her cigar finished and discarded. "Turning in," she said. "Idyllwild has a certain charm about it. I've never been up here before, but the sky full of stars surrounded by pine trees is stunning. I do believe I relaxed. Toby is making some memories out there. Good night, Miss Brown."

"Good night," I said, as she picked her way around the cat and disappeared into her room.

"Here it is," Karine said, coming in with the measure. We spent ten minutes moving it around, jotting down numbers and keeping our voices low. I went on and on about the catalog until Karine had had enough, and she peeked into it herself.

"Would you look at the kitchen section?" she whispered in reverence. "And all these years, I made do with a wooden spoon."

"I'll have to look into the budget," I said, "but why don't you take this with you, and see if there's something you can't live without? I'm not to be trusted with it anymore." I thrust the catalog into her hands.

"Well," she said, "no harm in wishing." She tucked it under her arm and went back into the kitchen.

With a sigh, I put the order blank into a desk drawer for tomorrow. My wish list was much longer than the little slip of paper. And some of the things I wished for weren't for sale.

I looked up at the sound of many hooves on the road and, through the window, I watched Lindley's coach go by, white as a ghost in the moonlight. I heard it pull up in front of the post office and wondered how I had summoned its fairy tale presence with only a wish.

16

HATTIE

L indley's coach had trespassed twice now in as many days, but at least it was after the regular stagecoach had made its appearance. Mr. Hannahs was gone for the night, and I was relieved. I was sure the affront to his nerves was bad for his health.

A girl stepped inside without knocking, hat and satchel in hand, and I looked behind her, naturally expecting either a husband or a chaperone. Another look into her young, freckled face made me stand up and peer over her head, expecting at the very least a governess. She looked around the room with curious green eyes.

"How do you do?" the girl said, and she bobbed a clumsy curtsy.

"Good evening," I said, trying not to overreact. Not to make hasty assumptions. "Can I help you?"

"I'm Hattie." The door opened again, and both Molly and Charlotte, Lindley's maids, came in to stand on either side of the girl.

"Hello, Miss Brown," Charlotte said. "Mr. Lindley sent us over to see whether you'd still be wanting a maid? He said to let you know that all of his applicants have withdrawn their names after what just happened, and only Hattie is willing to give it a try." She put her arm around the girl's shoulders. "We told her she didn't have to work for Lindley, if you wanted her. It's a smaller place, you see. No offense. We thought she might feel safer here."

Their faces were hopeful but scared. Not of me, though, I thought. Mr. Craven's death had them spooked.

"I'm very happy to see you all," I said, still standing. "I do have a need for a maid."

"I hope you won't take this the wrong way, Miss Brown," Charlotte said. She seemed to be the spokesperson for the trio. "But Hattie wants to make sure of the place before she agrees to stay, and we wouldn't let her go alone, what with the doings around here. The coach will wait for us. If your hotel doesn't suit her, we'll carry her away again and get her safe back downhill."

Hattie had turned bright red during the speech but, with a friend on either side of her, stood tall.

"You are certainly welcome," I told her. "By all means, wander the place and see what you think. We have four rooms upstairs occupied, all but the last door on the left, but if you look inside that one, you will have an idea of what's involved." I looked at Hattie. "I have a new cook in the kitchen, if you'd like to make her acquaintance, and she can show you the rest. I think everyone should meet first, don't you?"

Hattie nodded, and taking Molly by the hand, the two girls went up the stairs.

"Hattie seems very young," I said to Charlotte. "Does her family approve her working?"

"She doesn't have any, Miss Brown." She took a step closer. "Hattie seems to be all on her own. We took her under our wing immediately, she's a sweet thing. I do hope you like her."

"I guess I wouldn't know for a while. We will hope she likes me."

"Oh," she said with a smile, "your place is much quieter. There are so many people turning our place upside down right now, it's a relief to be away for a few minutes, if you don't mind me saying so." She perked up when the girls came back down the stairs, and with a mutual nod, the girls turned into the dining room for a look.

"Which reminds me," Charlotte said, "we've brought a hat that was left behind in one of the rooms. A large white hat with pink silk roses that belongs to Mrs. Fontaine. They are still here, aren't they?"

I shook off my stunned silence and said, "Mrs. Fontaine left a hat behind. But she brought it back herself this morning. Didn't you help her find it?"

"I never saw her." Charlotte turned to the two maids who were back in the lobby. "Did you see Mrs. Fontaine anywhere on the property today?" They both shook their heads. "I pulled it out from under the bed in their suite this morning, and Mr. Lindley said make sure she got it."

I had no idea what to think.

Charlotte frowned as the other girls went into the kitchen, and I heard Karine greet them cheerfully.

"The woman has a way of losing her things." Charlotte gestured with a hand for emphasis. "The other night, when—you know—happened, she yelled at me on the veranda. She said she'd misplaced her fan and wanted me to get it right away. It wasn't all that hot outside, you know, but I guess the dancing got to her." She huffed. "A dark blue fan that matched her ensemble, and I never did find it." She sighed. "Not that watching her dance wasn't beautiful."

"I wonder," I said, "did you happen to see Mr. Fontaine on the veranda as well?"

"Maybe." The cheerful voices in the kitchen distracted her. "I did see another gentleman at the far end of the veranda, but I was intent on the fan."

The two maids and Karine joined us, each eating a gingersnap, and Karine held out a tin containing more. I accepted one while I tried to understand what I'd heard. Why would Mrs. Fontaine make such a fuss over her hat, then not bring it back? Unless, of course, she couldn't find it and was finally embarrassed by her behavior and had decided to let it go.

She could have forgotten more than one hat, I supposed, without realizing it.

And why did she think her husband and Charlotte kissed, if both of them denied anything of the sort?

I reached for another cookie. The woman was impossible.

"The place suits me very well," Hattie said. "I can wash and dust, sweep and scrub. Will you take me on?"

Her hopeful face melted my reservations. I held out

my hand. "Yes, Hattie. Let's get to know each other for a while and see how we manage."

Her hand was very small in mine, and I wondered if I was making a mistake, but the collective feminine satisfaction in the room was impossible to defy.

"I'll bring your case," Charlotte said with a smile at Hattie. "And the hat," she added with a nod to me as she stepped outside.

I looked at Molly and said, "You both seem very content working for Mr. Lindley. How long have you been with him?"

She blushed. "Going on three years now."

"You won't mind my taking Hattie? I heard you have a lot of tasks now that you're shorthanded, including working alongside the chef."

She gave me a shy smile. "I've been there long enough that I know all the jobs, I guess. We'll make do until we find another maid."

"Even if the desserts go missing?" I waved my cookie at her with a conspiratorial smile and almost dropped it when she burst into tears. Charlotte walked in with a suitcase in one hand and an enormous hat smothered in roses in the other, but promptly dropped both and threw her arms around Molly.

Mrs. Fontaine's hat sat jauntily on the floor, conjured directly from page 126.

"Molly, don't," she implored.

"I can't help it," cried the maid. "He acts like I don't exist now."

"Who?" I asked, knowing full well it was none of my business. She cried like her heart had broken, and it was distressing to think I'd sent her into tears. I wracked my brain. "The chef?"

Charlotte looked at me apprehensively. "Mr. Lindley."

The rest of us watched while Molly pulled herself together. "I'm sorry," she said, "it's been a terrible week." She accepted a handkerchief from Charlotte and wiped her eyes.

"Are you in love with Mr. Lindley?" I asked in surprise.

"What's more important," answered Charlotte, "is that he's in love with her. Or at least, we think he is. He hasn't actually come out and said as much." The maid's tears started falling again. "But if a man kisses you, a good man, a gentleman like Mr. Lindley, then he ought to own it in public."

I couldn't get my mind around it.

"He kissed me Monday night." Molly was calm now. "I went to his office to get more instructions for those horrible newlyweds, and he laughed at me and told me not all couples in love are so arrogant. Then he put a finger under my chin, told me I was a kind heart, and kissed me." She twisted the handkerchief in her hands. "That's all there was to it, except I went dashing into his office Tuesday night, when the dessert went missing..." she trailed off in uncertainty.

"You may as well tell her now," Charlotte said.

Molly took a deep breath. "What was I thinking? The dessert was just an excuse to see him. I thought he'd be pleased to see me, even for that brief moment, and I ran into his office and put my hand on his arm. I —I wanted reassurance."

She looked at me in mild accusation. "He'd been dancing with you. It wasn't until the man stood up straight that I realized it wasn't Mr. Lindley by a long shot. A tall, thin man was in the office, bent over a big open briefcase on the desk."

Molly blushed. "I begged his pardon and ducked out again. When I ran into Mr. Lindley in the lobby, he caught hold of me and we went to the front doors."

She turned scarlet. "I didn't even get my message out before he kissed me again. Of course, I didn't tell the sheriff any of that. What would Mr. Lindley think? And now that that man got killed, I may as well be invisible again."

She looked at me through her tears. "I'm sorry. I saw the way he kissed your hand when you left. He's obviously smitten with you."

I was astonished. "Surely you don't think that I'm on the make with Mr. Lindley?"

"I don't know what to think, but if you do, tell me plainly, and I'll take a job somewhere else." She was despondent.

"You'll do no such thing!" cried Charlotte.

"Understand me," I said, and the whole room listened in rapt attention. "I am not romantically interested in Mr. Lindley. He's helping me with the business of this hotel, and I consider him an invaluable friend." I put a tentative hand on Molly's shoulder. "Leaving him would be a mistake. You're right about this terrible week. Why don't you wait until this case is closed and see where things are then?"

She wiped at her eyes and nodded.

"Are you saying that Mr. Peabody was in Mr. Lindley's office, going through my lawyer's briefcase?" I asked her.

"If Mr. Peabody is the man who's in charge of all those boys, then yes," she said. "I never saw him before the next morning, when we were all waiting for the sheriff."

"Molly, let's go," Charlotte said, her arm still around her shoulders.

She turned to Hattie. "If it doesn't work out here, send for us."

Hattie nodded, and I escorted the two girls out to the white coach and put them inside. "Thank you for telling me," I said to Molly. "I won't betray your confidence. Mr. Lindley is a good man. He's worth waiting for." With that, I secured the door.

The coach lamps threw a warm glow to either side of the driver, and I listened to the horse's harness as it disappeared around the bend.

I considered all the information, tried to sort through it. Had Lindley found love again? If so, I was happy for him. I would encourage him to remove Molly from her position at once and allow her a courtship on as even ground as there might be. I had no idea what kind of family she came from, but a servant dating an employer was anything but respectable for either party.

If, on the other hand, Lindley had only had a weak moment and taken advantage of a romantic girl, I would call him out on it. Lindley was an honorable man. But he was still only a man.

Through the window I watched Karine take Hattie's bundle, and together they stepped into the kitchen. A moment later, they exited the back door, and I heard their steps move through the lean-to and into the little room that they would share. There were a lot of servants back in El Paso on my ranch. Housemaids and stable workers and caballeros. I even had a manager who oversaw the daily operations, who left me to the larger tasks of choosing drapery colors or hosting fiestas when businessmen came calling. But I had never before felt such a weight of responsibility for someone the way I felt tonight for Karine and Hattie. They were every bit as between homes as I was.

We deserved a place of our own.

17

MUDDLED

I stood outside in the early morning air, a scarf wrapped around my shoulders. The crisp scent of pine competed with the savory one drifting from the kitchen where Karine was working her magic. I was grateful for the solitude. There was more privacy on the veranda than there was in the hotel.

The sunrise, when it finally tipped over Tahquitz Peak, sent inquisitive fingers of light into the tree line, and there it diffused into a color that was unmatched at any other time of day. A jay called from one tree, and a crow answered from another. Idyllwild was a place to appreciate details.

From far away, floating so lightly in the air that I wondered whether I imagined it, I heard the bugle. The boy with the yellow bandana was waking Tahquitz. I wasn't sure I liked that idea. We'd had enough mischief for one week.

My stomach had kept me up most of the night, a

niggle that came and went like butterflies. Or maybe bats.

Something wasn't sitting right, and I couldn't put my finger on it. Mack's presence only muddled my thinking. His impersonal directness had a way of pushing my apprehensions aside and leaving me with dark vague feelings where a solid hunch should have been.

I patted my pocket and frowned. It was empty, but I reached inside both skirt pockets, to be sure. Thinking carefully, I recalled putting my watch into my desk when I'd wrestled with the cat. I'd gone through all the desk drawers twice before Hattie walked through the lobby with a platter of muffins for the dining room.

"Hattie," I called to her, "have you been in my desk at all?"

"No, Miss Brown. I've been helping Karine all morning. Besides, I don't think you'd want me cleaning it, do you?" She looked at the dining room door with a sense of urgency. Noises overhead warned of impending hungry guests.

"Go ahead," I said. "It'll keep until later."

Breakfast was a drawn-out affair. Mack arrived at the same time Miss Alden did, and they discussed the weather until she went back to her room. The chauffeur appeared next, and the two men engaged in a friendly competition of sorts, to decide which of them knew more about steam engines. I hadn't the energy to put myself into the middle of the fray, although I was happy to watch Mack lose to the driver in the end, even if he hadn't the grace to admit it. Mack finally left for his office after singing praises to Karine on his way out. Karine popped her head out of the kitchen long enough to reply, and we both looked up to see the Fontaines coming downstairs.

"Next," Karine said, and disappeared back inside.

"Good morning," I said, and the couple smiled in reply. Mrs. Fontaine wore a simple day dress, perfectly coiffed hair wrapped in an eyelet headband, and her dapper husband followed her. She immediately saw her hat on my desk and froze halfway down the staircase.

"How did that get there?" she asked, staring at it.

"It was delivered last night," I said. "Found at Lindley's and returned. I didn't want to disturb you by bringing it up."

She closed her eyes momentarily. "Well. After all of my efforts and here it is." She continued down the steps. "The staff over there is abominable."

"Darling?" asked Mr. Fontaine, confusion in his tone, "hadn't you found it, then?"

"Obviously not. There it lies. There were other issues more important than that yesterday, wouldn't you agree?"

Her tone was icy, and he immediately dropped the subject and ushered her into the dining room.

I decided I'd had enough of listening to the happy couple and turned away.

I took advantage of the time by going back into my own bedroom and turning it upside down, looking for my watch. There was a chance it was in my other skirt or had fallen beneath a piece of furniture. I finally gave it up. My watch was gone.

After Hattie had cleared the last of breakfast away, I pulled her aside.

"Something of value is missing from a desk drawer," I said, trying to regulate my voice. I didn't want to scare her, but I was getting more upset by the minute. I should never have left my desk unlocked.

From the look on her pale face, Hattie understood the implications immediately. "What is it? I'll look for it." It was really all she had to offer.

"A pocket watch. Gold, with engraving on the inside of the cover." I tried not to tear up. "It has a short gold chain and a winding key."

"Don't cry, Miss Brown." Her voice was distressed. "We'll find it if it's here. I'll start right now." She began sweeping the lobby, peeking behind pine cones, and lifting the edges of the carpet as she went.

I went into the kitchen. "Karine, my watch is missing."

Karine stopped what she was doing and put her hands to her hips, frowning. "Your gold watch? The one I seen you pull out yesterday morning?"

"Yes."

"And where did you see it last?"

"In my desk. But I've searched it thoroughly. It's not there, Karine, or in my room, either."

"Are you thinking I've taken it?"

"No. Not at all."

"And Hattie?"

"I just don't know!" I let the tears fall then and reached for a towel to dry them. "The hotel is full of strangers, Karine. You've been here all of two days, and it feels like you've been here forever."

"I'll take that for the compliment it is." She took the towel from me and wiped her hands on it before hanging it from the sink lip. "You can't go around accusing folks of theft, especially your guests. Let me take a good look in my room first. Lil Hattie just arrived, but I don't expect to find any wrong doings on her part." She nodded. "But if I find it, well, there'll be a swift end to it."

She went out the back door, and I heard the door to their small room shut behind her. Despondent, I wandered back into the lobby to find Hattie held captive by Mrs. Fontaine.

"We do have a maid!" sniffed Mrs. Fontaine. "I'd begun to lose all hope. There isn't much to you, is there? You'd blow away in a stiff wind. Heavens above, how I'd love to hand you my washing. As it is, we hope to be leaving today. Tomorrow at the latest. Much too soon to expect everything to dry beforehand for packing."

Hattie gave me a questioning look as I walked up. "Certainly, she can help with what you need," I said. "She arrived from the resort last night along with the hat, but she's learning quickly how we do things around here."

"The maids at the resort were dreadfully inadequate, so I haven't much faith in you," she said, "but at the very least, you could clean up a few items today. I'll set them in the hall once I'm sorted." She nodded at the hat. "You can deliver that to my room, first."

Mrs. Fontaine swept past us and out to the veranda, magazine in hand. Mr. Fontaine followed.

I made up my mind. If I was going to trust anyone, I was going to start with my own people.

"Hattie," I said with my voice lowered, "you aren't

the only stranger in this building, but you're the only one I trust."

Her smile was fragile and grateful. "Thank you, Miss Brown."

Her eager face made me ashamed of myself for thinking she might have taken the watch. "I want you to keep your eyes open today as you clean all the rooms. Even if you don't find my watch," I took a breath, "perhaps you'll find something else that might be odd. Don't touch anything, though. If there is a thief among us, I don't want you to be swept into the ranks of the accused."

Hattie bobbed another of her awkward curtsies, "Oh," she said, "I certainly won't."

I was deep in the ledgers, trying to distract myself, when Karine came to me. She kept her voice low and informed me that she'd found nothing to report in either their room, the wash area, or the kitchen.

I closed the ledger and sat for some time with my hands folded over it, staring at the lush pink silk roses on the hat next to me. If my stomach rumbled at me any louder, they'd hear it clear to Hemet. I opened a lower desk drawer and pulled out a thin, leather-bound journal. It was something I kept very private. I ran a finger over the tooled design on the cover, the brand of my El Paso ranch. These pages held many stories about my past. Some heartbreak. Some victories.

I opened it now, hoping to find some answers. Occasionally, the pages brought me clarity.

Who killed Mr. Craven? I wrote.

I stared at it for another minute, then crossed it out and wrote, *Who didn't kill Mr. Craven?*

Karine, Hattie, and Spoon: not here then

Sheriff Fuller, Deputy MacDougall: obvious

John, Elizabeth, the Hannahs', Jim, the Keens, Carlos: not there/no motive/refuse to consider

Lindley, Charlotte, Molly, and the rest of Lindley's staff: there/motive?/doubtful

Fontaines: there/motive?/doubtful

Peabody, Boy Scouts: there/suspect!/but not the boys

Rose, chauffeur: not here then

Someone else: political rival, hired assassin, personal...

At this, I stopped writing. Personal? All along, I'd assumed Mr. Craven's murder was about him.

But what if it was about me?

Who would kill my lawyer in order to stop him from selling the ranch in El Paso?

The manager there?

I knew next to nothing about him or the employees. Hadn't communicated with them. It was very possible that they knew nothing about Billy's death or my intentions. I'd told no one there about my plan to flee to Los Angeles to live with my uncle; I'd simply vanished. Billy had chased after me. How long would it be before our continued absence was questioned?

It was a long shot. But if someone discovered my plan to sell the ranch and wanted to keep it, knowing that neither Billy nor myself was ever returning, it could form motive.

"Squatters, Miss Brown," Mr. Craven had said.

I thought about that for another few minutes. Then I shook my head. If someone in El Paso wanted to thwart the plan, all they had to do was wait for Mr. Craven to walk through their door. It made no sense to climb a mountain to kill him. I put my pencil to the page again.

Uncle Orin?

I laughed out loud.

"No stone unturned, Miss Brown," Mack's voice echoed in my head.

Only if he was involved with a mobster and felt the need to scare me out of Idyllwild and into his home.

There wasn't a person on my family tree inclined to that level of drama, thank goodness, even if he were desperate for my help in raising young Maria. I liked to think that the little girl was as practical as the rest of us, but only a trip to Los Angeles would answer that question.

I looked over my page of notes and felt better. My stomach was behaving, and a new thought had occurred to me. Mack and the sheriff were thorough and methodical, but there were some conversations that men would never have. And that's where I needed to investigate.

I closed the journal and carried it into my bedroom. I had just locked it into my trunk when there was a sharp rap on the lobby door. A moment later, Hattie called for me.

18

PAPERWORK

"Loveda, I need to speak with you at once." Lindley stood on the veranda, and a man next him in a brown suit took off his hat when I stepped out to join them. The sheriff and Mack stood further behind them. But they kept their hats on. Lindley's buggy stood hitched out front and gripped tightly in the sheriff's hand was Mr. Craven's briefcase.

I knew that Hattie was watching through the window, but my attempt at keeping Lindley at arm's distance was immediately foiled as he removed his hat and took my hand. "We've stumbled upon another tangle. Where can we speak in private?" He wore a familiar smooth expression on his face I'd witnessed enough to know that he was beyond angry and holding himself in check.

All my guests were on the veranda, waiting. Waiting for someone to arrive or something to happen so they could leave Idyllwild. None of them had gone so far as to begin pacing this morning, but the arrival of law enforcement and the look on Lindley's face arrested their complete attention. The tone of his voice was unnerving. The magazine lowered. The fan stopped moving.

"I run a tiny hotel, Lindley, you know there isn't anywhere here."

"In the post office, maybe?" He glanced next door.

"I'm sure there's nothing you can tell me that Mr. Hannahs won't keep in confidence." I glanced at the sheriff, but he didn't offer an opinion.

"It'll have to do." Lindley tucked my hand possessively into the crook of his arm and led me away, and I didn't have to look behind me to know four pairs of eyes followed us, and that Hattie was forming her own opinions on my relationship status.

"Lindley," I asked, "you're making me uneasy. Have they have caught the killer?"

"Not yet. But I'm afraid my news is going to upset you." He opened the screen door for me, and Mr. Hannahs looked up from his paper as I stepped inside.

"Miss Brown," Mr. Hannahs said from his position behind the counter, "I need to speak with you right away." Then he saw all the men file in behind me. He fell quiet and waited to see what was happening.

"Hello, George," the sheriff said. "Mind if we use your place here for some official police work? I don't need to tell you it's confidential, but if it makes you uneasy, you can step outside. I'll cover for you if the phone rings."

"Why sheriff," Mr. Hannahs said, baffled by the group, "go right ahead, and don't mind me."

Now that we were more or less in private, Lindley was visibly shaken.

"Loveda, may I introduce my lawyer, Mr. Plink. To clear the air, you did give me permission to show your paperwork to my lawyer?" he asked.

"Of course," I said, confused. All the men looked at me as though the question was of the utmost importance. "I had already asked you, personally, to do so. I would be grateful if he did, especially as I'm without a lawyer entirely now."

The lawyer sat down at Mr. Hannahs' typing table and opened the briefcase clasps with a firm click. I couldn't bring myself to look inside at my little pile of dreams.

"Good." Lindley looked at the sheriff. "You see, the speed with which we were able to open and understand these files was legitimate from a privacy standpoint. No laws were broken. And it's brought fresh information forward for your investigation."

"What do you mean?" I asked, though I was already afraid of what he might say.

"I had Mr. Plink take a look at your estate papers yesterday afternoon," Lindley said. He'd kept his hat off and was running his fingers through his hair. "Do you need to sit down, Loveda?"

"No." At this point, I was braced for almost anything. What could be worse than a man murdered?

"These are the papers you signed for Mr. Craven," Mr. Plink said impassively, lifting the sheaf of familiar pages. "So far as I can ascertain, these papers give away all of your claim to a property in El Paso. You do have an estate that you wish to liquidate?"

I nodded.

"With these signatures, Mr. Craven would have been able to do so and legally keep it all himself. You've given him permission for it and signed away all your rights to him. The paperwork you filled out turned everything over to Mr. Craven, down to the last penny."

"No. No, I didn't."

The men were looking at me with a mix of sympathy and anger.

"The man was nothing but a shark, Loveda," Lindley said. His eyes were bitter. "He came up here to swindle you out of everything."

"He does seem to be a real estate attorney, an inheritance lawyer of sorts," droned the lawyer, shuffling the pages back into place. "Not the first rumor of fraudulent activity or even accusations of bribery connected to his name. Mr. Craven has contacts in very high places, and some of those have recently been called into question."

"I can't believe it!" I finally said. "Dr. Prost gave him a glowing recommendation."

"I placed a phone call down the hill," the sheriff said, "and these papers will end up in prosecution proceedings—although now the man's dead, not sure what will come of it next."

"It will bring down the other crooked men," Mack said. "Where there's one bad egg, there are others."

The full impact of what they were saying hit me. "The dirty rat," I said. "He was in my house! I trusted him, and I was just another target to him!" I felt violated and crossed my arms, hugging them tightly.

The sheriff scratched the whiskers on his chin

thoughtfully. "More to the point, who else wanted to kill Mr. Craven?"

I turned on him. "Sheriff, you don't think for a minute…"

"No, Miss Brown. But someone did."

I stared at the briefcase as though it held snakes. Each stroke of a pen was a lie or a cheat.

"Sheriff," I said into the silence, "what if I'm not the only one who wanted their paperwork double-checked? What if someone else smelled a rat?"

"I am all attention, Miss Brown," he said quietly.

"Mr. Peabody was caught alone in Mr. Lindley's office when the murder occurred, searching through this briefcase. What was he looking for?"

"Where did you get this information?" asked the sheriff, taking a step toward me. "How do you know? Was the briefcase moved from the office at any point?" He went over the facts. "Mr. Peabody claimed to be in the campground until he accosted the boys stealing doughnuts and returned with the boys to the camp after the murder occurred. You, yourself, gave witness that he was on the veranda chasing them."

He shifted back and forth on his feet. "You gentlemen remain under strict confidentiality," he reminded Lindley and his lawyer, "but this puts a new perspective on our findings yesterday."

Mack was visibly upset but said nothing.

"If Peabody was in the office, who murdered Craven?" the sheriff continued. The room was silent. "And why did someone plant evidence under his tent?" His eyes bored into mine. "Miss Brown, is this witness reliable?"

I only hesitated a little. "Yes. A maid discovered him doing so. Apparently, he was in the office prior to chasing the boys. It gives Mr. Peabody a firm alibi…but an entirely new question in my mind about his presence on the mountain." I refused to look at Lindley, although he gazed at me steadfastly, and I felt myself flush from my hairline to my shoulders.

"So far as I know," I continued, "there was only paperwork in the case. But if money or something of value went missing, we may never know." The niggle in my stomach was on full alert. Whatever Mr. Peabody was looking for felt somehow more acute than my own fraudulent paperwork.

The sheriff stood beside the open case, and together, he and the deputy went through the case again. The lawyer stepped aside and feigned aloofness, but I could see my question buzzing around behind his eyes and already, I suspected several ideas had suggested themselves before the case was abandoned again with a shrug.

"No false compartments," Mack said. "Name clearly engraved near the handles. Heavy but honest. We collected Mr. Craven's personal effects from his pockets and your room, Miss Brown. His money, tie stick, cufflinks, and such appear to be accounted for."

"Unless our Boy Scout leader was in dire need of a stamp," the sheriff said, "I can't imagine why he was in the heart of the resort, alone, rifling through it, when he had ten boys to supervise." He frowned at the incongruity.

The lawyer sat down again and pulled the case toward him. "I've been through the contents," he said, "and may I suggest that a person who goes through a lawyer's papers is, in fact, looking for a piece of paper? As this is the first time I've heard about a Mr. Peabody, it falls on me to tell you that one file in particular," he sifted through a stack and pulled some papers from it, "does, in fact, mention a Mr. Peabody."

We gathered near, and Mr. Hannahs leaned over his counter far enough to risk a fall off the other side.

"Normally, of course," he said primly, "such paper-work is strictly confidential." He looked at the sheriff. "In this case, I assumed the entire contents were commandeered for the investigation and can be used accordingly?"

The sheriff had his hands on his hips, and his mouth was a thin, straight line. His eyes squinted at the lawyer and I noticed a thin sheen of sweat form on Mr. Plink's forehead.

"Get on with it," the sheriff growled.

"It appears that," continued Mr. Plink, "a Rose Geyser, in the settling of her estate through Mr. Craven, won a custody issue. A boy she adopted. Heavily contested by the boy's father." He shuffled the pages. "Says Miss Geyser is the boy's aunt. Yes. She paid Mr. Craven a considerable sum for his assistance in the adoption and the changing of the boy's name. The size of a hefty bribe. Most unorthodox to award a child away from its own parent. Father goes by two names. One of them is Jasper H. Peabody."

The room had gone so silent that we could hear the wind in the trees outside.

"What was the boy's name?" I asked.

He looked at the pages again. "Tobias Alden."

My stomach was in knots.

"What is it, Loveda?" Lindley put a hand on my shoulder as I leaned against the desk edge.

"Tobias Alden's mother is sitting on my veranda. Toby is in the Boy Scout troop."

There was a general hush in the room.

"I wonder if you would invite her to our little party, Miss Brown?" asked the sheriff.

I'd never felt more like a traitor than during the steps I took between the post office and my veranda. Miss Alden sat looking at the pines across the road, absentmindedly tapping her closed fan on the arm of her chair, waiting.

"Excuse me, Miss Alden," I asked, "would you please join me next door? There's a matter that might interest you, so long as you have to wait, anyway. And it may be something you can help me with."

Rose frowned. The others on the veranda seemed to be cut from marble, they were so still. "The fact is," she finally said, standing up, "if I can do anything that will help get any of us off this mountain, I'm happy to volunteer." She walked down the boardwalk with me. "But I'm looking forward to going home."

I held the door for her, and when she stepped inside and saw the men waiting for her, she looked over her shoulder at me, agitated.

"Miss Alden?" began the sheriff. "I'd like to ask you some questions."

Ten minutes later, Miss Alden, nee Geyser, was sitting in the chair that the lawyer had abandoned, sobbing into her handkerchief, head in her hands. The little black feather danced above her hat.

"You're telling me that Mr. Peabody is Mr. Ecton?" She moved her head back and forth in denial.

"Yes," Mr. Plink said. "That is the other name on the paperwork."

"He's taken him," she gasped. "He's taken my Toby!"

"Can you tell me anything else that I need to know?" The sheriff had had enough, and his voice was cutting.

"He's a terrible man," she said, "relentless. We moved three times. How did he find us? My poor baby sister. It was her dying wish. She'll never forgive me for all eternity."

"So you admit to bribing Mr. Craven to gain custody of the boy?" asked Mack.

"I had to. It took all of our parent's estate to do it. That man has been hunting us ever since." She blew her nose. "When I read in the paper that it was Mr. Craven who was killed, I nearly fainted. Oh, I should never have let Toby out of my sight!"

The sheriff shook his head. "Miss Alden, this child custody matter is beyond my jurisdiction, but it's my duty to tell you that, once the paperwork gets to the proper authorities, your custody proceedings will be called into question. I'll have to bear witness to the confession. You won't be able to take the boy and disappear again. And I don't need to tell you that the courts are against awarding a child away from its father."

Miss Alden broke down beyond recall, and I stared helplessly at the sheriff. Lindley nodded at me, and I took it as an indication that, as I was the only female in the room, it was squarely on my shoulders to deal with her. I raised my eyebrows back at him, but he put his hands behind his back, and the other men all took the smallest shift backwards. Even Mr. Hannahs had retreated behind his counter. I let them all know, with a look, exactly what I thought about being put into the awkward position, and, reaching down for Miss Alden's heaving shoulders, nudged her to rise from the chair.

Slowly, we left the post office and went into the hotel. Her driver stared, open-mouthed, as she passed, and the Fontaines were hard at work guessing what might have happened to upset her. Karine and Hattie watched me take Rose upstairs, and I called over my shoulder, "Hattie, bring up some tea for her, please."

It took me some time to calm Rose down. She asked me questions that I had no answers for and hurled accusations against Mr. Peabody that I had no idea what to do with.

When I stepped from her room, Hattie was in the hall with a tea tray in her hands. "Thank you," I said. "See if she wants anything else. She's had some bad news, but she will be all right."

Hattie nodded. "I'm up here cleaning as it is," she said. "I'll be right here if she needs me." She leaned closer. "No sign of a watch yet, though."

She stepped in with her tray, and I went back to the lobby where Lindley stood, waiting for me. His face was a perfect storm.

19

WATCH

"Lindley," I said, coming down the stairs.

"Loveda. We need to talk."

"Yes. We do. Where?" I looked through the window, and no one had moved. Rose was upstairs crying. Karine hummed determinedly in the kitchen. "Why don't we go for a walk?" I suggested.

He ran his hand through his hair one more time, then nodded and reached for the door. "The sheriff and the deputy have gone on to his office with the briefcase. They are reconsidering the case, looking over their original notes." He opened the door, and as I passed by him, his eyes looked deep into mine. "They asked me some hard questions just now. And I'd like to ask some of my own."

We stepped onto the veranda and Mr. Plink was now seated where Rose had been, looking for all the world as if he were on a summer holiday. No one was speaking but they all looked up. Lindley nodded to his lawyer as we walked away, down the middle of the road, toward Strawberry Creek. Lindley didn't offer his arm.

We walked in silence, passing the post office, the blacksmith shop, then the sheriff's office. At the turnoff to the creek, he motioned for me to precede him, and we stepped gratefully into the deep shade of the trees. I followed the sound of the water, stopping at last next to the creek where it formed its little waterfall, tumbling cheerfully over the lip of granite, and splashing in the small pool below before meandering away again.

"Loveda," he finally said, "what do you know about the night Craven was killed? How did you find out about Peabody being in my office?" He was distraught. "Because I had no idea he was in there."

"I suppose you didn't," I said, dipping a finger in the falling water. "Molly said she found you out in the lobby. According to her, you never made it to the office." I didn't want to face him. Didn't want to see his discomfort. But he put a hand on my arm, and I turned.

"Molly saw him?"

"Yes. She thought at first, he was you. She was looking for you."

He flushed beneath his tan face. "Why?"

"Lindley, I think you know."

"She told you? When?"

"Last night, when the girls dropped off Hattie. Thank you for her, by the way. She's perfect so far."

It was Lindley's turn to stare at the water. "Why would Molly tell you about us?"

"There wasn't much to tell, on her part. But she thought you and I were an item and told me plainly that, if I had my sights set on you, that she would leave at once."

"She what?" He spun around. "She won't."

The demanding tone in his voice told me everything I wanted to hear, and I smiled. "I suppose that depends a lot on what happens next."

"She thought you and I were together, did she?" Now it was his turn to smile. "Well," he said, straightening his jacket, "we are."

I raised an eyebrow.

"Loveda, we are business partners, no matter what, but it will always be a little more than that between us." He took my hand. "I want you to stay, and I want you to win." The sincerity in his face made me bite my lip to keep from tearing up.

"Mr. Craven almost took away everything from you. I won't let that mistake happen twice. I'll make sure it works out." He kissed my hand. "I feel particularly responsible for you. But," he said, relinquishing my hand, "it's not of a romantic nature." He frowned. "Have I led you believe otherwise? Do you have your sights set on me?"

"No," I said, smiling, "and thank you for clearing the air. While we are being frank, you should tell me what happened on the veranda the night Mr. Craven was killed. I'd like to hear your honest version of that." I hesitated. "And I'd like to hear your honest version of Molly's...relationship."

"I've turned out rather foolish today," he said. "I had to admit, in front of my lawyer, in front of Mr. Hannahs no less, that, instead of being in my office when Craven was killed, I was on the front veranda steps, kissing Molly." His hat was off again, and his fingers were about to stand his hair on end permanently. "I'm ashamed of the lie. But not of the kiss."

"Lindley, did you see Mr. Fontaine walking anywhere out there?"

He smiled. "I did, but only after I'd kissed her properly. I heard steps, turned to see him down the way, but he continued around the corner of the veranda, and I considered myself lucky that he hadn't seen us. Not," he insisted, "that I would have turned her loose if he had."

"That sounds as if you like it."

"I was on my way to my office, of course I was, but when I saw her standing in the lobby, well…" he trailed off and stared at the waterfall. "We're having a bit of… something…and I scarcely know myself what it is, it's been coming on so slowly."

"You can't just keep going like that," I said. "The girl needs clarity."

"I won't be questioned about it," he said with a bit of rebellion. "I'm a grown man, Loveda."

"Excuse me," I said, "but no partner of mine is going to be unhappy or confused. It's bad for business. I won't stand for it."

"She's a sweet girl. I would never trifle with a woman. You must believe that my intentions are noble. Bit of a cliche, I suppose." He hung his head. "What is your professional advice on it, then?"

"Dismiss her the minute you get home."

"What?"

"Tell her you care for her, and her only, then give her

a chance to see you as an equal. Actually," I said, "you must treat her as your superior."

"She is. She told the truth." He looked miserable. "What if she leaves?"

"She'll leave you, regardless, before the week's out, if you don't."

"I can't lose another maid!"

"No. You can't lose this chance at happiness. You can find more maids. You won't find more Mollys."

After another minute, Lindley offered me his arm again and we walked back to the highway. "The sheriff had better wrap up this investigation soon. Mr. Plink tells me there are other lawyers on their way up here. Newspaper reporters and deputies have swarmed my place. They have the body. They have the knife. Where's the killer?"

"I suppose it's not Mr. Peabody anymore?"

"The sheriff thinks he was looking for his kid. Peabody—or whatever his name is—did nothing more criminal than what I was going to do," Lindley said. We walked toward the buildings. "I want you to be careful, Loveda. That only reduced the suspect list by one."

I stopped at the post office landing and turned my back to my guests. They had watched us from the minute we'd reappeared on the road.

"Was Mr. Fontaine alone when you saw him on the veranda?" I asked quietly.

"I believe so, why?"

"I'm wondering if you were the only person stealing a kiss that night."

"Miss Brown!" Mr. Hannahs hollered at me from inside the post office and I jumped.

"Mr. Hannahs?" I asked, trying to peer through the screen door. "Are you okay?"

"Need you for a minute!" he called.

I shrugged and said goodbye to Lindley.

"Thank you for our talk," he said, kissing my hand. "I have to get Mr. Plink on his way. After this case closes, I'll have him work up some fresh papers for you. Don't give up on El Paso, Loveda."

I smiled as he went to collect his lawyer, and the two of them climbed into the buggy. I watched them drive away and turned to enter the post office.

"Miss Brown, I've been waiting for you all morning!" Mr. Hannahs was red in the face and pounded the counter hard enough I was afraid that he'd damaged his fist.

"Mr. Hannahs," I said, crossing the room to join him, "lower your voice." I'd never heard him yell like that unless he was angry at Lindley, and I fervently hoped his anger wasn't about the walk I'd just taken.

"Only look at what's in today's headlines!" He thrust the *Hemet News* in front of me and began to read it aloud, anyway.

"Notorious Tucson lawyer, Mr. Milo Craven, was staying at the Nelson Hotel on the night before his murder. Look!" Mr. Hannahs interjected, "How do they have a photo of you standing in front of the hotel?"

"I have no idea, Mr. Hannahs!" I leaned over and scrutinized the grainy image. Although I wasn't facing the camera in the photograph, there was no mistaking my face. I thought back to the reporter who had barged into the lobby. "He must have taken that from across the road, from the trees." I hated the idea that someone could do that without my knowing it. Once again, I felt violated and angry.

"The hotel proprietor, that's you, I suppose," continued Mr. Hannahs, "claimed to have no knowledge of the mysterious actions of Mr. Craven, but it's clear that nefarious doings followed the fraudulent lawyer in his last days. Is this the person responsible for his murder? Was a trip to the mountainside the final undoing of a man with many enemies? Mr. Craven left behind a wife and two children. Although his pocket watch speaks for him most eloquently, the esteemed Dr. Prost has denied any business relations with Mr. Craven and declined further comment. When will the murderer be caught, and will the public denounce or applaud him?"

Mr. Hannahs frowned at me. "This other picture looks very familiar. Don't you have a watch like this one?"

My hand flew to my throat. There, below the narrow column full of slander and fabrication, was another photo. Papa's watch, cover open, engraving clear enough to read. "To my dear colleague," read Mr. Hannahs again, "from Dr. Prost!"

I was silent for some time. Long enough for Mr. Hannahs to slide the newspaper beneath his counter, pour me a cup of his exceptional coffee, and make sympathetic noises. I looked at him over the steaming mug, ignoring the tears on my cheeks, my hands gripping the edge of the counter.

"Perhaps...Dr. Prost also gave Mr. Craven a watch?" he suggested.

"No. Mr. Fontaine stole my watch." I tried to keep my voice steady and failed. "Is he also a murderer?"

I WENT DIRECTLY to Mack's office.

"Miss Brown, please calm down." Mack had offered me the chair in his little room and poured a pale liquid from a flask he kept in a desk drawer into a cup for me. "You must be able to have proof before you fling accusations around. What has Mr. Fontaine done, besides be a bore, that makes you feel he is capable of murder?"

I sipped the drink and felt it burn down my throat. I knew better than to sip again.

"And can I remind you that he is sporting an eye that shouts from the rafters that he isn't overly athletic?"

"What does that have to do with it?" I asked.

"To be blunt, slitting a throat is not the easiest trick to pull off in one blow. Amateurs could bobble the job in any number of unfortunate ways. It takes strength and skill." Mack sat down behind his desk.

"Or luck and passion." I didn't want to go into details, but I felt that perhaps Mr. Fontaine had both.

The sheriff was gone, and I'd treated my guests on the veranda to another view of me hurrying from one place to another like a billiard ball.

"I left my watch in my desk drawer," I said, "early yesterday morning. The reporter was in my place after that. The only place the reporter could have laid his hands on the watch is when he ran upstairs. The only way the watch could have gotten upstairs into Mr. Fontaine's room, is if Mr. Fontaine put it there."

"The maid?"

"I didn't have a maid yesterday."

"Your cook?"

"Was making a cake."

"Mrs. Fontaine?"

"Gone to Lindley's on my horse. Mack, none of these people would have stolen a watch, only to place it in the upstairs room."

"All right, Miss Brown," he said, "I hear you. Let's see whether Mr. Fontaine has something to say for himself."

He left me sitting in his office while he walked down the way to my veranda. I was filled with dread and wished Mack hadn't moved so many things into the tiny space. Accusing someone of theft—or worse—while sitting twelve inches away from him seemed like madness.

When I heard footsteps returning, I stood up and moved away from the door. It opened, and Mr. and Mrs. Fontaine stepped inside.

"Apologies," Mack said from outside, "it's a tight fit. How about the Fontaines take a seat on my bed, and Miss Brown can take the desk chair, there? Make yourselves at home."

Everyone arranged themselves, and Mrs. Fontaine saw the questioning look on my face. "I wasn't going to let him come alone," she quipped. "The last time someone was invited for a chat, she left in hysterics." I was thankful Mack had placed a desk between us.

"Darling," objected Mr. Fontaine, but from the

sound of his voice, he hadn't been consulted on her decision and had not a shadow of argument left in him.

"Mr. Fontaine," Mack said from his seat by the door, "in an effort to be quick, I will be blunt. Have you read any newspapers this morning?"

If that was Mack's way of being direct, we were going to be here for a while.

"No," Mr. Fontaine said, as puzzled as I was.

"Do you personally know any newspaper reporters, or have you come into contact with one lately?" He had his notebook in hand and jotted down answers as they came.

"No."

"Well," interrupted Mrs. Fontaine, "we did place a newspaper notice about the wedding."

"That, however," Mack said, writing, "is impersonal. Did you know the people in the office?"

"No," Mrs. Fontaine said and ignored the irritated look from her husband.

"A newspaper reporter was in your hotel room yesterday." Mack put it as a statement.

"Yes." Mr. Fontaine took the lead again.

"Did you know him?"

"No."

"Would you be able to identify him if you saw him?"

"Doubtful. He was in and out very fast and ran out the door and away."

"And did this person remove anything from your room when he was there?"

"No." If Mr. Fontaine was lying, he was very good at it.

"Then why," I interjected, "did you yell 'stop thief' when he ran?"

Mr. Fontaine looked at me. "Anyone who comes into a hotel room like that is looking for trouble. I was lying down, groggy, with this," he pointed to his eye, now almost healed. "It was a normal reaction to the situation, if you ask me."

Mack nodded as he scribbled something else into his book. "Very good. Did you notice anyone else behaving in an unusual manner around the hotel yesterday?"

I could have sworn Mr. Fontaine considered naming his wife and mentally wrestled with the temptation. "No. Afraid not," he said.

"Thank you, Mr. Fontaine. Now, you see, Mrs. Fontaine," Mack said with a smile, "nothing to worry about. Miss Brown has reported a missing item, and we thought we'd ask everyone about the reporters, as we have reason to believe a newspaper person is our thief. If the item was not stolen from your room, we can narrow it down to other places." He stood up and opened the door. "It's a nice warm day, isn't it?"

The Fontaines stood up, and without a glance in my direction, stepped outside next to him.

"It is," Mrs. Fontaine said. "We're packing up, deputy, in great expectations of leaving for home. Please tell me we can go today?"

"I'm sure we are very close to closing the case," he said with a little nod.

The Fontaines walked away, and Mack stepped back inside in time to see me pick up the cup and drain it.

20

KIDNAPPED

"What was that?" I choked out, wiping my mouth with the back of my sleeve.

"Miss Brown," he began.

"You didn't even ask him if he stole the watch. You didn't even tell him it was a watch we were looking for!"

He had to sit down in the other chair, and it felt nice to be sitting in the seat of power for once. "Mack, he took it, I know he did." My lip quivered. "I want my watch back."

"And you shall have it." Mack reached over and patted my hand. "I will 'phone down to the paper at once and demand it."

"He's lying."

"Perhaps. All we have to do is dust your watch for fingerprints to find out. If he touched it, they'll be there. Either way, we've caught the reporter, and he will confess, whether he took it from Fontaine's room or not."

"What if he's our killer?"

"Miss Brown." His voice became very patient as he stood up. "I must ask you to refrain from wild accusations."

"Someone did it," I said, "and it's not Mr. Peabody." It was awfully warm inside, and I started to ask Mack to open the windows, then realized that they already were.

"About that." Mack sounded angry. He pointed to Mr. Craven's briefcase sitting solidly on the floor next to the desk. "If you knew Mr. Peabody didn't kill Mr. Craven, why didn't you say so yesterday when we were looking at the knife? Why would you let me look like such a fool? Even you agreed that Peabody was our killer! I made a classic blunder and chased the obvious suspect."

I didn't like his tone and implied as much. "I didn't find out until late last night, and as Mr. Peabody is definitely not the killer and most definitely out of reach regardless, I thought it might keep overnight. When was I going to speak to you? In my sleep? You needn't make such a fuss over your reputation."

"It's man hours, Miss Brown," he said. "Last night the sheriff made plans for a stake-out today. To make sure Mr. Peabody wouldn't escape once he realized we were on to him. Those hours could have been better spent going over other suspects."

"Well, he's still a bad egg, as you say. Maybe someone should be here when Miss Alden gets a hold of him."

Mack wanted to pace, it was clear, but three steps to

each side was all he had to work with. The thought made me giggle.

Mack frowned at me. "A custody battle is fought in the courts, Miss Brown. If there's a skirmish, it will be verbal. But I've been given directions to allow the boy to go home with his aunt. Mr. Peabody has no reason to suspect that she's here, so I'm counting on their encounter being over quickly. Miss Alden will leave as soon as the scouts return." He put a hand on the gun in the holster on his hip. "And if Mr. Peabody needs a reason to walk away, I'll have one for him."

I sat there staring at Mack's gun until he was uncomfortable.

"Miss Brown?" he asked, "let's step out for some air." I took his hand and let him help me from the chair, and he put it in the crook of his arm as we stepped outside. "It's past noon, we'll see what Karine made for lunch."

"Mr. Fontaine killed Mr. Craven," I said.

Mack pulled on my arm, and we stopped. He looked around us in every direction, but everyone was inside. "Miss Brown," he begged, "please stop. Until we know for sure and have someone behind bars, you simply can't go round saying things like that."

"What was he doing on the veranda?"

"Miss Brown, are you going to stop?" He looked at me like he might toss me over his shoulder and plant me in a tree unless I did.

"Yes." I stood up as straight as possible. "I will." My stomach was protesting both the liquor and Mack's demand.

"If you must ponder things," he said, somewhat

relieved, "ask yourself who wanted to frame Mr. Peabody. The knife did not land under his tent by accident."

We continued down the boardwalk in silence. I needed to get to Lindley's. I needed to find Charlotte.

Lunch was exceptionally quiet and vaguely tense. The Fontaines were resentful of Mack's questioning and probably mine by implication. Rose came down, having cleaned herself up fairly well, paid me for their rooms, and she and the driver were prepared to leave as soon as the boys returned. Mack ate a hearty meal, and the rest of us picked at it with indifference, which made Karine fussy in the kitchen and Hattie try to blend into the walls as she delivered trays.

The Fontaines had only just risen from their chairs when we all heard shouts outside. The cries brought us all quickly out of the hotel, and we saw the Boy Scouts, riding their mules triumphantly down the road toward us.

"Hurrah! Hurrah! Hurrah!" they shouted, the mules pacing, unconcerned, below them.

I found myself counting heads and started running to meet them. Nine boys. And no Mr. Peabody.

"Where is he?" called Mack, running next to me.

"What's happened?" I shouted.

The boy on the lead mule hopped down and hitched it to the post in front of the blacksmith shop, and the boys behind him did the same, scrabbling down and securing animals in front of whichever post was handy. We had mules up and down the boardwalk, and a Boy Scout gang tramping the length of it, clapping each other on the back, each talking over the others. Carlos and Mr. Hannahs both came to their doors and gaped at the confusion. Karine popped her head out from behind the kitchen door.

"We did it!" cried the twins.

"Wait till Mr. Peabody sees us!" a freckled boy said. "We got our badges for sure! Wahoo!"

"Boys," I yelled over their excited heads, "where is Mr. Peabody?" I grabbed the nearest scout and made him look me in the eyes. "Where is he?" I repeated.

"He's coming behind us," he said with a grin. "We had to find our way back down the mountain all by ourselves to earn our explorer badge."

"But who's missing?" I said, and my stomach felt like lead.

"Toby stayed with him on account of he needed the bugle, but we got here easy! We did it!" he crowed, and the other boys scattered. Some went directly for my apple trees, and a couple went to brag to Carlos.

I looked around. The Fontaines had gotten no further than the veranda. The driver was standing between his car and the boys who spied it first, trying to keep them away from it. But Rose had run into the middle of the road, looking in every direction, spinning like a gray top, and her wail grew louder and higher as she did.

"Mack!" I called. He was heading for his office and turned. "Miss Alden!" He wasn't going to leave me alone with her twice. I marched after him. "Mack, you have to talk to her."

"I need to go for the sheriff," he said. "Maybe Mr. Peabody's coming still or maybe he's not, but that's a

really big coincidence, don't you think? That he's disappeared with the boy?"

"If he shows up, you have to be here!"

He realized it was true and for once didn't argue
with me, but stood on the boardwalk shaking his head
over the tumult. "He could. But if he's figured out that
Toby is his kid, he could be halfway to Mexico by now."

"Mexico!" Miss Alden screeched behind me. I
almost jumped into Mack's arms.

"My Toby is up there," she said. "I demand that you
find him at once!"

"Miss, we can't form a posse unless it becomes a
missing person's case," Mack said. "At the moment,
we've been told that your son is on his way and could
arrive at any minute. Let's wait and see."

"What if there's been an accident?" Rose clutched
her hand to her heart. "What if this wretched man fell
from a cliff or was bitten by a snake?" Her face was
ashen. "What if Toby was?" At this, she collapsed, and
three Boy Scouts rushed to her side. One took her wrist
and felt for a pulse, one lifted her feet, and one called
for the first aid kit.

I took one look at Rose's bloomers and ran. "I'm
going for the sheriff," I called over my shoulder.

Carlos saw me coming and went to get Blue. I went
into his shop and found her saddle.

"Thanks, Carlos," I said, as we both went to work on
Blue.

I RACED Blue past the two cars and handful of tents parked along the road and ignored the men lounging beneath trees at Lindley's. When I galloped up to the entrance, a stable boy saw me coming and was there to take Blue's reins. I ran up the stairs and into the lobby shouting, "Lindley! Where are you?"

Lindley, his lawyer, two deputies, and the sheriff streamed out of the office and took in my wild eyes.

"They're back," I said, catching my breath, "and Mr. Peabody took Toby."

"What?" the sheriff said.

"All the scouts came back except Toby. The boys said Mr. Peabody kept Toby and sent them back on their own. I left Mack with them, and Miss Alden is beside herself."

Sheriff Fuller remained calm and took a minute to rub the back of his neck. "Custody issue isn't something we need to pursue," he said, with a glance at the lawyer. "But is it a kidnapping? Missing persons?" He considered it, then put his hands on his hips. "Hell, boys, could be we misjudged the man. Convincing act. What about this hypothesis: the man knows Craven has information, he gets what he needs from the briefcase, kills the man responsible for giving away the kid, ditches the knife, plans an expedition, takes off with the kid?" He frowned. "Question is, what's he doing with the kid?"

No one spoke. I couldn't breathe.

"That depends," continued the sheriff, reaching back into the office for his hat, "on whether or not the kid went willingly." He put his hat on and tamped it down. "If the kid didn't want to go, or if the kid fought back, and the man's already done one desperate deed of revenge..."

I gasped, but the other men remained grim and went back into the office for their things.

"Let's go find out." The sheriff and his deputies went out the lobby doors.

Lindley put a hand on my arm. "I'm sure the boy will be okay."

I smiled weakly. But I knew from experience that people weren't always what they told you they were, and I had more faith in the boy's honesty than the man's. I desperately hoped the boy was safe.

"Lindley," I said, "before I go back, I need to speak to the maids." I looked over at Charlotte, sitting at her desk. She had been listening the entire time, and in her face I saw fear, sadness, and anger.

"What is it, Loveda?" he asked. "It's all we can do to not fall apart around here."

"Have you spoken to Molly yet?" I asked quietly.

He leaned back and darted a look at Charlotte but said clearly enough, "We just returned. No."

I turned to the lawyer. "Would you mind stepping into the office for a few minutes? We need some privacy." I smiled at the incongruity. "After all you've heard this morning, I imagine that's silly. But it's a personal conversation. Nothing that could help you with the paperwork."

Mr. Plink gave me a little bow. "Of course," he said, "I need to finish writing up my own reports so I can leave today, myself." He reentered the office and closed the door behind him.

"Lindley," I said, looking into his eyes, "do you still stand by our conversation?"

"Loveda, what are you up to?"

"Lindley, it's important. There's something I need to know, and I need your help, but you must tell me first, if you do."

He gave me a half smile. "You really do drive straight to the point, don't you? Yes. I trust you. What do you need?"

"I'm sorry," I said, "but this is the fastest way to know for sure."

"If you would please," I asked Charlotte, "fetch Molly? We need you both." Charlotte looked from me to Lindley, who nodded, and then left the room.

"What are you up to?"

"There's no way that Mr. Peabody could have been physically in your office and been murdering Mr. Craven at the same time."

"You don't believe he did it?"

"No. But we need to find out who did."

The two girls came into the lobby with wary faces. Molly looked down at the floor, and Charlotte kept her head up and her arm around Molly's shoulders.

"Thank you, ladies," I said. "Molly, please come stand in front of the office door."

She complied, passed us without making eye contact.

"There. And Lindley, please go stand in front of the ballroom door." He did so.

I turned to Charlotte. "And where were you right before the screaming began?"

She pointed behind Lindley. "On the back veranda."

"You were coming or going from the Fontaine's suite?"

"Yes."

"Well, which one is it? We need a very accurate picture."

"Going."

"You mean to say that you had already searched for the fan and left without it? Returned to the veranda to tell Mrs. Fontaine so?"

"Yes."

"Was there anyone in the Fontaine's room?"

"No." Her frown was growing. "I've already told you this."

"I know. Thank you." I turned to Lindley. "Now, Lindley, if you would come toward your office. And Molly, if you would walk away from the door into the center of the lobby."

They both did so and stopped when they were inches apart from colliding.

"There," I said, "and what happened next?"

Lindley looked at me. His eyes narrowed in accusation, but mine held a challenge and, not one to back down in a gentleman's duel, he made up his mind at once and took Molly in his arms.

Molly looked up and put her hands against his chest, but he brought his face down to hers and said, "Blast them all. Let's tell the truth, Molly."

Charlotte inhaled sharply when they kissed, and I turned to her and said, "I think, given the quickly changing circumstances around here, that you should step forward and tell the truth, too."

She kept her chin up but began to wring her hands. There was a struggle on her face.

"Do you care about Lindley or not?" I insisted.

Lindley looked up at her as well, but never moved his arms from around Molly. They both waited with me for whatever Charlotte was trying to say.

"Please." It was Molly's small voice we heard, and she was talking to Charlotte.

Charlotte hung her head, and I walked over to her. "We don't know who's in danger," I said, "but whatever you've done can be fixed right now. If you tell the truth."

21

TRUTH

"I wasn't alone in the room." Charlotte twisted her hands together in anguish. "Mr. Fontaine was there."

I tried to sound sympathetic. "And you kissed him on the veranda?"

She looked up at me, angry. "No! I would never! He's a scoundrel!"

Mrs. Fontaine's accusations were fresh in my mind. I tried again. "What happened, then?"

She kept her eyes firmly on the carpet. "He did come up to me on the veranda. At the back corner. I thought he needed something, but he approached me very intimately and tried to ask me a favor." She shook her head. "I didn't even have time to react. Mrs. Fontaine was at the other end of the veranda and called out his name. He jumped away and left me standing there, feeling like a fool." Her chin came back up and she looked me in the eye. "I'd done nothing wrong. I went up to Mrs. Fontaine and asked whether she needed anything, and she sent me to find her fan."

She paused here, so I nudged her. "Which you did?"

"Yes. There was a lamp on in the room, and the minute I went into it, Mr. Fontaine came in behind me and closed the door. I determined to slap him, scream if I needed to, but he smiled and told me he had a proposition." Her hands clenched into fists. "He wanted me to steal for him."

She turned her eyes to Lindley in an agony. "He asked if there were any valuables hidden away and told me if I didn't cooperate, he'd seal my fate." She teared up. "My reputation, my career, my virtue…he, he took me by the arms, and what else could I do? I was terrified and agreed to find him something. I said whatever he wanted me to say so he would let me go."

She pulled a handkerchief from her pocket and wiped her face. "I'm so sorry."

Lindley's voice was very quiet. Very calm. He kept Molly's hand firmly in his but asked, "What did you take?"

"Nothing!" she cried. "The minute he left the room, the screaming began, and he ran for it. I left their room, crying, and never went near him again. They left the very next day."

She was miserable, and I put a gentle hand on her shoulder. "Why didn't you tell somebody?"

She glanced at Molly. "Mr. Lindley, you were acting strange to begin with. I thought maybe the idea of my virtue wouldn't stand up against the idea of having a thief on staff. I was sure you'd turn me out. Why would you believe me instead of a gentleman? And the look on Mr. Fontaine's face was plain that he'd be after me if I mentioned it to anyone."

Molly had placed her hand on Lindley's sleeve, and he looked down at her without smiling. "Did you know this?"

She trembled. "Yes."

"Do you think I'm a gentleman?"

Almost a whisper. "Yes."

He looked into her eyes for another minute, then turned to us. "I've given you a promotion, but that's not enough. I apologize. I'm going to put protection in place for my staff. It's outrageous that a guest can accost you at any time." He looked at Molly. "Or anyone, for that matter."

"Lindley," I said.

"I've been a fool." He stepped away from Molly and took both of her hands in his. "Please, Molly, forgive me."

Her smile was timid but authentic, and Lindley brushed the tops of her hands with his lips before letting them go.

"Tell me how this plays out at once, Miss Brown," he said. "I have many things to see to. And a killer to catch."

I stepped away from Charlotte, and she wiped her face again. "What's the fastest route from this door," I indicated the office, "to the corner of the veranda where Mr. Craven was sitting?"

Everyone agreed it was going through the front doors and turning left.

"And who was standing between him and the front doors?"

Molly blushed.

"Any other route is complicated, especially if you're trying to avoid people and carrying a knife. He simply would never have had time to kill Mr. Craven."

"And you are suggesting," Lindley said harshly, "that our killer is Mr. Fontaine?"

"He was in the immediate vicinity, with no one watching him, without scruples, and is obviously capable of violence." I turned to Charlotte. "I have to go. Did you tell Hattie any of this?"

She blanched. "We didn't want to frighten her any more than she already was. Your place is so small," she hesitated, "nowhere to hide. Nothing to steal." She saw the reaction on my face. "She's safe, isn't she?"

"I hope so," I said, turning on my heel. "There are four deputies with guns around her. Lindley, thank you."

"Loveda, be careful," he called after me. I bounded down the steps, and a stable boy darted into the stable for Blue.

A man came up to me and asked, "Hey lady, where's everyone off to today? Anything going on inside? Sheriff and his boys looked pretty worked up when they left. What's happening?"

I looked at the newspaper reporter so fiercely that he took a step back.

"Don't take my picture," I said. "Don't ask me any questions." I took Blue's reins. "And if you work for the *Hemet News*," I said, swinging up on Blue, skirt pulled up to reveal my stockings and high-button shoes, "tell your boss that I'm bringing charges of theft to his doorstep unless I get my gold watch back!"

I took Blue into a canter and headed for home.

As I rode around the last bend, I slowed to a walk and took in the sight. Mrs. Keen's buggy sat parked next to Miss Alden's automobile in front of my hotel. The two women were on my veranda, pacing the length of it, arms wrapped around each other, an aura of volcanic tension in their wake. The Fontaines sat in chairs up against the plate glass window, craning their necks in an attempt to see and hear what was happening next door. Rose's driver was seated in his black machine, now quite thick with dust, staring directly ahead at the hotel at nothing in particular.

Under the oak tree, sitting in the shade, were half a dozen reporters, pencils scribbling furiously into notebooks. Mack and a deputy stood between them and the post office. They all looked my way briefly as I rode up, then went right back to what they were doing. Beyond the post office, past the blacksmith shop, the other deputy stood, blocking the road from that direction.

I dismounted next to Mrs. Keen's buggy and hitched Blue, trying not to distract anyone. After thinking about it, I walked around the back of the hotel, passed my garden, and crept up the side of the building to the open kitchen door where I'd counted on Karine standing. She did not disappoint me.

She held her finger to her lips as I joined her on the wooden porch. The sheriff was standing on the post office landing, facing the front door. Sitting along Mr. Hannahs' bench at the doorway were all nine Boy Scouts. I wondered how long it had taken him to accomplish the feat. Behind the sheriff stood seven mules, hitched to the post, patiently watching him work. I imagined Mr. Hannahs and Carlos were somewhere close by.

"Boys," began the sheriff in a voice meant to encourage trust, "I need to know what happened up on the trail this morning. I need to know anything you want to tell me about what Mr. Peabody said or did, anything at all."

"We just went camping," one said. "The usual stuff. I can't wait to tell my Ma about it!"

"Was there anything *un*usual, then, son?" The sheriff's impatience was showing beneath his thin veneer of calm.

"We heard coyotes," offered another. "If you howl real loud, they answer you back."

"What about Toby?" asked the sheriff. "Did he act any different this morning?"

"He was mad he had to stay with Mr. Peabody," a boy said, swinging his legs. "Thought it was real unfair."

"You can't walk in the wilderness alone. Everybody knows that," offered another.

"Mr. Peabody said he needed Toby on account of his bugle."

"Yeah, that way if anything went wrong, he could blow his bugle for help."

"But he didn't get his explorer badge," a scout said, "so that's not fair. He shoulda got a chance."

"Hey sheriff, can you shoot your gun for us?"

"Yeah, shoot at a tree or something so we can watch."

"Can we get our picture in the newspaper?" One boy tried to jump up, but the sheriff caught him by the shoulder and directed him to sit back down again.

"Where did you see Mr. Peabody and Toby last, before you headed back to town?" Sheriff Fuller was breathing deeply.

"At the campsite," a boy said.

"Toby was on the mule and Mr. Peabody had the rope, and they waved and watched while we went ahead down the trail."

"How long did Mr. Peabody say he'd be before following after you?"

"He said he was gonna be right behind us. In case we got lost." The boy laughed. "We never get lost."

"Yep. Told us to hurry, in case he did catch us. That would be cheatin', if we let him help."

"What time was it when you left them?" The sheriff was pulling at straws, I thought. How would the boys know?

"Seven this morning," a boy promptly said. "I got my Ma's watch."

One boy punched him. "Bet your Ma don't know you took it."

The sheriff rubbed the back of his neck. "Boys, did you ever see or hear Mr. Peabody or Toby again, after you left?"

"Nope. Hey, when is lunch? We need to start a fire."

"Boys," commanded the sheriff, "sit still for a few

minutes more. Don't anybody move." He nodded toward Mack, who came forward to join him. The deputy stepped up and stood next to the boys on the landing, and the sheriff and Mack stepped up to the hotel veranda.

Mack looked my way, then ignored me. Miss Alden and Mrs. Keen stepped to the veranda rail and spoke to the sheriff on the other side of it. The Fontaines and the reporters strained to hear.

"You're going after Toby," Miss Alden said.

"Yes. I'll form a search party and head up the trail. I recommend you go on home, Miss Alden. There's nothing more to be done here."

"But I want to be here the minute there's news!"

Mrs. Keen added her emphatic nod to Miss Alden's declaration.

"I understand your concern, Miss Alden," he said, glancing over to the reporters. "But we will be bringing Mr. Peabody and the boy to Hemet once they've been located. They won't return to Idyllwild."

"I don't understand," Miss Alden said, reaching for her handkerchief. "What if Toby is hurt?"

"Whether this is a medical crisis or a criminal activity is yet to be determined," he said firmly, "but the boy will end up in Hemet, no matter what. If you must be on hand, wait for him there. Either the courthouse or the hospital will be able to direct you."

"Oh!" she said and fell into Mrs. Keen's embrace.

The sheriff noticed me then and said, "Miss Brown, if I may have a word?"

I gave Karine a brief look as I stepped down and joined them. He motioned toward the garden, and we walked behind the post office, out of sight and, I assumed, out of earshot.

"Miss Brown," the sheriff said, "it's been six hours since Mr. Peabody or the boy was seen last. That's a mighty big head start. I don't need to tell you that they won't be coming back. I've got to get men on the trail and hope it's still fresh enough to track."

"There'll be clues," Mack said, "footprints, mule droppings. We'll have to hurry to use the daylight."

"You aren't going," the sheriff said. "I'm taking Carlos."

Mack waited a beat then said, "But, sir, I'm more than qualified to lead a posse."

"I'm not doubting your abilities, MacDougall. I have an invaluable asset in Carlos Peyote and he'll find them fast."

Mack was silent and looked out at the trees.

"Now then." The sheriff turned back to me. "These boys have to stay at your place." He held up a hand when I opened my mouth. "They can't be put back at Lindley's. Not safe to camp alone, and the place is still a crime scene. You'll be well compensated for your time, Miss Brown. They only need to be safe until Lindley takes them back to Banning in his coach in the morning. No other way to get them downhill."

Mack and I stood there, thinking of all the things we didn't dare say out loud.

"That's settled, then. Lotta trails up there." He jabbed a thumb at Tahquitz Peak. "He could cross the saddle and head east for the desert or take one south where it drops to the Anza Valley. But I'm hoping we catch them fast enough to haul 'em into Hemet. I'll be in touch after we get there. If we lose the trail, or if we find a body…it might be sooner rather than later."

He looked at Mack. "I'm counting on you to keep this place quiet till I'm back." The sheriff walked toward the blacksmith shop. Horses came to the corral rails in greeting.

Several minutes afterward, we watched the sheriff, his two deputies, and Carlos loading up their saddled horses. Rifles, blankets, canteens, rope. The sheriff threw first aid supplies into his saddlebags, but there was no way of knowing whether they would use it or pack out a body instead.

The scouts watched, fascinated, and Carlos had clearly risen to hero status among them. They bombarded him with questions that he didn't have time to answer and offered nonstop advice. The sheriff took advantage of their collective attention and told them they were staying at the hotel overnight, and to implicitly obey the lady in charge. When he pointed in my direction and nine pairs of eyes took my measure, I went weak in the knees with fear.

The reporters were spread out from one end of the boardwalk to the other, peeking around corners and scribbling down their opinions. By the time Carlos finally led the band of men down to Strawberry Creek and turned into the tree line, the reporters were in front of Mack's office, pushing their pencils as fast as they could go.

"Okay, boys, the show is over," Mack said from the middle of the road. "Get going. Maybe you'll reach Hemet before they do."

The reporters walked down the road, hesitated in front of the boys.

"Get!" hollered Mack. They saluted him and kept walking, laughing, headed for Lindley's and their automobiles, off to get the next story.

My heart sank for the bugle playing boy with the yellow bandana.

22

THIEF

I stood on the post office landing and looked up and down the road. Carlos and the men had disappeared in one direction, the reporters in the other. Mack shook his head and went into his office, shutting the door behind him. Miss Alden and Mrs. Keen were deep in conversation on the veranda. The Fontaines were still seated near them, and I wondered what they would say when they realized the Boy Scouts would be sleeping upstairs with them. It made me smile despite myself.

I turned around slowly and sure enough, Mr. Hannahs was standing behind his screen door, watching.

"What did you make of all that?" I asked him.

"I have a list of complaints," he said. "The first is that there are mules tied up where my stagecoach will be. The second is that no one is minding the blacksmith shop."

He was right. I dug deep into my memory and thought back to when I was a governess in Boston. The twin boys there had given me grief on occasion, but I had always managed to stay one step ahead of them. I looked around me. Nine boys wandered in various states of mischief. I shuddered. It had been awhile.

"Boys!" I belted it out from my diaphragm.

Apparently, the stern governess voice I'd cultivated back in Boston was as chilling as ever. I had everyone's complete attention, even the people on the veranda.

"There are seven mules tied up out here," I said. "You need to get them unloaded, cleaned up, and out in the corral in the next thirty minutes." They stared at me.

"Go!"

The boys ran to the mules and began untying bundles, flinging parcels up and down the boardwalk in a race to see who could beat the rest.

I marched along the side and pointed into the black-smith shop. "You get the brushes," I said to a boy. "You get a hoof pick," I said to the next. I nodded at the first scout who was leading a mule toward the corral. "Make sure he's brushed. Don't let the horses out when you open the gate."

I pointed to a boy who was standing aside. "Start gathering the supplies. When they're in a tidy pile right here, we'll move you all in upstairs."

The boy pulled a face at me. "Lady, I'm tired. I'm takin' a break."

"You want your horsemanship badge?" I asked, bending down and looking him in the eye.

He nodded.

"Then get going." I stood up and hollered at the retreating backs. "First man who gets his mule done and the packs ready gets a dozen cookies!"

The boys tripped over each other and nearly lost a mule in the process of finishing the job. When they were all lined back up on the boardwalk, parcels on their shoulders, I led them to the hotel. Mrs. Keen and Miss Alden stood aside, mouths open, as they passed into the lobby.

"Upstairs, three doors on the left, three boys to a room," I called after them. "Then report back here."

Mrs. Keen goggled at me. "Miss Brown? Have you ever considered leading a Girl Scout troop?"

"Never once," I said. What she was witnessing was self-preservation.

She turned to Miss Alden. "Such a quiet, unassuming thing," she said. "I never guessed she had it in her."

Mrs. Keen hugged Rose and said, "I'll say goodbye now, and good luck. It's a terrible business, but we know how to keep our chin up, don't we?" Rose nodded. "Good. I know it will all turn out for the best, and I hope you and Toby come back for a visit sometime. We must remain positive! We must see things through! Have a safe drive down the mountain, dear."

Mrs. Keen climbed into her buggy and rode away in the afternoon sunshine.

"I must hurry if I'm to make it to Hemet in the daylight," Rose said.

She went to the driver and asked him to start the automobile, then reached into the back seat to retrieve her veil and came back to the veranda with us. All the boys clambered back outside and gathered around to watch the driver work his magic. I was as spellbound as they were. We watched him shift gears, push buttons, pull levers, adjust the choke, prime the cylinders, and crank the shaft. It was an amazing process. The engine came to life, and the boys cheered for him. The driver smiled for the first time.

"Well," Rose said, "I'm off. Thank you." She bumped into me as she hurried past us, and the driver opened the door for her to climb aboard. She had a word with him and he nodded, then he got himself into his seat and backed the car into the road. I saw at once that the boys were about to run behind the car and quickly shouted, "Who wants cookies?"

It was enough of a distraction, and I held the lobby door open for them. They piled inside. The Fontaines were stuck to their seats, still, and had yet to utter a syllable. Mrs. Fontaine looked at me and said, "Are those ruffians staying in this hotel?" Her eyes despaired and her tone was tragic.

I nodded and went inside.

Karine stood in the kitchen doorway, surveying the group of jostling boys, hands on her hips, the door held open by her ample backside. "Now then," she was saying, "you'll have to have better manners than that."

"Let's sit in the dining room," I suggested. "We have enough chairs there."

The boys gathered around the table and I said, "Karine, I'm sorry. This was very last minute. Sheriff's orders."

She smiled. "On a moment's notice, the ad said. I haven't forgotten. I can feed a pile of boys, don't you worry."

"But do you have cookies?" I asked. "Any ginger-snaps left?"

I heard Rose's car drive by.

She laughed. "Yes, and more are easy to whip up. Boys don't worry none about quality nor variety," she said, moving back into the kitchen. "They are all about volume. Send them out for apples to go with the cookies, and maybe we'll pop corn tonight."

The idea made me smile. I hadn't had popped corn in years.

"Miss Brown! Miss Brown!" The calls were muffled but clear, even over the boys' voices. I dashed outside again.

I looked at the Fontaines, and they pointed toward the blacksmith shop. Mr. Hannahs was out on his landing, and I ran past him, calling out, "What happened?"

Mack had his horse out of the corral and tied up for saddling.

"What is it?" I asked.

"She took it!" Mack said. "She bloody held a gun on me and took the lawyer's briefcase!"

"Who? Rose?"

"Why didn't I jump over my desk and tackle her?" He cinched the saddle tight, and his horse shifted uneasily.

"She took the papers?" I was dumbfounded. "What gun?"

"I'm going after her. That contraption can only go so fast on this road." He leapt onto his horse and gathered up the reins. "And this time, I won't be caught flat-footed!"

He clapped his legs against his horse and bolted from the blacksmith shop in pursuit of Miss Alden's automobile. I followed onto the boardwalk and joined

Mr. Hannahs on his landing. He watched Mack disappear down the road. The Fontaines were on their feet watching as well, and Mrs. Fontaine actually looked amused.

"Complaint number three," Mr. Hannahs grumbled. "I've about had my fill of nonsense. How did we go from all the law enforcement to none?"

I shrugged. "Where did Rose get a gun?" My head was spinning. "Mack can't go after her all alone. There are two of them, even if he does catch up to them."

Mr. Hannahs grunted and said, "Come inside."

He went to the telephone and rang it. After a couple of turns, someone picked up at Lindley's, and Mr. Hannahs told them to rouse the stable boys and back up the deputy. "They could be anywhere on that twenty-mile switchback," he said as he hung up. "But at least he won't be alone."

He stood behind his counter and asked, "How're you holding up, Miss Brown? Awful sorry to hear what I had to hear this morning. Lot of snakes in this world."

"Isn't that the truth?" asked Mr. Fontaine, coming into the post office. "How do you do?"

Mr. Hannahs nodded, and I stepped aside, feigning interest in a stack of postcards.

"We'll be leaving on the morning stagecoach, my good man," Mr. Fontaine said. "I'd like to purchase the tickets now and save us some fuss then, you know." He reached into his trouser pocket and pulled out his billfold.

Mr. Hannahs looked him up and down. "Don't recall you arriving on the coach."

Mr. Fontaine smiled. "We didn't. Came up in Mr.

Lindley's beautiful white coach on Monday. Apparently, it's been commandeered for other purposes. Our honeymoon isn't at all what we'd hoped for." He glanced my way. "The regular coach is just another nail in the coffin, really."

"Murder has a way of doing that," agreed Mr. Hannahs somberly.

I slowly edged away from Mr. Fontaine.

"Glad to see justice upheld in this fine community," continued Mr. Fontaine. "What are things coming to when apparently upstanding clean cut American men turn out to be good-for-nothing murderers? Using children, too." He handed his money to Mr. Hannahs, who was writing out the ticket. "I hope the sheriff gives him his due."

He looked at me. "No offense, miss, but a man who will slit another man's throat deserves the death penalty, and I see no reason why the courts need to be involved." He took his ticket and nodded his thanks to Mr. Hannahs. "Prison's too good for him. Good day."

It seemed to me that Mr. Fontaine was overplaying it a bit.

"Complaints four and five are the Fontaines in particular," Mr. Hannahs said. He ducked behind his counter and came back up with a stack of newspapers. They had been sorted and opened to different pages.

"I keep papers, Miss Brown. They're an education."

"What is it, Mr. Hannahs?" I asked.

Mr. Hannahs shook the paper on top at me.

"I've found it. It's in here." He held it under my nose. "From last month's pile, an article in the *Arizona Daily Star*."

He plunked his finger down, as if pinning the newspaper to the counter and read the headline. "Wife of Railroad Engineer L. H. Cooper Sentenced for Murder of Husband."

"What?"

"Mrs. Louis H. Cooper," he continued, "sentenced to hang for the murder by poison of her late husband. Judge Moore passed judgement after key testimony provided by distinguished attorney, Mr. Milo Craven, Esquire, of local prominence."

He stopped reading and asked, "This the same lawyer as you had in here Tuesday? Same one you all had a powwow over in here this morning?"

I put a hand on my stomach. "It must be."

"But that's not all I found," continued Mr. Hannahs. He reached behind the counter. "Asked myself why that name was familiar. Not the lawyer, mind you, the woman. This one's from last week." He pulled a newer copy of the same *Daily Star* and read the article inside.

"Mr. J. Fontaine Marries Railroad Bride. Miss Lucy M. Cooper, daughter of the late Mr. and Mrs. Louis H. Cooper of Tucson, Arizona, and Mr. Jonathan Fontaine, son of Mr. and Mrs. Erik Fontaine of New York, New York, were wed by the justice of the peace in a private ceremony out of respect to the deceased parents of the bride and were received by a small group of intimate acquaintances for a wedding breakfast at the Hotel Adams before leaving on their wedding trip. The newlyweds will honeymoon via railway to a mountaintop resort and plan to set up housekeeping in Riverside, California."

I found myself, once again, gripping Mr. Hannahs' counter in an effort to stay upright.

"I'm thinking, Miss Brown," he said quietly, "that you and Miss Rose weren't the only ones unhappy with this particular lawyer."

"Mr. Craven was responsible for Lucy Fontaine's mother's death." I whispered it out loud, hoping it would click. Hoping my brain could process the implications without making me faint on the spot. "I think, Mr. Hannahs, that could induce Mr. Fontaine to murder."

"I can't let you stay here tonight," he said, folding the papers back up.

"I can't leave," I said. "Mr. Hannahs, I have nine boys and two other women in that hotel. I have to keep them all safe."

"We have no way to capture or question him. The Fontaines can't leave tonight, and I won't just ride home and let it be." Mr. Hannahs was very upset, but trying not to be heard outside the building. "That fool deputy took the last able-bodied men in town with him."

"We'll let him think he's won." I said it matter-of-factly and almost convinced myself. "Why not? Mr. Fontaine thinks we're all looking in the opposite direction. They'll have an evening distracted by the boys and get out of here first thing in the morning. We can tell the sheriff about it when he gets back and let some other lawmen go after him." I put my hand on his sleeve for a minute. "Off the mountain. Far away from here."

"Miss Brown, you're a fool." Mr. Hannahs said it with a grim smile, because he knew I was right. There was nothing else to be done. "Can you act like nothing is wrong until then?"

"I'll have to. Maybe Mack will be back before then."

"Maybe. He's complaint six. Never seems to contribute in the places as need it."

"He's new. He'll get better."

Mr. Hannahs grunted noncommittally. "Didn't see you place an order for ammunition today."

"I have the order in my desk drawer." I froze as an appalling thought formed in my head. "Um. I'll go get it."

"Better late than never." His voice was many shades of disapproval. "I'll leave you my gun. Sarah would skin me alive if I didn't."

He put a Smith and Wesson revolver on the counter. There was an old saying that I believed in. A man wasn't a man without his horse, his gun, and his hat.

"Mr. Hannahs," I said, "I can't take your gun. You need it as much as I do."

"Miss Brown," he said, "if you don't, I'll have to go over there and shoot him myself in front of everybody without letting him say a word first. Take the gun. Don't use it unless you have to." He slid it over to me. "But if you do. Aim."

"Thank you, Mr. Hannahs."

I slid it most of the way into my pocket and folded part of my skirt over the rest with my hand. I remembered carrying a gun down the boardwalk yesterday. In front of Rose's driver.

I dragged myself outside and down the boardwalk. The Fontaines sat in their veranda seats, too warm, rather content with themselves, and out of entertainment. They sensed my shared ennui and didn't look my way as I passed them to go inside. The boys were done in the dining room, and I could hear them somewhere out back. Karine was hard at work, humming in the kitchen.

With reluctant footsteps, I went to my desk. I slid the top drawer open. My gun was gone.

"Oh, Rose," I muttered.

23

COZY

S upper had the desired effect. It roused the Fontaines to motion and engrossed the boys for fully a half an hour as they sat around the dining room table, going over the week's events. I would much rather have stayed in the kitchen with Karine but, for all Mr. Fontaine was a thief and a murderer, he and his wife had an abject horror of children, and my presence was a buffer. I didn't need one bit of drama until the Fontaines cleared out in the morning.

As I sat there playing with my food, I heard the sounds of Jim's stagecoach arrive at the post office, and, after a few minutes, I heard it leave. I knew without looking that Mr. Hannahs was locking up the post office for the night and going for his horse, putting out feed for the others, since Carlos wasn't there to do it.

Hattie came and went with tray after tray of food. The boys ate with devastating speed. Once in a while, a boy would look at Hattie with calf eyes. She didn't seem to notice, but dealing with puberty and crushes was absolutely not on my agenda. Getting through the night, one hour at a time, consumed me.

"Sure beats our trail chow," one of the twins said, shoving cornbread into his mouth. I was trying to keep the names straight. The twins were Herbert and Harry, but who was which was beyond me.

"Miss Brown," Cap, the boy with the missing front tooth, said, "we have lots of vittles in our packs still."

"You can't make any fires," I said, heading him off at the pass. "After we eat, we'll have a look at your things. Maybe you can give the food to Karine and she'll make it for your breakfast."

The freckled boy, Frank, perked up. He reached for another potato and said, "Swell! We have lots of camp-fire cocoa left. Hey," he asked, stuffing a bite in his mouth, "do we have to sleep inside tonight? It's our last night."

"Absolutely." I put as much firmness into my voice as I could. Once they were upstairs for the night, I had only to post myself at the foot of the staircase to assure they stayed there until dawn. None of their three rooms had windows, but I didn't plan on getting any sleep, regardless. There was a collective moan, but no outright rebellion. I thought I heard the Fontaines groan, as well.

Each boy ate more than I'd seen any grown man swallow, and finally, the scouts slowed to a halt. I assigned three of them to help clear the table and help Karine wash up in the kitchen, and three of them to make sure the horses and mules were settled for the night and the blacksmith shop locked up. The last three were to come with me and sort their packs.

"You can bring us back a basket of apples, so long as you're there," I called to the boys heading outside.

The Fontaines watched me follow the three boys up the stairs and decided to return to the veranda. The sun was setting and taking the heat with it, but it still felt airless and cramped in the little rooms. I watched as the boys opened all the packs and dumped the contents over the floor.

"Oh, look," one said, "there's Marvin's *Adventure* magazine." He stopped to thumb through it, but I gave him a look and he put it on the bed.

"Here's the pack with the cocoa," another said, "and there's the biscuit mix."

"Let's put anything that's food out in the hall," I said, "and we'll put all the blankets on the beds." It was a lot to sort, and I started feeling sorry for the mules.

The third boy had opened a pack and was piling up weaponry. Hatchets, knifes, slingshots, a hacksaw. "Why would you need all of that?" I asked.

"We wanted to bring bows and arrows, too," the boy said, still unloading, "but Mr. Peabody said enough was enough."

The door was open, and I saw Hattie pass by in the hall, her arms full. "Hattie," I called, stepping from the room, "how are you?" I had observed nothing out of the ordinary in her behavior during supper, and I was fairly certain Mr. Fontaine had not been inside the hotel for most of the day, but I was unsure how to approach her to keep her safe without scaring her.

"Keeping up," she said shortly. "Thank you for sending help. That was a huge pile of dishes."

"I see you've only traded one task for another," I said. "What have you there?"

She set her pile on the hallway carpet and began sorting items. "These are Mrs. Fontaine's lace gloves. Used boiling water to get the dirt out. These are Mr. Fontaine's dress shoes…" She placed the other small items in a tidy row against their door and stood up.

"Miss Brown," she said quietly, "I know you said to look for a watch, but I wouldn't know where to begin in those rooms." She pointed to the two closed doors. "When the missus asked me to take some things, these doors were open, and every square inch was covered in frocks or hats or gloves or shoes." She looked in at the boys in their room. They sat deeply engrossed in the errant magazine.

"Miss Brown," she whispered, "one of these shoes," she pointed to the white men's dress shoes, the ones Mr. Fontaine wore in the ballroom, "had blood on it!"

I looked down at the gleaming white patent leather.

"It was smeared," she said, "across the side, like someone had picked it up with," she made a face, "bloody fingers."

"You're sure it was blood?" I asked.

"Yes." She shook her head. "You weren't here to ask, and Mrs. Fontaine told me to hurry, so I cleaned it. You might not believe me, but I need to tell you. I'm not very comfortable around them." She squeezed her hands together. "Are you all still looking for a murderer?"

"Yes." I let her see some of my distress. "But I found the watch. It's in a newspaper office somewhere in

Hemet. I know that Mr. Fontaine stole it, but we aren't going to tell him so."

Hattie's eyes were huge.

"We aren't going to say anything to anyone because we are all alone tonight, and I want them to leave first thing in the morning and never come back. You needn't be afraid, Hattie, we are all perfectly safe as long as we're together."

"Safe from who?" asked a boy behind me.

I whirled around and saw three pairs of eyes taking in the scene. "You boys weren't supposed to be listening. It's bad manners." I was so frustrated. "I want all of you to leave the Fontaines completely alone. They aren't used to children, and I can't stand much more excitement myself." I put a hand on my forehead. "Is this all the food?"

The boys nodded, and I told them to pack it all down to the kitchen and turn it in.

Hattie stood there, waiting. "Hattie," I offered, placing my hand gently on her small shoulder, "truly, as long as you aren't alone in a room with him, you're safe. He has no reason to interact with you at all. Help Mrs. Fontaine with whatever she needs and then stay with Karine for the rest of the night."

She nodded and went back down the staircase. The cat passed her on his way up, and I closed all the doors. "You are as nosy as the rest of them," I said to him. It offended him, of course, and he wouldn't let me pet him, so I went back to the lobby.

I locked Mr. Hannahs' gun safely into my desk, and hung the key on the thin, gold chain around my neck, tucked inside my blouse. I was looking forward to returning it to him in the morning. Unused.

When I popped my head into the kitchen to make sure the food had arrived, I found three boys holding dish towels and clearly upset about their prolonged duties. "Go on outside," I told them, taking a towel from one of them. "Enjoy it while you can."

The boys dashed through the door and I took their place at the sink, drying the last of the dishes alongside of Karine, and listened to her hum for another minute. The cries outside in the gathering dusk sounded happy for the most part.

"What's goin' on?" Karine asked at last. "Lot of running around today. But where's this killer we all been looking for?"

She kept her eyes on her work, but the tone of her voice implied she knew I was keeping something from her.

"You don't think it's Mr. Peabody?" I asked.

"Not from the way you're acting," she said wryly. "You're as jumpy as a cricket. Hattie told me what she saw, and she told me where the watch is."

I took the last dish from her and wiped it. "There's no proof," I said. "It's frustrating. They'll leave tomorrow, and all I really know for sure is that he's our thief."

She gave a dissatisfied humph. "Maybe our deputy will be back in time for some last questions."

We both sighed. "It's dark now. He can't be galloping in the dark. Automobiles are slow, but they don't need to stop. And they have lights. If Mack was going to catch them, he did already." I looked out the open kitchen door to the night sky. "All we have to do is wait."

We hung the damp towels to dry as Hattie walked in. "Mrs. Fontaine wants me to help her pack her things." She looked at me. "Is that all right?"

Karine was waiting for my answer as well.

"Where is Mr. Fontaine?"

"Still sitting on the veranda."

"Yes, then." I looked at both women. "We have to act like everything is fine. So it will be."

They both nodded, and I went outside to collect the boys.

Twenty minutes later, the boys sprawled across every inch of the lobby floor, looking at magazines in the lamplight. Mr. Fontaine was smoking a cigar on the veranda, and I'd closed the lobby door firmly against the smell. From upstairs, I heard Mrs. Fontaine giving orders and Hattie's small voice answering.

"Get this cat out of the way!" cried Mrs. Fontaine. The cat came bounding onto the staircase without ceremony, and some of the boys immediately vied for his attention. I sat down at my desk and pulled out my ledgers. Perhaps if I stared at the tiny numbers hard enough, they would make sense. And keep me from getting hysterical.

The boys seemed docile under their house arrest, and I felt relieved. A couple of them were poring over their Scout Handbook, tallying up their various badges from the week. One had a *Boys Life* magazine and one had a *National Geographic* that I planned on reading myself after they went to bed. One boy, Marvin, had three issues of *Adventure* magazine and led a discussion about someone called Captain Kettle and his friend McTodd.

"Stranded on a desert island," Marvin said. "That really happens, you know."

"Left on their own, like us?" asked a boy who may have been Jakey. "Real men can handle it," he said with confidence. "We have to know what to do when things go wrong."

"Like Amundsen going to the South Pole."

"What about this one?" asked a twin. Herbert or Harry, they were interchangeable. "It says here this lady was stolen by Indians and grew up in their tribe."

"Let's see," Marvin said.

They kept their heads down over the magazines and didn't notice the look on my face. I knew a woman who had been stolen by Indians far away and long ago. Elizabeth Nelson had been stolen as a child for her beautiful red hair and escaped years later, but not before they had partially scalped her. I looked around the hotel. This had been her last home before she'd gone to live, once again, in the forest, this time, on her own terms. I didn't think the magazine story had anything to compare with the tragedies of real life, and certainly I wouldn't relabel them as adventure.

The conversations skipped quickly from baseball to volcanoes and back around to camping, and I wondered at the life of ten-year-old boys.

One boy on the staircase got up to stand at my elbow.

Another boy behind him shoved him forward. "Go on, Robin," he said, "ask her."

"Um, Miss Brown?" he said timidly, "is this yours?"

He held out a small, polished stone, the size of my fingernail and almost aglow with a white and blue sheen. I took it from him and held it under my lamp, turning it gently and admiring its color variations.

"No. Where did you get this?" I asked.

He turned around and punched the boy behind him and said, "Told you so, Chuck! I could've kept it!"

"From the other place," Cap said. "It was on the ground. I guess we thought it was yours because…"

He was reluctant to continue, and another boy stepped up and whispered, "Because you're pretty and you smell like flowers."

Poor Robin blushed to his hair and said, "I knew it wasn't her."

But Chuck smiled wickedly. "Had to be you," he said, "we saw you right where it dropped." This statement had all the boys moving closer to me, and I wondered what conversations had been going on outside.

"Boys, what are you talking about?" I demanded. "And make it quick."

Most of them looked ashamed, and I couldn't begin to imagine what lay on their collective conscience.

"We gave it back. So we aren't thieves." The boy who had handed me the stone waited for my confirmation.

"Yes. That's true," I said. "But I think there's a story behind it. Maybe you'd better speak up and make Mr. Peabody proud of you."

They all hung their heads, then.

"Mr. Peabody is the last person we're gonna tell. He didn't know we were there."

"We sent Herb and Harry in."

"And Billy went because he's a show-off." The boy on the stair started to punch the speaker, but I caught his arm.

I thought back to the night of the murder. "Three boys went into the kitchen?" I asked. They nodded.

"But we all followed 'em," Frank said. "We dared them to steal the doughnuts, then we were all gonna take 'em back to the camp."

"Yeah. Mr. Peabody was gone, and we were hungry."

"So, we did," finished Frank. "But then…"

The entire group squirmed with distress.

"Boys, where were you when Mr. Craven was killed?" The parents were going to see red if they found out their boys witnessed a murder.

"Under the veranda," Frank said in a whisper, "behind the rail."

"And we saw you do it," Cap said.

24

TREED

"Why in the world would you think I killed someone?" I asked in shock.

"Did you?" asked Cap. "Sure looked like you."

"Absolutely not." The boys were as quiet as I'd ever seen them, and I stood up, motioning them to sit back down to their magazines. "I was there, but after it happened. I'm sorry you had to be anywhere near that. I'm sure it was traumatic and frightening."

"No, it wasn't," Marvin said. "The veranda was really dark. We only heard the footsteps and stuff."

"But the vomit was disgusting!" Frank said. "We ran for it, then."

"You didn't throw up?" Cap was disappointed. "You didn't kill that man?"

I thought about who was on the veranda that night. About what the boys were telling me.

"Mrs. Fontaine threw up," I whispered to myself. I glanced at the stone on my desk. "And she lost a moonstone against the rail when I ran into her."

Robin reached out and picked it up. "Nope. It rolled across the veranda and fell into the grass when that man got killed. He fought back." He turned the colored stone over in his palm. "Can I keep it, then?"

"Yes." I hardly knew what to think, but the boys were satisfied, albeit vaguely crestfallen, that I was not the killer.

"Boys, this is very serious." I waved at their magazines. "Real life isn't glamorous. It's dangerous. You should be ashamed of yourselves for taking it so lightly."

They wandered back to their seats, but I could see the interest in reading had paled next to my words of admonition. I stood at my desk, weak in the knees, wondering how I could keep them occupied for another hour so I could send them to bed in peace. Wondering how I had missed looking in the right place for clues.

The voices upstairs had continued unabated during our conversation, and after more prodding, I had the scouts sitting back down when Mr. Fontaine poked his head in. If he noticed that I was upset, he rightly concluded it was due to being surrounded by boys and ignored me. He cocked his head, listened, then shook it and went back outside and sat in the circle of light cast from the bulb overhead. His cigar was almost finished.

"Miss Brown?" asked Billy. "Can I go to bed? I don't feel too good."

"Is it your stomach?" I asked.

He suddenly threw his arms around my waist. "I want to go home," he said, muffled in my elbow. "I miss my mom."

I nodded. "Lock your doors behind you."

If the subject matter in the lobby was too stressful for me, I didn't think it would sit very well with the boys once they realized how serious it was. Several of the boys joined him, and the two that remained gathered up the magazines and flipped half-heartedly through the pages. I hoped no one would have nightmares.

Hattie came down the stairs, passing the boys, and her face was so pale that even they paused to look at her. Her green eyes were wide, and she held tightly to the hatbox in her hands.

"Miss Brown!" I knew from the tone in her hushed voice that she was panicking and pulled her quickly through the dining room door and into the darkened room. Whatever it was, Hattie was about to bolt from the building.

"Hattie, what is it?"

She dropped the hatbox on the table and stepped away from it. "In there. It's all in there." Her breath was coming faster and faster. I put a hand on her shoulder. "She has a hat. The big one with pink roses. We brought it last night…" She glanced at the door. "I went to put it into the hatbox. Of course, it goes in there."

I needed to know what was in the hatbox, but Hattie made me too afraid to turn on the lights and look.

"When I opened the box…it had blood all in the bottom. Dried blood. Dark. It's torn where she tried to get it off. The paper must have stuck to…"

I felt a wave of nausea hit, and we both swayed for a minute. "I thought it was the gloves." She shuddered. "There's a pair of gloves covered in blood stains inside, and they smell something awful, and when I started to lift one out, it occurred to me what I was looking at. Well, I don't know what I was thinking. Mrs. Fontaine had her back to me, and I closed the lid again quick. Oh, Miss Brown! She's the one you're all looking for! She'll kill us!"

There were whispers behind the door and a shuffle of feet. When I opened it and looked out, the two boys were going up the stairs to join their group, and I couldn't decide whether it was a retreat to bed or the next ploy to avoid it. But at least they were contained.

"Hattie, did she see you take it?" I strained my ears for any sounds upstairs.

"No. I left right away and came down the stairs." She moaned. "I took it before I could think."

"You have to put it back before she sees you."

"I can't climb the stairs with it, Miss Brown! I feel faint!"

"Then I'll try. She might not notice with all the boys around. Tell Karine you must both go to your room and lock the door behind you."

"But what about you? What about the boys?"

"We all have locks on our doors. The Fontaines don't care about us. There's no reason why they won't just go to bed and leave in the morning."

It was at this juncture that we both heard the scream. We dashed into the lobby at the same time that Mr. Fontaine did. Up the stairs, we heard Mrs. Fontaine scream again and the sound of scuffling in the hall.

"We've got her trapped, boys," called out a boy in the hall. "Spread out and keep an eye sharp!"

Karine opened the kitchen door, and I shoved Hattie toward her. "Stay together!" I hissed.

Mr. Fontaine reached the bottom of the stairs, and three scouts came forward and blocked the way up.

"Halt!" the boy in front said, brandishing a knife. "We've got a dangerous criminal up here and we're holding her for when the sheriff arrives!"

"She's under arrest!" the boy next to him said. He held an ax overhead.

Mrs. Fontaine screamed again. "Get out of my room! How dare you! Go away! Get out!"

Mr. Fontaine whirled at me. "Call off those ruffians at once! This is an outrage! How dare you accost my wife?"

"Frank!" I called. "What are you doing? Stop!"

"Get the rope," a voice said. "Tie her up."

"Gag her!" another hollered.

I heard another scream, but anger was quickly overshadowing the fear in it. "You horrible little cretin! Touch me and you'll see what happens!" Mrs. Fontaine sounded like a cornered beast, and I made it up two stairs before the twins aimed their knifes at me.

"Stay back, Miss Brown, she's desperate! All criminals are desperate! She's likely to do anything!"

"Johnny!" cried Mrs. Fontaine, and her husband spun on his heel and ran out the front door.

"She's going for the window!" cried a boy upstairs. "Head her off at the pass, men!"

The three boys charged down the staircase, and I backed away from their flailing weapons, smashing against Hattie, who was frozen in place against Karine. Three more boys barreled past us and out the door, and I ran outside after them.

"Boys!" I cried, having no idea what I wanted to say.

My original plan, and the one that had followed it, was going up in smoke.

I came out to see my ladder at the end of the building, flexing under the weight of Mrs. Fontaine. She had come through the window and grabbed it, but once she was aloft, she realized that scouts had surrounded the bottom rung.

"I've got her!" cried a boy leaning out from the window, and Mrs. Fontaine went up the ladder and scrambled onto the roof. The boy never hesitated. He leapt from the windowsill onto the ladder at the same time that Mr. Fontaine grabbed hold of it from below, and simultaneously, the two followed Mrs. Fontaine up to the roof.

Scouts stood in the window, back lit by the hotel room lamp. As Mr. Fontaine passed them, he growled, "Just you wait until I get my hands on you!" It was enough to keep them from reaching for the ladder once he was above them.

The moon had almost risen over Tahquitz, but there wasn't enough light to see what was happening on the roof. There were muffled cries and lots of fumbling over the shingles.

"Oh, no!"

"Get away from me!"

"Lucy!"

"Johnny, where are you?"

"Ouch!"

The Boy Scouts lowered the ladder and laid it down in the grass. "We've got her now," Cap said. "She's treed."

"Spread out, boys, and make sure it's secure!" the

boy in the window cried. He put both hands on the window and slammed it shut. A minute later, all the scouts had surrounded the hotel, making sure there was no other way down from the roof, howling like wolves.

I watched the debacle in horror. Hattie and Karine and I stood huddled on the veranda under the light, trying to decide what to do. The boys had the element of surprise, but there was no way of knowing whether either Mr. or Mrs. Fontaine had a weapon.

"Cap!" I said, "Who's on the roof?"

"The villain, Miss Brown! We got her!"

"No," I said, putting a hand on his shoulder. He lowered the ax in his hand, and I was glad I wasn't considered part and parcel with the enemy. I was unbearably grateful the boys had determined my innocence earlier. "The boy. Which boy followed her up?"

He looked around and shrugged.

"There she is, go that way!" shouted the boy on the roof. I paced the veranda, craning my neck, trying to discover where he was.

Karine and Hattie joined the scouts who were circling the hotel in the shadows. Light came through the front windows, and the open kitchen door threw a square of light over the back porch and onto the grass beyond it, but the other two sides of the hotel, and anything above it, were in complete darkness. I started to go inside for a lantern when the moon summited and rose into the sky. It cast everything in a wintery glow.

"Hey, where'd everybody go?" the boy on the roof said. It was quickly followed by, "Hey! Lemme go!"

There was a brief scuffle and Mr. Fontaine's angry voice floated down to us from the chimney, "I don't know what's going on around here, but you're in a lot of trouble."

"Ouch! That's mine!" hollered the boy.

"Miss Brown?" Mr. Fontaine said. "Disarm your band of thugs, and let us off the roof. The sheriff is going to hear about this. Lucy, darling, are you hurt?"

Mrs. Fontaine's voice came from the kitchen side of the roof. "I'm going to make those wretched little beasts pay!" she spat. "Everywhere I go, there they are."

"Lucy, are you hurt? I can't see you from where I'm sitting. Are you safe?"

"I'm fine. There are two brats staring up at me from the ground, and my dress has been torn, and I've gotten a splinter under a fingernail because I wasn't wearing gloves. I'm dandy."

Cap tapped me on the arm. "It's Marvin," he said. "Marvin went up after her. He's a hero!"

I lifted a hand to my forehead. "Marvin!" I called. "Marvin, are you safe?"

"Marvin, is it?" asked Mr. Fontaine dryly. "Marvin is definitely not safe. I am holding Marvin's knife and pointing the part that hurts at him right now. He's sitting against the chimney not moving because if he does, he will get hurt."

"Marvin," I said, "you can answer me. Tell me if you are all right."

"Yeah," I heard him say. "I guess so." He sounded disappointed.

"Good, don't move right now. Sit still until we get you down." I didn't receive an answer, but I didn't hear him crying, either. I was livid now. It was one thing to let them get away if it meant the safety of the people in my charge, but a man who used a child as a shield was the lowest of the low. Mr. Fontaine wasn't getting away with it.

He wasn't getting away with any of it.

The general howling had stopped, and Cap stood next to me, looking up at the roof. "You're going to jail," he called out. "That's what happens to criminals."

"I'm not a criminal!" Mr. Fontaine said. "Miss Brown, we need that ladder now. And get those boys away from it."

"You are a criminal," I said. "You stole my pocket watch, and the reporter stole it from you. You're a thief and a liar."

"You can't prove anything!" he said, startled.

"I can." I marched out under the oak tree to make sure Mr. Fontaine could hear me. "There's a way to identify your fingerprints on it. And I know what you were doing with the maid in your suite, back at the resort!"

Mrs. Fontaine took a very loud intake of breath, and when she released her words, an owl nearby flew off, startled. "I knew it! Oh, I knew it! You swore to me! You swore on my mother's grave!" Her voice cracked. "How dare you? How dare you betray me the very week of our honeymoon! I'll never forgive you! Never! I wish I could slap your face!" Mrs. Fontaine was furious. "You can't trust maids. Not with laundry. Not with husbands."

She was telling the gospel truth, but I wasn't going to say so out loud.

"Now, then," he stammered, "I thought we'd put that behind us."

"I want a divorce. I'm getting an annulment. This was all a horrible mistake!"

"Lucy!" pleaded Mr. Fontaine. "Darling, listen to me! I've done nothing with the maid. Nothing, you hear? It's all a lie!"

"Mr. Fontaine," I called up agreeably, "I can bring over the maid and let her tell your wife for you, or you can come clean." I was bluffing. I wasn't going anywhere.

"I saw what I saw," declared Mrs. Fontaine, "and you lied to me."

There was a pause overhead, and I looked around me. Cap and Hattie were still in front of the hotel with me. The others, I assumed, had set up a circle and watched the other walls. I had no idea what time it was, but surely Mack would arrive soon. I wasn't sure what I would do if this went on all night.

"Lucy." Mr. Fontaine's voice had changed to one of a man who weighed his words carefully. "Darling. I love you more than any woman on earth. Please believe me. I would never, under any circumstances, be with another."

"Save it," she declared. "I've heard that one before."

"Fine! You win!" He was angry again. I could picture him waving his arms in the air. "You want the truth? Okay! The truth is, I am a thief! Are you happy now?"

"You what?" Mrs. Fontaine said.

"I steal things. I steal them and sell them because," he choked, "because I'm broke, Lucy. Dead broke."

25

CONFESSIONAL

There was another pause while the unhappy bride tried to process the information.

"Explain broke," she said.

"Lucy, you know I came directly from my business in New York to marry you in Tucson. I wrote to you about my urgent affairs, and you replied not to worry, that the justice of the peace suited you. I knew your parents just passed."

Here, he paused and listened, but she was deathly quiet.

"I am not altogether as rich as I'd represented myself," he continued. "I am, in fact, penniless. My business ventures have dissolved, and the creditors took what was left. I went through with the wedding because you were so terribly distraught over your parents' death. I couldn't let you down. We might have waited, but darling, you needed me!"

"You have nothing?" she asked, incredulous.

"Nothing but your love, my dear, and I would give my life's blood to have that." He was miserable.

"But I bought all these clothes," she said. "I spent a fortune on wedding clothes." Her voice trailed off.

"It doesn't matter," he said. "Hang the bill. I want to know if you love me still?"

"What were you doing in the suite?" she said.

"Demanding that the maid tell me where the valuables in the resort were located," he said. "I don't even have enough for our train tickets to Riverside yet."

I wondered if Mrs. Fontaine's silence was due, in part, to her internal debate over asking me to confirm his statement. She must have decided that his words rang true because she finally said, "And did you manage to steal anything before we landed in this dump?"

He didn't hesitate. "No," he said with a tinge of bitterness, "There wasn't any time. You insisted that we leave immediately after the murder. I had some luck here, though," he muttered.

"Johnny," she said, "I had no idea. I don't know what to think."

"I spent the last dollars I had on this trip. I wanted our honeymoon to be a wonderful memory. Something we could hold on to it in the lean times. Until I could get back on my feet again. You deserved it after all you've endured. You're the light of my life, Lucy. I'll try again. I'll work three jobs and be an honest man for the rest of my days if you'll take me back."

I'd had enough. "Mr. Fontaine!" I called up, "Don't pick out any curtains yet. You're going straight to jail."

There was an echoing "Hurrah!" around the hotel.

"Damnit, woman!" he said, "I'll get your watch back for you. I've stolen nothing worth going to jail over. It's just a watch!" I heard him shift around on the roof. "And speaking of that," he said, "what possible use is a revolver without cartridges, even one with a mother-of-pearl handle? I would have taken it to protect myself from the murderer, but it was empty!"

"As it turns out," I said with every bit of sarcasm I could muster, "the gun was stolen, *anyway*. The watch was stolen *twice*. And you would have had no chance at all to protect yourself from the killer because the killer is your *wife*!"

Another resounding "Hurrah!" circled the hotel.

There was no answer from the roof. Finally Marvin said, "Can I get down now?"

There was more silence.

"Hattie," I said quietly, "go inside and turn off every light. We need to be able to see."

After the lights blinked out, and my eyes adjusted to the moonlight, it was possible to make out the top of Mr. Fontaine's silhouette on the roof next to the chimney. Marvin must have been tucked above the chimney. I couldn't make out any body parts beyond the stones, but Mr. Fontaine faced that direction, straddling the ridgeline above it.

"Lucy?" he called at last. "I won't believe it. Love? Talk to me."

There was nothing for several minutes, and then she said, "Mr. Peabody killed him. They found proof."

"He didn't," I called up. "We have proof."

"You don't. We all heard the sheriff. That man is a murderer and a kidnapper, both," Mrs. Fontaine said.

"You can't talk about Mr. Peabody like that!" Marvin said. "He took us adventuring!"

"Yeah!" cried Cap next to me. "He and Toby are prob'ly fighting mountain lions right now!"

It was beyond me how these boys could combine fantasy and reality into one continuous truth in their heads. Life was what they intended to make it.

"Mrs. Fontaine," I said, "my maid has your hatbox. We know what's inside of it." I saw Hattie shrink back into the lobby doorway.

"What are they talking about?" asked Mr. Fontaine. "What hatbox? The one you fussed so much over?"

"I don't know what you're talking about," she said.

"We know Mr. Craven was a dirty politician. He hurt a lot of people. He hurt your mother," I said.

"Don't you talk about my mother!" she screeched. "You don't know what he did to her!"

"Who, Lucy?" asked Mr. Fontaine. "What is she saying?"

"These boys were there when you killed him." At this point, I needed her to understand. She wasn't going to get away with murder. Even if she murdered a nasty crook.

"I hate you!" she shouted. "You stupid kids ruined everything! What were you doing down there? I should have thrown the knife at you instead of dropping it!"

Her confession was full of venom, and there was deep silence in the mountain night as everyone absorbed the words.

I knew what I had to do. I didn't have the maternal passion of Miss Alden, the empty arms of Mrs. Keen, or the casual assumptions about children that Mrs.

Hannahs had, but Marvin was in danger, and I was going to save him.

I motioned to Cap, and he leaned in close. "You have to get the ladder up against the house again. But quietly. Don't let Mr. Fontaine catch you. I have to get Marvin out of there."

Cap disappeared, and soon he and several boys were stealthily lifting the ladder to the far edge of the building in the dark. The bump of the ladder against the roof could have been mistaken for the whisper of the oak leaves.

"Mrs. Fontaine," I said, "these boys had nothing to do with it. You did it." I kept my voice calm and reasonable.

"Lucy," Mr. Fontaine said, "please. Tell me it isn't true. Tell me. I'll believe you."

"It doesn't matter any more." It was Mrs. Fontaine's turn to be bitter. "He killed my mother. I killed him. It's justice."

"But…you told me that your parents died from the flu." Mr. Fontaine was clearly confused.

"You don't read the papers out West, do you, Mr. Fontaine?" I asked.

I motioned to Cap, and the boys spread out again. Cap tugged at my sleeve, and I whispered, "No. I won't trap another boy up there. I'm going. Wait a minute." If I could get the couple fighting again, I might have enough time to pull Marvin down. I needed to distract Mr. Fontaine.

"Mr. Craven was the one who gave the testimony that sent her mother to the gallows. For poisoning her husband!"

"Lucy!" Mr. Fontaine said.

"She didn't!" cried Mrs. Fontaine. "What lies! My father died from too much liquor. He drank too much. Ma about died from a broken heart!"

"But poison!"

"No, Johnny! The alcohol!" She was crying now. "Mr. Craven was partnered up with another lawyer to sell our property after Pa died. Everything about that place reminded Ma of years of fighting and drinking. I encouraged her to get rid of it. Our wedding was coming soon, and..." Here she broke down long enough for me to reach the highest rung of the ladder.

I didn't dare look down. I kept my eyes on the roof until I could peek over the edge. From this side, I could clearly see Marvin against the chimney. Mr. Fontaine was beyond him and had turned around to face the voice of his wife. I waved at Marvin, but he was looking toward the Fontaines.

Mrs. Fontaine was done crying. "She signed the papers. The very next day, they arrested her." Her voice was icy. Feral.

"But why?" Mr. Fontaine asked.

"They accused her of poisoning Pa, and Mr. Craven had a signed confession with her name on it." There was a sliding noise, and I saw the figure of Mrs. Fontaine pulling herself up to the roof line. "It happened so fast. They hung her. I wasn't there. I was at Mr. Craven's house, trying to find my way inside to kill him."

She had managed to perch herself on the same peak as Mr. Fontaine, but she was at the far end of the ridge. I ducked back down out of sight, hoping she wouldn't notice me, that I blended in enough with the oak tree spreading around me.

"He never leaves his house," she said. "He never travels." She inched her way toward him. "They almost caught me once, but I've figured out how to survive, Johnny. I know how to keep living when there isn't a reason to."

"I won't believe it," Mr. Fontaine said. "You couldn't have killed a man. You, you don't have it in you."

"It was so easy once I found out he was leaving. I went through his mail and found his itinerary. I didn't even know this place existed." Her voice cracked, and she yanked at her hem where it caught on a shingle.

"I sent you the letter to come. Planned the wedding for the date of his train ticket. Insisted we needed to honeymoon in Idyllwild." She was closer. I couldn't make out the features of her face when Mr. Fontaine dropped his head, but her tone was ugly and she was far from remorseful.

I waited until he started speaking and then hissed at Marvin. "Marvin!" I whispered, "Hey!"

"This trip was because of that lawyer?" Mr. Fontaine's shock turned to wrath. "You said it was the most romantic thing, a dream come true, you could hardly wait to leave! You wanted mountains, you said. Dancing till dawn and…and…white horses!" He took Marvin's knife and stabbed the roof shingles, hard enough that I could see it quiver as it stuck there.

Mrs. Fontaine froze, and so did I. I was halfway to Marvin, slithering on my stomach, on the roof. My shoes were the last things touching the ladder, and if the Fontaines had eyes for anyone else, they would surely have seen me. Marvin had frozen in place until Mr. Fontaine put the knife into the roof. When Marvin jumped, he looked frantically around and finally saw me. I waved at him to come toward me.

"Lucy!" cried Mr. Fontaine, "I thought you loved me! I thought you cared!"

"I do."

"You only married me because you needed me to get you here. It was the lawyer. Not me." He had no idea he was crying.

"He killed her."

"You used me."

Marvin was slowly coming my direction. He kept his eyes firmly on mine and held onto the ridgepole with one hand as he crept along the sloping surface. I could almost touch him.

"It was my only hope. You were my only hope. Can't you see that?"

"We danced in the ballroom. We laughed. Then you slit a man's throat? Who are you?"

"I'd do it again." Her voice was hard, bitter.

I had Marvin's hand and pulled him back toward the ladder, guiding him. My feet touched the ladder, but this time it stayed blessedly in place. I motioned Marvin to pass me and go down first but he shook his head. I thought about shoving him right off the roof. Instead, I yanked on his arm and half pulled, half dragged him to the ladder. We had to hurry.

"You were never supposed to find out," continued Mrs. Fontaine. "It was perfect. Someone else took the blame. Even if he didn't, I made sure not to leave any evidence. If those rotten little fiends hadn't been under the veranda, we'd be long gone by now."

"Oh no, you don't!" cried Mr. Fontaine behind me.

"Go!" I yelled at Marvin. I didn't look back. Marvin scrambled onto the ladder, and I had my arms around it, ready to follow him. I felt someone grab my foot and pull hard.

"Catch him!" Mrs. Fontaine said.

Marvin's head disappeared down the ladder. I kicked at the hands on my foot. My other foot was captured, but not before I felt a solid connection between my heel and Mr. Fontaine. He grunted in pain, and his knee came down on the back of my leg. I clung to the ladder, and the boys below it began to shout.

"You can do it, Miss Brown! Fight! Get him!"

My legs began to drop down the side of the roof with Mr. Fontaine attached to them. He scrabbled to grab the ridgepole without losing his hold on me. I had a viselike grip on the ladder and felt it shudder. Someone was climbing up to help.

Fingers curled into my hair and gathered it up in a fist. It snapped my head up hard and I released the ladder in shock. I reached up to grab at the arm above me, and Mr. Fontaine held still, one hand still firmly around my ankle.

"That's right," Lucy Fontaine said in a deathly calm voice. "Don't move."

The boys were doing war whoops out of sight on the ground, and they didn't hear her say, "Sit up nice and slow. Johnny, let her go."

The knife point pressed into my throat, just below

my ear, and I was too terrified to move. I heard her heavy breathing. Her knee was in my back.

Staring into my eyes from the edge of the roof was John.

"Get down!" hissed Mrs. Fontaine. "I'll slit her open like a sack of flour!"

John squinted his eyes at her a little and slowly dropped back down out of sight.

"Get everyone away from here!" screamed Mrs. Fontaine. "All of you back away! I want you all lying face down in the middle of the road where I can see you, or I'll kill your precious Miss Brown!"

Three things happened simultaneously. Mr. Fontaine pulled on my legs to get himself back onto the ridgeline but instead, dragged us both downward. Mrs. Fontaine screamed like a banshee, released me, and kicked me firmly in the side.

And I slid helplessly down the side of the roof, winded, attached by the foot to a screaming Mr. Fontaine.

26

CAUGHT

The fall should have hurt so much more than it did. Between my terror and the fact that I couldn't breathe in properly for a good scream went a long way toward my becoming a hero of epic proportions in the eyes of the Boy Scouts.

I may have fainted on the way down. It was hard to tell.

Mr. Fontaine caught his jacket in the oak tree on his descent, thereby slowing mine to the point that, when John caught me, I didn't, in fact, squash him. Mr. Fontaine's jacket ripped and brought him to the ground soon after. But the boys told me he suffered with humiliation, first, and rightly so.

I was on the ground and examined for broken bones while the screams of Mrs. Fontaine continued unabated for several more minutes. They had removed the ladder after John came down, and it took some time before I understood what had happened.

"I saw it," John said with a chuckle. "It was coming

out of the chimney while you two were wrestling up there. Huge. Furious. It was coming up behind Mrs. Fontaine when she grabbed you and, all in all, I think justice was nicely served."

I stayed flat on the ground. I liked it there. Several faces gathered over my head, and they all talked at once.

I heard Karine's voice mingled with John's voice and Hattie calling something from the veranda, but whenever I started to lift my head to see what was going on, dizziness hit. The moon filtered through the oak tree branches above me. I could trace its bright orb behind the leafy canopy, and everywhere else it bathed the boughs in soft whites and blues, like the moonstone.

Karine lifted the cool cloth she had been holding against my forehead.

John's face came into view. "How are you feeling?" he asked.

"Is Marvin okay?" I replied. The night was quiet now, too quiet. "Where are the Fontaines?"

"That sounds like business as usual," he said and offered his hand.

I let him help me up. I was battered, but miraculously, not broken. Karine and Hattie each took an elbow and helped walk me up to the veranda chairs, where I sat down gingerly.

John sat next to me. "Mr. Fontaine is back in his room for the night, tied to his bed with some knots that, frankly, have me envious. Those scouts sure know their stuff."

Hattie handed me a cup of mint tea, and I took it gratefully.

"Mrs. Fontaine remains on the roof, held hostage by the biggest coon I've ever seen. Did you know you had a raccoon living in your chimney?"

I shook my head over my teacup. It hurt.

John smiled. "I told her I'm down here, waiting, if she would rather be safely tied up and out of the breeze. But she thought better of it and chose wisely, in my opinion. She said she wanted to enjoy the open sky and the starlight one last time."

"What?" interjected Karine.

He laughed. "Well, her exact words were, 'Go to hell.' But I understood what she meant."

"That, and you have a rifle," Hattie said.

"That, too," he agreed.

"When did you get here?" I asked. "How did you know? And what took you so long?"

"Mr. Hannahs came to see me. It's a long ride for him at his age, but there was no other way to reach me. Told me about the crazy lady and the automobile chase, the deputy and the Fontaines. It was a lot of information, but I finally got out of him that you were here with a hotel full of people and only his old gun between you and a murdering vamp. I had to come find out for myself, didn't I?"

Karine and Hattie weren't sure who he was or what to make of him, but the peaceful way John and I teased each other put a smile on their faces, and for a little while, we all sat together like old friends.

A voice overhead broke into our conversation.

"Awfully free and easy, how you're sure I'm the villain."

We all looked up at the eaves. "Are you ready to

come down, now?" asked John. He picked his rifle up and laid it across his lap.

"She hated him as much as anyone," Mrs. Fontaine murmured from the roof.

Hattie frowned at me, and Karine said, "Let me get my fry pan and hush her up."

"It could've been her next," continued Mrs. Fontaine. "The only reason he left Tucson was to rob another woman blind. He'd have found a way to make her swing afterwards, to cover his evidence." Her voice came floating around our ears. "You all would've done the same. He was the villain. I'm the savior. He won't destroy another family. It's over."

"Mrs. Fontaine," I said, "come down out of the night air. I'm sure if you explain things to the sheriff, they'll go easy on you."

"You won't put me in jail," she said. "You'll have to burn the place down before I let you touch me."

"Is this really the honeymoon you wanted?" I asked. "What about your husband?"

There was a pause. "He's not going to jail, is he?"

John put a hand on my arm. "That depends on whether he's guilty," he said.

"He's the only one who didn't do anything wrong," she finally said. "You have to let him go."

"I suppose we might, if we had a good reason to." John shook his head at my puzzled look. "Do we?"

"I told you. The only thing he's guilty of is being poor."

"My dear Mrs. Fontaine," John said, "someone has to go to jail."

There was a long silence.

Karine stood up and said, "I'm going to get those boys some food. Don't want them to faint away with hunger while they're on patrol. Come on, Hattie, you can deliver." The two went into the dark hotel, and the kitchen light flickered back on.

"What'll we do?" I whispered. "These boys can't stay up all night, staring at the roof."

"You underestimate boys," he said with a smile. "They've never had such adventure."

It occurred to me that he looked very nice in moonlight. Electricity had its place in the modern world, but it was no substitute for a moonlit night.

"Still want to run a hotel?" he asked.

"Yes. But there's a long list of guest qualifications forming. It eliminates all but the most cooperative people."

"You draw the line at killers?"

"And thieves." I reached up and touched his cheek. "Your eye is healing."

He caught my hand. "And Mr. Fontaine has a completely black one, again. You kicked him, right in the face, up there." He tossed his chin toward the roof and leaned his rifle back against the wall next to him.

He sat back in his chair with a sigh and enclosed my hand in both of his. "Tell me something, Miss Brown. How is it that, without a gun or a man, without a deputy or a call for help, you managed to catch our killer, save a boy, and dodge the criminal mastermind who wanted to take everything you had, including, so I understand, your life?"

His hands felt nice. "Rubbish. I didn't do anything. Even the raccoon was braver than I was, and you know it." I shifted in my chair. "I know you'll think less of me, but all I wanted was for them to leave and never come back. That was the sum total of my plan."

"I guess you didn't need me for it, then," he said.

I didn't have time to figure out the strange tone in his voice. We turned at the sound of three horses coming down the road. John and I stood up and walked out to meet them, and the riders pulled up short when they saw John's rifle.

"It's us, deputy," John called out. "Been some trouble here."

The horses carried flecks of lather from their pursuit, and the look on Mack's face showed his exasperation. Even the moonlight didn't soften the hard lines in his face. The two men with him were Lindley's stable boys.

"Mack, what happened?" I asked.

"We caught up to them," he said, and he and the other men dismounted. "They made it halfway down the mountain before they ran out of gas. By the time we arrived, they had abandoned the useless contraption. No sign of either of them." He spat in the dirt. "There was an avalanche of papers floating among the treetops, where the briefcase had been dumped out over a cliff."

Mack was bitter.

"I don't suppose you found her gun?" I couldn't help asking.

Mack reached into his shirt and pulled out my Colt. "I did." He stared at it in disgust. "Sitting on the seat. She never fired it, but there aren't any cartridges in it. Makes no sense."

I kept my mouth shut. I would explain some other time. Maybe next year.

John pointed up to the hotel roof. "Maybe what's sitting up there will make you feel better." All the men turned to squint at it, and only I caught the hint of sarcasm in John's voice.

"What's that?" asked Mack.

"The woman who murdered Mr. Craven," I said. "It's Mrs. Fontaine, and she's trapped up there."

I looked at Mack. "I'm so glad you came back."

He stood a little taller. "What? I thought the sheriff went after the killer. Mr. Peabody."

"I'll have to explain," I said, "but in the meantime, we have to get her off the roof and into jail. She confessed. You have at least a dozen witnesses to that. But she isn't going to come without a fight. We need you."

John turned to look at me but had nothing to say.

"She killed a man?" Mack was trying to picture it, to add up the pieces, but I could see he was exhausted.

"Boys," he finally said to his companions, "the mules are that way." He motioned beyond the blacksmith shop and they rode toward the corral. "They're going to take the mules and their harness and tow that machine the rest of the way down the mountain in the morning. Take it to the station in Banning and file my report. If that crazy woman shows her face anywhere, or tries to get her car back, we'll have her."

He dragged his hand over his face a few times. "If this is the murderer, then I need to get her down the other direction, to the Hemet jail on the morning coach." He looked at the hotel. He looked at John's gun. "How do you propose we get her from here to there? Is she not cooperating with the usual persuasions?"

"I think she's decided to go down fighting." John said. He didn't seem to care.

"What's keeping her on the roof?"

"Nine Boy Scouts are surrounding the place," I said. "They chased her there. They're keeping her there. But this can't go on forever."

For the millionth time, I cursed Mr. Fontaine. I had no way of knowing what time it was. I only knew it was past everyone's bedtime.

"Wait," I said. "What if we negotiate?"

"You caught that, did you?" asked John.

"Yes," I said, "in all fairness, I think you're brilliant."

He didn't exactly smile, but he took a step back and motioned his gun toward the hotel in an invitation. "Go ahead."

"Mack, if I get her to come down, will you lock her up in your place?"

He grunted. "Where else? I'll clear out the boxes right now." He led his horse to the blacksmith shop and hitched it there. "Give me a minute," he called, and went to his office.

John returned to the veranda with me. He sat back in his chair and nodded, ready to watch the show.

"Don't you have somewhere else to be?" I hissed and got a smile in reply.

"Mrs. Fontaine!" I called up, "Won't you come down now? The deputy is back. He said you can stay in his office, there. It's nice, with a bed and privacy and everything."

"Jail is jail. Don't act like it's a resort."

"It is compared to the rooftop."

"I'm not going to jail."

"You must be sore and bruised. I know I am. I'm getting cold. I'm getting hungry. Come down. We'll get you taken care of."

"You'll have to shoot me. No point in jumping. That obviously didn't kill you."

"Mrs. Fontaine, we don't want any more people hurt."

"Then where's Johnny?"

"He's not hurt. He's inside, safe."

"You've tied him up."

"And we're taking him to jail in the morning."

"He didn't do anything."

"That's up to the system."

"The same system that let my mother die!"

"I can't help it. He's a thief."

"You can help it. You can let him go. He doesn't have it."

"If I let him go, he'll steal again."

"He only stole for me! He only did it because he wanted to take care of me!"

"Mrs. Fontaine, don't let him go to jail because his only crime was loving you."

Silence.

"Mrs. Fontaine. If you come down quietly and let the deputy lock you in his office, I'll let your husband go."

More silence.

"I'll let him go. And when the judge finds out what happened, all the horrible things Mr. Craven did, you will be okay. He'll know you aren't the villain. You will be their chief witness against the crimes. You will help take down the other wretched people in the system."

Nothing.

"You will stand for real justice, Mrs. Fontaine. You can beat them at their own game."

After an eternity, Mrs. Fontaine said, "Bring the ladder."

John stood up and put a hand on my shoulder briefly as he passed me. He called for the boys, and they swarmed beneath the oak tree, hefting the ladder back into place. Karine and Hattie joined me.

"Mrs. Fontaine," called John, "the ladder is here. Do you want me to come up and help you?"

"Stay away from me!" she said. "I'll come on my own terms, thank you."

"Not quite," John said, holding the bottom of the ladder, "but I'll let you start that way. Nice and slow, if you please."

Mack walked up the boardwalk, and I met him at the end of it. He had his gun holstered and held a pair of handcuffs.

"The place is cleared out again," he muttered, as we watched the backside of Mrs. Fontaine dangle over the edge of the roof. "I don't think the sheriff expected a criminal to need it so soon."

"Probably not," I agreed.

"You'd better have some evidence for this," he said, walking toward the ladder.

John stepped back from the ladder and trained his rifle on Mrs. Fontaine's back. I held my breath. She was almost to the bottom when John said, "Stop there. I want to see the knife. I want you to keep your hands over your head, right where they are on the ladder. Tell me where it is, and give it to me."

"It's in my hand," she said, and dropped it to the ground. Marvin ran in and grabbed it.

"Good," John said. "Let's go now."

When Mrs. Fontaine reached the bottom, she allowed the deputy to put the handcuffs on her small wrists and walked quietly down the boardwalk with him. The boys began to cheer, and John's voice rang out like a shot. "No!"

In the instant silence, Mrs. Fontaine completed her walk and was locked inside the building. Mack tucked the key in his pocket, dragged his chair over in front of the door, and sat down with a groan.

"Karine, can you bring him some supper?" I asked. She nodded and went into the kitchen.

"Hattie, he'll want a blanket. He'll deny that he does. But leave him one, anyway." Hattie ran inside for it.

I looked at John. "Have you ever considered leading a Boy Scout troop?"

"Never." He was still staring at Mack.

"But," he said, "I think I'll stick around and back the boys up, anyway."

27

COACHES

M r. Hannahs arrived for his usual five in the morning shift to find a welcoming party. I woke up on the front veranda, my head on John's shoulder, as Mr. Hannahs rode by in the early dawn. He was trying to take in everything at once.

The Boy Scouts had relocated their bedding to the landing and were spread out in various forms of repose. They littered the place with apple cores, stale popcorn, and empty cocoa-stained mugs. Mack waved at Mr. Hannahs from his chair in front of the office, and I wondered what Mr. Hannahs thought about all of us being outside so early.

The horses whinnied a welcome from the corral, and Mr. Hannahs' horse answered. It seemed to be a wake-up call for everyone.

I sat up and stretched, yawning ferociously, and then looked at John. "I smell coffee."

Sitting in front of us on the veranda rail were two cups of coffee. The steam was still rising from them.

"God bless Karine," John said, standing up. "Give her a raise." He reached for a cup. "Give her anything she wants."

"I heard that," called Karine from around the corner. She and Hattie had come from the kitchen with trays of breakfast for Mack and Mrs. Fontaine. The boys had a whiff of it going by and quickly roused from their blankets.

"Leave the place better than you found it," I called. Cap saluted me, and they began clearing out.

Mr. Hannahs had turned out his horse and was at the post office door with his keys in his hand. "Miss Brown?" he called, "still two for the morning coach?"

I stepped out to meet him. "Yes. But they're in handcuffs."

"It was mighty polite of them to pay for their own tickets. You didn't use my gun, did you?" he asked, and he didn't even wait for me to shake my head. "No," he said, unlocking his door, "I'm sure it's been put somewhere safe and secure. What are we going to do with you?"

"We'll start with sending everyone off the mountain."

"Amen," he said, and flipped on the lights inside. "Coach'll be here in a half hour. Glad to see you got some help."

"I'll fill you in after they're gone," I promised. The damning hatbox was still hidden in my bedroom. It made little sense to send it on the coach, but all the same, I wished the sheriff were back.

That half hour was spent feeding the boys, John, and Mr. Fontaine. Mr. Fontaine wore a pair of handcuffs, and the boys sat at the table, fascinated, watching him manipulate his fork and cup. He was surly and sore, sans jacket. His black eye looked vividly painful, and after ascertaining the whereabouts of his wife, he remained firmly silent.

"You understand the arrangement?" John asked him. "You go peacefully and never return. Your wife made this possible when she turned herself in. Otherwise, you'd be going straight to jail for theft and worse."

Mr. Fontaine pushed his eggs around on the plate and hung his head.

"We don't take kindly to using child hostages," John said. "I never want you to show your face around here again."

Marvin nodded his head and scooped a huge forkful of fried potatoes into his mouth, and a twin on either side of him clapped him on the back. It was a wonder he didn't choke.

Hattie stuck her head into the dining room. "The coach is here," she said.

John and I stood up. "Stay where you are and finish," I told the boys. "Your coach is coming right after, and you still have to pack your things and pile them on the boardwalk."

Mrs. Fontaine and the deputy stood together on the post office landing, ready for the coach. Mrs. Fontaine's dress was the worse for the night's escapades, and her hair stuck out in odd places around the knot on her head. As her hands were cuffed behind her, there was no help for it.

"Where's Johnny?" she spat at me when I walked up.

"No closer, please," Mack said. "Give us space." He had a hand lightly on her elbow.

"Having breakfast," I said. "He's going to be fine. He's coming on the coach with you, but up top."

"You said he wouldn't go to jail!" She strained at the cuffs, and Mack gave her a shake.

"He's not. But he's going somewhere. He can't very well stay here."

She held still when Mr. Fontaine came out of the hotel with John.

"Lucy," he said softly.

"Johnny! What's happened?" Mrs. Fontaine took in his appearance with shock.

"I'm all right. As well as could be expected after this wretched week." He gazed at her solemnly. "You look like an angel." Mr. Fontaine was completely spent.

The rumble of the stagecoach caught everyone's attention, and Jim brought his fresh team to a halt, his expertise matched with an energetic air that signified the last day of his work week.

He didn't ask any questions when he saw Mack with a handcuffed woman. His gaze swept over the rest of us, and he said, "Just the one?"

"Yes," Mack said. "The other sits on top until we're safely inside the Hemet courts. Then he'll go about his own business." Mack held out the handcuff key. "You can take care of it."

Jim pocketed it, then took his lock box into the post office.

Mack opened the coach door. "After you, Mrs. Fontaine," he said.

Mrs. Fontaine stepped to the door and looked back

at her husband of a week. "I'm sorry it had to be like this."

He stared at her, then closed his eyes and shook his head.

"I love you, Johnny."

She stepped inside, and Mack joined her, closing the door firmly in place behind them.

Jim reappeared and stepped up to put his box into place. Once he secured his rifle, he turned and offered a hand to Mr. Fontaine, who awkwardly stepped between the spokes and clambered into place beside him.

"Have a good day, folks," called Jim, and took off the brake. His horses turned the coach and headed for Hemet.

The dawn was fast moving into the full sunshine of a summer morning. Mr. Hannahs swiped his hands on his pants a couple of times and went into the post office. I turned to John.

"Are you sticking around for the grand finale?" I asked.

"I wouldn't miss it."

BOY SCOUTS WERE in the rooms. Boy Scouts were in the kitchen. They were in the oak tree, the lobby, and the corral feeding apples to the horses. We had a pile of camping supplies stacked up on the boardwalk that looked bigger than an actual elephant, and I wondered how it was all going to fit in Lindley's coach.

When the gilded white extravaganza appeared at the bend in the road, boys converged from all directions to meet it. They stayed on the boardwalk as the prancing white horses pulled up and, for the first time ever, Mr. Hannahs remained inside of his post office and steadfastly ignored its presence. I imagined he was holding his breath, waiting for blessed peace—continuously out of reach this week—to descend.

Karine and Hattie joined John on the veranda to watch.

The driver, resplendent in his white suit, climbed down and begged the boys to stop touching the horses.

"Boys!" I said. They snapped to attention and gave me a salute. The driver stood gaping, and I turned to him and sweetly said, "Where would you like the luggage stacked? Inside or on top?"

Before he could answer, the door to the coach swung open, and Lindley himself stepped out, dressed in his best suit. His every hair was in place. There was a small sprig of holly in his lapel. It was my turn to gape.

He doffed his top hat and bowed over my hand. "Good morning to you, Miss Brown. How elegant you look on this beautiful new day."

I laughed outright. "Oh, Lindley! What's the occasion?" I reached up and smoothed at my hopeless hair despite myself.

"I shall perform my magnum opus today," he said, popping his hat back on. "I'm going to convince nine sets of parents that their children have, in fact, had the best, the most important, week of their little lives. The Idyllwild Inn must be on the camping list of every scouting group in America! These lucky boys have had a unique opportunity for vigorous personal and character growth. They've discovered the rewards of being model citizens. Mr. Peabody, who was called away on a sudden family emergency, left his charges in the gifted care of a governess imported directly from Boston's finest, the lovely Miss Brown."

"You're ridiculous." I pulled my hand away.

"I'm a visionary, Miss Brown. I am a new man today, full of new possibilities. And you, my talented partner, are directly responsible for it. How will I ever thank you?"

"You can start by taking these scouts home." I nodded to the driver. "Boys, form a chain gang and pass the luggage up to the driver. Let's go!"

As they jumped to obey, Lindley pulled me aside. "When I return tonight, I perform my swan song."

"Lindley!"

"She knows it's coming. Loveda, I'm more frightened of two little words from Molly than of every screaming parent on earth. I don't know what I'll do if she tells me she's leaving."

I put a hand on his perfect, pressed sleeve. "She won't."

His hand rested on mine for a minute, and then he straightened and turned to the boys. All the luggage was stowed, and with a salute in my general direction, they piled inside the coach.

"Adieu, my dear," Lindley said, and climbed into the coach behind them. He closed the door and rapped on the wall. The driver gathered up the white reins, spoke to his horses, and pulled out for the Banning road.

"Wow," breathed Hattie, watching it vanish around the corner.

"Are you going to change your mind and work for him, Hattie?" I asked.

"No," she said with a small smile. "I've seen all I need to see. That Mr. Lindley is too much for me." She opened her hand and held up the moonstone. "Your place is full of surprises, though."

"How did you get that?"

"The boy is sweet on red hair," she giggled. "And he wanted me to have it to remember him by."

I rolled my shoulders and wished the scouts good riddance.

"You'd best get hold of that Mrs. Keen," Karine said. "The kitchen's been emptied of supplies by half."

The two went into the hotel, and I was alone at long last on my veranda. There were no guests upstairs. No voices coming from the gardens or the corral. Or the roof. The temptation to go to bed for a week was very strong.

"John?" I looked in all directions and saw him saddling his horse in front of the blacksmith shop. He didn't look up as I stepped forward, lifting my palm to his horse's gentle muzzle. "John, thank you. Thank you for being here."

John seemed lost in his own thoughts. When he didn't comment, I said, "I wouldn't have made it through the night without you."

He finished tightening the girth and rested a hand on the saddle. "I think, Miss Brown, that you underestimate yourself."

The sun was rapidly moving overhead, and the day was warming. I needed a hat. I needed a bath. I needed to sit down.

"Thanks. But if that raccoon had come at me, I would have pitched myself off the roof head first." I smiled, but he didn't join me.

"I also think that Lindley should have been here instead of me." The way he said it hinted at disdain.

"How would he have known what was happening here?"

"Isn't that what partners do? Know what's happening? I somehow managed it."

I didn't like the underlying tension in his vague accusation, and I was beyond too tired to guess his meaning. "What are you talking about?"

He reached for the rope and unhitched his horse. "From the way he looks at you, he's decided to be much more than your dance partner." He mounted. "My personal opinions on him aside, you should stop teasing the man."

"Teasing?" I almost laughed out loud, but the disapproval on his face stopped me short.

He moved his horse forward. "If we're all going to be neighbors, the sooner you sort yourself out, the better. Glad I could help. Good morning, Miss Brown."

He rode off, and I closed my eyes against the bright sunshine and pulled the scent of warm pine and road dust deep into my lungs. I listened to the sound of hoofbeats fading away and the scrub jay that scolded from above the blacksmith shop. I slid both hands into my skirt pockets, and my fingers automatically felt for my watch.

One of the most frustrating things about John was his tendency to look below the surface and deduce things from keen observation. Living off the land demanded the understanding of different behaviors, intuition about what people or animals might do next. His ability made it possible for him to interact with Elizabeth Nelson, somewhere out in the forest. On the other hand, I was someone who continually took things and people at face value, and it regularly landed me in hot water.

I sighed because I knew John was right. I needed to get myself sorted.

I sighed because I knew John was wrong. Lindley already had a new dance partner.

I walked past the post office and wondered if everyone else thought Lindley and I were together. Hopefully after tonight, that rumor could be put to rest. I thought briefly about what Molly might do next if she were unemployed. Whether she would stay in Idyllwild or move down the mountain. My hands went to my desk, slid open the drawer. I laid eyes on my ledger at the same time I felt around in the empty space where Mr. Hannahs' gun should have been.

My heartbeat reached panic speed as I reached to the chain around my neck, pulling it out, making sure the key was still there. I'd locked it. I knew I had. But the ledger on my desktop mocked me. Reminded me that I'd pulled it out in a moment of desperation and as quickly abandoned it for larger problems.

And left the desk unlocked.

I dropped to my chair and buried my face in my hands. What was I going to tell Mr. Hannahs?

I heard Hattie came down the staircase behind me and she cried out, "What is it, Miss Brown! Are you hurt?"

Karine came from the kitchen. "Mercy, this place," she said.

"This is going to sound very bad," I said, "but have either of you seen an old but highly functional Smith and Wesson revolver around here? I seem to have lost one." I dropped my head back and stared at the ceiling. "It belongs to Mr. Hannahs. And I left it here, in this drawer."

"A gun, Miss Brown?" whispered Hattie.

Karine and I took in her pale face, innumerable freckles beneath her teary green eyes.

"I never saw it," Hattie said. "You told everybody last night that your gun was stolen. Miss Brown, everybody's walked by this desk a hundred times since then."

"But you know something about it?" I prodded.

She shook her head. "Only that sometime this morning in the dark, when all the boys were shifting beds next door, the conversation was detectives, and a boy mentioned that Mr. Fontaine told him he was a real live undercover detective, like in the books. I didn't think anything about it, Miss Brown. If you had a gun, why didn't you use it? When the boy said he'd made secret plans and traded weapons, I had no idea it was anything but tall tales."

The three of us looked through the window to the clear greens, browns, and blues of Idyllwild.

Who had the gun? A Boy Scout? Or Mr. Fontaine?

28

SILKS

Two weeks later found me alone on the veranda watching the sun set against the stony crags of Tahquitz Peak. The quiet was palpable. My ears strained to catch a bird call or the heavy drop of a pine cone to the forest floor. Even the kitchen was subdued behind me. Supper was ready.

Mr. Hannahs stepped out of the post office and locked the door. He nodded at me and had a hard time disguising the smile across his face. I turned back to the sunset, but the granite had cooled quickly to ashen shadows. A few minutes later, Mr. Hannahs rode by and tipped his hat.

"Lovely…" he began. "…evening, Miss Brown."

"Good night, Mr. Hannahs," I said, waving a gloved hand.

His new Smith and Wesson was at his side, the finest my money could buy. I had retrieved my Colt, at great expense to my ego, and it was currently hidden in the safest spot in the hotel: under my pillow. I watched in satisfaction as Mr. Hannahs walked his horse for home.

I reached up to make sure my hat still balanced squarely between my ears. With gloves on, it was hard to tell if my hair tucked into it properly, and I stopped myself from running back inside and resetting the hat all over again. Between the hairpins and hatpins and my rebellious curls, it had taken Hattie almost an hour to get it perfect, and I didn't have that kind of time now.

The blacksmith shop was silent. Carlos had led the sheriff as far as the Anza Valley, where they'd discovered a deflated Mr. Peabody and a tearful Toby. Although Mr. Peabody had explained his history, Toby wanted to go back to Rose. Mr. Peabody went with Carlos to take him home.

In front of the blacksmith shop, Mack finished saddling his horse. He was heading to Lindley's for supper, but he stopped in front of my veranda and looked me up and down with an approving smile.

"Aren't you a picture?" he said. "Still have your watch?"

I smiled and patted my pocket watch. They had returned it along with the fingerprint card that Mack had made for me. Mr. Fontaine's prints were inconclusive, but they had identified mine. It helped that the newspaper editor-in-chief had put the fear of God into that skulking reporter.

My watch hung from its short gold chain at the waist of my white silk dress where the wide navy sash bound it. Embroidery draped along the front of my top and continued in panels along the skirt line. Beneath my dress was a new-fashioned corset that forced me to stand up straight. From its lacy edge, the corset held up my embroidered navy stockings, and those tucked into white, heeled, patent leather and cloth high-buttoned shoes. Between my shoes and my white silk hat covered in pink roses, I was at least a foot taller than usual.

But I still wouldn't be able to look at John eye to eye until we sat down for supper.

"Good," Mack said. "Any hints of trouble around here?" His casual sweep of the area included my roofline, and I laughed. There were some things neither of us were going to take for granted ever again.

"I don't think they'll come back," I said. "Their egos couldn't stand it."

"Neither could mine," Mack said.

The Fontaines had escaped the stagecoach, some-where along the road to Hemet. According to Jim, hangdog Mr. Fontaine had sprung to life, put a gun in his face, and demanded he pull over. In the wrestling match that ensued, the horses took a wheel off the road and lodged the coach against a massive tree, releasing both passengers. The Fontaines were at large. Jim had a nasty scar over one eye where he landed in the road. Mack had a badly bruised ego.

"Sheriff'll be back tomorrow," Mack reminded me as he moved his horse forward.

"So long as he comes back alone!" I called after him. The sheriff was in Banning, awarding a custom Boy Scout badge to each of the scouts for their bravery. He called it an honorary deputy badge, an embroidered star that would make any boy proud. I sincerely hoped he would never have reason to make more.

In the dusk, I watched John Wyman ride around the

bend in the road and pass Mack. They exchanged greetings, then each went their separate ways.

Karine stuck her head out of the lobby door. "He here yet? Soup's on." She flicked on the light in the lobby.

"He is now, Karine, thank you."

She went back inside, and John rode up and stopped at the post. He stared at me long enough to make me blush, but I counted on the distance and the light at my back to keep that knowledge to myself.

"Well," he said.

"Hello to you, too," I said. "Are you going to come sit down? Karine's not the patient type."

He thought about it. I suppose he had options. Then he swung down from the saddle and hitched his horse. He stepped across the boardwalk and took off his Stetson. "How many flowers did you put on that hat?" he asked.

"All of them," I said. "It's heavy."

He looked uncomfortable. "It's just supper, right? Who else is coming?" He tapped his hat against his denim pants and rolled a shoulder under his clean, buttoned-up work shirt.

"Nobody. John. I told you. I want to thank you properly. It is just supper, but it will have to do. Karine outdid herself. Be sure you compliment her."

As he appeared to have no idea what to do with himself, I turned and led the way into the dining room. The cat sat on my desk, and I reached for him as we passed. The thing dodged my tentative gesture, clearly still not impressed with me.

The dining room glowed with candles in candelabras, lace over linen, fine china, and crystal goblets.

John paused at the display, then helped me into my chair. Something he did effortlessly, as though some old memory had finally come to his rescue. He hung his hat on the door and sat down.

"I borrowed it from Lindley. Most of it," I said. "He insisted on giving us this, too." I pointed to a bottle of champagne. "He's celebrating." I couldn't hide my happiness.

"Is he, now?" John began to thaw, and when Hattie came in with a hot tureen, he smiled at her.

"If you've been under a rock for two weeks, and maybe you have," I said, picking up my spoon and pointing it at him, "then I'll tell you that his Molly has decided to remain in Idyllwild so that Lindley has a chance to woo her properly."

He reached for the bottle. "I'll drink to that."

"Good. I thought perhaps every shred of civilization might have been wrung from you."

"This may come as a shock, Miss Brown, but I hosted more than one dignitary at my estate in Virginia. It was a lifetime ago, but I do know how to serve champagne."

John filled the tall, narrow flutes, and we clinked them together and took a sip. I reminded myself that I could admire the sweet and bubbly treat in the glass. I didn't need to drink it to enjoy it.

His face was guarded, but relaxed. "It brings back my complicated days," he said. "I spend a lot of time forgetting them."

"Hear, hear," I said. "Only the good parts are worth

remembering." I patted my watch. It was comforting to have it back again.

"And you, Miss Brown, are you celebrating something?"

"Yes." I couldn't refuse another sip of champagne. "Here's to home." I lifted my glass.

"Home? Did Lindley find a new lawyer for you?" He raised his glass to mine.

"No. I've decided to drop it for now. All I have to do to get what I want is to hold still." I clinked my glass to his. "I'm squatting." I sipped and laughed. "That sounds so ridiculous out loud, but there it is, and here I plan to stay."

"You could have any future in the world with that money." I saw plainly that it was a question.

"I have everything I want. Right here. This is where I belong." I sipped more sparkling bubbles.

He pondered it and admitted, "Me, too." I saw the same decision cross his face, a memory from another lifetime. "I don't think I've tasted champagne since Cleveland was president. When was that?"

"I wouldn't know. I was a child."

My quip was drowned out by a tremendous racket in the lobby. Snarls, yowls, growls, and screeches brought us running into the room.

The cat was in the fireplace, spinning like a top, fighting a raccoon. The coon hung down from the chimney, and the top half of the cat disappeared after it. Together, they churned up the fireplace in a cloud of ash, soot, and black coals that spread over the hearth and onto the carpet. With a violent hiss, the cat clawed his way higher. The rumble in the chimney was terrifying.

Hattie cried out, and Karine rushed from the kitchen with a broom. "Spoon!" she shrieked, "Out of there! No! He'll be eaten!"

"Oh, no!" I said, coughing, and made one lunge for the bottom of the cat. "How many are in there?"

I stepped back, and she swatted at the animals with her broom. As more and more of the fireplace debris went into the air, I realized that one solid object remained, and it wasn't moving at all. It was a cash box.

"Karine! Look!" With one hand covering my nose and mouth, I reached toward the box with my other.

At that moment, two raccoons came shooting out of the fireplace and ran straight up my arm, scrabbling for a perch among the flowers on my hat. I staggered backward, clutching at my hair, as the top-heavy tornado sent me swaying across the room.

"Hattie, the door!" Karine called out.

I shrank into myself, shrieking, and braced as Karine took her broom and aimed. Hattie threw open the front lobby door and flattened herself against the wall and, with a baseball-worthy swing, Karine sent the hat and the raccoons flying through it. The cat came from behind, and with a savage growl, chased them into the night.

"Spoon!" cried Karine, and she and Hattie ran after them.

It was surprisingly hard to breathe while wearing the corset, but several pounds had been swept from my head. I staggered as far as the doorway and leaned against the jamb. The women were under the oak tree, pleading with the cat to come down.

What was left of my hat was on the veranda. Pink silk roses drifted across the wood like moonlit nymphs.

When I turned back to John, he was standing perfectly still next to the desk, a champagne flute in one hand. His eyes were wide, but he kept his face smoothly indifferent, waiting to see which way the wind would blow.

My hair had pulled out of the knot on my head, and half of it fell around my shoulders. Every inch of me was filthy. With a sooty glove, I lifted a scrap of lace on my sleeve and examined its torn edge. I could still feel the little claws on my dress and shivered.

Across the room, the cash box stood defiantly in the fireplace and I walked to it. It had been banked. Of course it had. It was the perfect summer hiding spot in this ridiculous hotel. I picked it up and brought it to my desktop. John watched as I flipped the catch and opened the lid. Paper bills, coins, a couple of small keys, and silver dollars mingled inside.

The absurdity of the situation struck me, and I laughed. I laughed so hard that tears came.

I held out my hand to John, and he stepped closer, but instead of taking his offered hand, I took the glass from his other and drank it all, leaning back against the desk.

When I could breathe again, I said, "I don't know what it is, but I am destined never to wear a clean, pretty frock. Lucy Fontaine tried." I gestured to my dress. "There are plenty more where this came from.

She left me drifts of beautiful clothes. But she never, I am certain, tried living in Idyllwild."

John reached out and tucked my hair behind my ear. "It all comes out in the wash."

"That's true." I was happy. "I wouldn't trade this for any mansion back East." I wiped at my eyes.

"I don't know," John said. He was much too close for manners. "Every time I'm around you, I start feeling complicated."

"What?" The champagne was giving me a comfortable, warm feeling in the pit of my stomach. It was nice for a change, but it made John's words sound low and gentle. Which made no sense.

"You have a way of complicating my life without coming anywhere near me, now that I think about it. Those crazy Fontaines might've had one thing right."

"Um. Sorry?" I hiccuped.

He traced the soot on my cheek. "My God, you're beautiful."

And he kissed me.

MYSTERY, HISTORY, OR POPPYCOCK?

These three elements combine to make Loveda Brown's fictional world come to life. But which parts are history and which are poppycock? A great deal of research goes into making these books, and most of it never ends up on the page. If you're the curious type, read on.

I pulled many of the characters in this series from real Idyllwild history. John and Mary Keen ran Keen Kamp, a campground where Hole-in-the-Tree (at the fork in the road) was a popular photo spot. The area was not known as Mountain Center until after World War II. The Keens retired in 1911 and sold the camp to Percy and Anita Walker, but I needed them to stick around for my series.

I used a fictitious Mrs. Keen to introduce the

national politics of the day. The National American Woman Suffrage Association formed in 1900 and gained momentum over the next decade. In 1912, Arizona, Kansas, and Oregon joined the handful of states in the Wild West giving women the vote. But the 19th Amendment wasn't passed until 1920.

Apparently, women had to prove their mettle during a global war before men could take them seriously. And this is my idea of poppycock.

The Boy Scouts of America program was founded in 1910 in Silver Bay, New York, modeled after the Boy Scouts Association in Britain. By 1919, there were troops in every state. The Girls Scouts of America (originally Girl Guides) was founded in 1912 in Savannah, Georgia. The cookies arrived in 1917.

Scouting promotes service, leadership skills, and character. It seemed to me that a murder mystery would provide ample such opportunities for a troop of rambunctious Boy Scouts. They didn't let me down.

National Geographic remains one of my favorite magazines to peruse. First published in 1888, the iconic golden border became a hallmark in 1910. In their efforts to promote cultural understanding, the inclusion of nude or semi-nude photographs occasionally offended readers. In a time when women were arrested for wearing one-piece swimming costumes, it might easily have been a taboo magazine for children.

THANK YOU

I hope you enjoyed reading about the little mountain paradise of Idyllwild, California. My family can be found there every summer, enjoying the sunshine, pine trees, and legend-worthy Tahquitz Peak. Loveda Brown's world is completely fictitious, but the spirit of her Wild West lives on. Thank you for riding along.

Please drop a couple of lines to review this book. It only takes a minute and it lasts forever. You can shop, leave reviews, subscribe to my newsletter, and find me on all the fun book-loving things at JolieTunnell.com.

Want to know what happens next? Here's the opening chapter of *Loveda Brown Sings the Blues*...

LOVEDA BROWN SINGS THE BLUES

There are kisses, and then there are kisses, and each of them means something quite specific, unless, of course, the kisser is a man. It's my experience that a man kisses for only one reason, to lure a woman into his arms where she becomes utterly vulnerable.

When a woman kisses, it can be anything from a question to a rebuke, so it's hard to blame a man for wanting to be the kisser instead of the kissee. He simply doesn't have the vocabulary for the other way 'round.

These were the thoughts that kept me company as I rode my mare, Blue, along the dusty road, breathing the scent of fresh pine and admiring the early morning summer sunshine. I gave Blue a couple of happy pats on the neck as we walked along the tree line.

"You always understand my kisses, don't you, Blue-girl?"

She nodded and blew a raspberry.

We headed around a little ridge that separated the only two hotels on the top of our mountain range. Idyllwild was just a dot on the California map, consisting of my tiny hotel, a post office, a blacksmith shop, and a deputy's office on my side of the ridge, and the Idyll-wild Inn on the other.

Mr. Walter Lindley owned the Inn and with visions of the future shining in his eyes, he'd filled Foster's Meadow with his sprawling resort, put a saloon up next to the road, built pretty little gingerbread-decorated cottages in the back, and rounded his place off nicely with an extensive tent area for campers.

As we rounded the last bend and I turned Blue in at Lindley's resort, I decided once again that, all things considered, I had the better arrangement between the two of us. My hotel was a converted home that had five rooms up top for guests. Cozy, quiet, and friendly, it didn't offer the razzle dazzle that Lindley loved, but provided a clean bed and good food for the travelers who arrived via the stagecoach.

The city of Hemet was twenty miles southwest from my hotel, and the city of Banning was twenty miles northwest from Lindley's. This single road connected us all. I looked over my shoulder as we left it behind and sighed.

If I rode further on to John Wyman's solitary cabin, I could ask him myself about his kiss and its implications. It irritated me beyond words that he'd kissed me out of nowhere and then carried on as though it hadn't happened. No explanation. Men were ridiculous. For now, it satisfied me to investigate a different kiss. One that Lindley had given Molly, his former maid.

"Loveda!" The cry came from the wide veranda that encompassed the resort building. A girl with bright hazel eyes started down the front stairs to meet me, and I laughed at both her enthusiasm and the hobble skirt she was attempting to negotiate the steps in.

Two bassett hounds acknowledged my arrival with half-hearted bays. They remained lounging on the veranda, thumping their tails on the wooden deck, and by this Juno and Biscuit recognized me as family.

"Molly, stop!" I called. "You'll just have to go up again!"

She waited obediently half way down while I dismounted and handed Blue's reins to a stable boy. He gave me a nod in welcome and led Blue away, and I dashed up the stairs and took her arm in mine. Together, we made it back up the steps.

"I'm so glad to see you," Molly said as we each took a seat in rocking chairs. The view from the veranda was gorgeous no matter which direction you faced, but this one was my favorite by far. Tahquitz Peak rose in morning glory and presided over the mountain like the legendary Cahuilla chief it was named for. I admired its craggy face while Molly launched into her morning news.

"Mr. Lindley's been such a gentleman, Loveda, arranged things just so. I'm still sharing the cottage with Charlotte—the receptionist, you know—we get on so well it didn't make sense to shift. But Charlotte gets up every morning before dawn to arrange the resort schedules and it was dull very quickly, so Lindley agreed I could manage the new maids."

She hesitated.

"My replacements. How strange. We've hired on three and I've been showing them the ropes, you know, bringing things together. We'll have to work well as a team before the big show this weekend." She took a flustered breath. "I mean, they will. It's odd to not be officially part of the staff anymore."

Molly's cheeks were flushed, and her smile showed an endearing little gap between her front teeth. Her pretty clothes were becoming and a big change from the normal maid's uniform of drab gray dresses and white starched aprons, but Molly wore them well.

I ran a hand over my full, deep green riding skirt. I was five foot four inches and wore sensible day dresses that befit a sensible hotel proprietor. Hobble skirts were only an option for taller ladies who had no use for staircases. Or really, anything at all.

"I know how you feel," I said. "When I went from being a governess in Boston to the wife of a wealthy El Paso rancher, I hardly knew what to do with myself. Of course," I amended, "I went as quickly from a wife to a widow to a hotel owner." I rocked in my chair a little. "Change is something you have to get comfortable with, or you will never know what you've missed."

"I would hate to miss Mr. Lindley," Molly said with a sigh.

"There you have it," I said. "You adapt and find out what the future has in store for you." I took up my pocket watch and checked the time. "Speaking of your beau, he told me to be here at nine precisely. Where is he?"

"We breakfasted at seven, and I haven't seen him since. And don't call him my beau."

"I will. It adds color to your face and a smile, too. Has he kissed you since he fired you?"

"What a blunt question. You make it sound so silly. No. He takes my hand and barely passes his face over it."

"And this displeases you?"

"He can't very well take liberties with a lady."

"You would rather stay the maid and be kissed? I don't think so. There are enough stigmas attached to the question of class and sex."

"Loveda!" She looked left and right, to see if anyone had overheard.

"I mean women's rights, Molly. It's 1912. If women can have the vote, women can make independent decisions on whether or not they will kiss a man and when. Why does the man decide these things?"

"Since when are you a suffragette?"

"I'm not. But the lines aren't drawn very fairly on some things, in my opinion." I sighed. "And the idea of an employer taking advantage of an employee is insufferable. What if a lady could kiss a man and still be a lady?"

Molly gasped.

"You see? It never hurts the man, the other way around. We are all caught between the old and the new. You two will have to find a way to navigate it."

Molly leaned closer and lowered her voice. "I do think Mr. Lindley arranged this event for my personal enjoyment. All I did was mention—mention, mind you —that I loved Mozart and he sends Charlotte on a wild goose chase, looking for an opera singer to come up and perform."

Her smile was part embarrassed and part pleased. "He already insisted I have access to the piano in the ballroom at any hour and told me to order up all the records I wished for our collection."

"Molly, I didn't realize you were musically inclined. I'm more interested in how the piano is put together and tuned. I've never tried playing one."

"I haven't played since I was a child," she admitted, "and I'm afraid to play in front of anyone, especially Mr. Lindley, but it was sweet of him to offer. Will you come to the show on Sunday? I'll make sure you get a front-row seat."

"I wouldn't miss it. But the front row must be for Karine. The woman nearly scorched a meal when she found out André Bernardi was coming up to sing her favorite songs. She's been going on about opera ever since."

"Then Mr. Lindley's done a good thing. Even if it's for your cook." Molly sounded pleased. "And is there anyone in particular you'd like me to seat next to you? Besides Karine?" She cut her eyes at me but rocked in her chair with an air of indifference. "I'd love to see you in your silks."

"I'm sure I don't know what you mean." I kept my eyes on Tahquitz.

"You're fairly surrounded by single men, Loveda. Take some of your own medicine, and tell me which one you'd prefer…dressing up for."

"That isn't fair. A woman should be able to wear what she pleases and when without everyone ascribing an agenda to it."

"So, is there something to the rumor or not?" Molly's chair stopped, and she addressed me frankly. "You dressed like an angel and invited John Wyman to supper. Borrowed our crystal and china for it. Sounds like an agenda, Loveda."

"Maybe I miss pretty things sometimes." I fidgeted with my riding gloves.

"Maybe you prefer John Wyman."

"That's nonsense." I looked at my watch again. "Didn't it occur to you that Lindley doesn't want you to miss pretty things, either? That he wants you to be content up here in this remote place? Now, there's a man with an agenda. I won't make a fuss again, if people are going to talk about me like that."

No one knew about John's kiss, and I was going to keep it that way. It wasn't the first time it had occurred to me that perhaps John thought I'd had an agenda that night, and it chafed. I had in no way provoked him. It wasn't my fault, and it didn't need to be repeated.

I was saved from outright quarreling with Molly by the appearance of Lindley, riding up and looking very pleased with himself. He smiled and lifted his little goatee higher when he noticed us sitting on the veranda. Lindley kept his tidy, pressed appearance, even on horseback, even when his temper flared, his every oiled hair in place. I envied him his composure and had only seen him without it when confronted with Molly.

Which seemed perfectly reasonable to me.

"Lindley's Summer Musical Extravaganza!" he said, lifting the bowler hat from his head and placing it over his heart with reverence. "Presenting the triumphant tenor, the famous operatic voice, direct from Los Angeles, ladies and gentlemen, André Bernardi!"

Molly and I rose from our chairs and clapped on cue, as Lindley beamed up at us.

"I've almost perfected my speech," he said, dismounting. "Nothing like a ride to clear your head." He nodded to the stable boy who materialized to collect his horse. Lindley came up the steps and gave my offered hand a hearty shake. He had been running this property for many years, and I was new to the hotel business. Lindley had taken me under his wing as a business partner of sorts and was as interested in my success as his own.

"Lindley, thank you so much for your help," I said, as we shook hands. "I'll repay your kindness one day."

He lingered over my hand for a minute and turned his eyes to Molly. "I believe you've paid in full, Miss Brown."

He took up Molly's hand and bent over it briefly, releasing it much sooner than Molly might have wished.

"How are you ladies on this fine morning?" he asked. Then, he looked out across the meadow and added, "We're about to have company."

"I would guess so," ventured Molly. "We've sold over eighty tickets."

We followed Lindley's gaze and watched a horseman coming our way.

"He didn't come from the road?" I asked.

"I was just out there checking the cabins," Lindley said with some curiosity. "I didn't see him."

The lone rider approached the veranda steps and halted his horse at the bottom of them. He swept the Panama from his head, revealing long black waving hair tied back loosely at his neck. I could see his bright black eyes set in a swarthy complexion taking in the details of everything around us, but the easy grin beneath his heavy mustache withheld his opinions.

"How do you do?" the man said. "Am I correct in thinking this is a hotel with rooms for hire?"

"You are," Lindley said, stepping forward. "Do you have a reservation for the weekend gala?"

The man blinked once. "Gala? I'm sure I don't know what you mean, sir."

"We are sold out of rooms, I'm afraid, for a Sunday event," Lindley said. "It's quite a production. Miss Brown has a hotel further down the road." He looked over his shoulder at me, and I nodded. "A quiet spot, but close enough to attend the gala if you wish."

"I have no desire to be thrust among crowds. In fact, thank you for letting me know. I came up with the explicit goal of peace and solitude." He swept his eyes over the veranda and stopped to stare at me. "The beauty of the mountain called to me."

His eyes were fascinating.

"Miss Brown," Lindley said, returning to our chairs, "my apologies. Shall we attend our business later? I have to oversee the rearrangement of the stables and convince my chef that cursing in French is not going to help with his pantry navigations. I confess, I'm swamped."

"I understand completely," I said, "and I'm happy to hear it. Don't worry about my things until after this weekend is over." The stable boy who had appeared next to the veranda looked from the stranger to me and decided correctly to bring my horse around.

"I'm Loveda Brown," I called to the man on his horse. "I'll show you the way myself."

"Morgan Bell. At your service," the man said, and replaced his hat. I watched his gloved fingers adjust it and return to gather the reins in one flowing, fluid movement. In addition to the usual working tack on his horse, he had a large, narrow box over the saddlebags behind him. Before I could catch myself, he noticed my stare and said, "Painter. I work in oils and chalks."

To my annoyance, I blushed and covered my embarrassment with a smile.

I turned toward Molly. She joined me briefly as Lindley walked to the front doors of the hotel and held the handle, waiting for her.

"He's devastating," whispered Molly at my elbow. "I'll keep that seat open next to you."

"Poppycock." I reached up and smoothed my brunette curls beneath my hatband. "Find something useful to do."

"I haven't any idea how to be a lady of leisure. What does one do without employment?"

I shrugged. "The first thing I did was learn how to shoot rattlesnakes at ten paces."

She put a gloved hand over her mouth, and I started down the steps.

"You might find something more useful, I suppose. But it came in handy at the time."

Don't stop now! Get the rest of the book at
https://jolietunnell.com/shop

Made in the USA
Columbia, SC
10 October 2024

43439811R00183